W9-BOM-179

good
catch

Discarded by MVCL

ALSO BY JENNIFER BARDSLEY

Genesis Girl

Damaged Goods

The Harper Landing Series

Sweet Bliss

Writing as Louise Cypress

Shifter's Wish

Shifter's Kiss

Shifter's Desire

Bite Me

Hunt Me

Slay Me

Slayer Academy: Secret Shifter

Mermaid Aboard

The Gift of Goodbye

Books, Boys, and Revenge

Narcosis Room

good catch

A Harper Landing Novel

JENNIFER BARDSLEY

Mount Vernon City Library
315 Snoqualmie Street
Mount Vernon, WA 98273

This is a work of fiction. Names, characters, organizations, places, events, and incidents are either products of the author's imagination or are used fictitiously.

Text copyright © 2021 by Jennifer Bardsley
All rights reserved.

No part of this book may be reproduced, or stored in a retrieval system, or transmitted in any form or by any means, electronic, mechanical, photocopying, recording, or otherwise, without express written permission of the publisher.

Published by Montlake, Seattle

www.apub.com

Amazon, the Amazon logo, and Montlake are trademarks of Amazon.com, Inc., or its affiliates.

ISBN-13: 9781542029797
ISBN-10: 1542029791

Cover design by Letitia Hasser

Printed in the United States of America

To creative spellers everywhere.

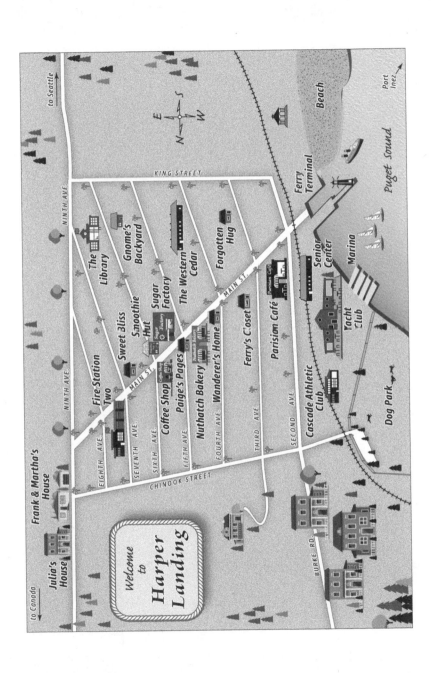

CHAPTER ONE

Attending a wedding was the last thing Marlo Jonas wanted to do the day after a breakup, yet here she was in the middle of the Harper Landing Yacht Club sitting next to the empty seat where her boyfriend, Ryan, was supposed to be. *Ex*-boyfriend. Last night after she had finished teaching spin class, Marlo had driven over to Bellevue to surprise him with a Halloween gift. As she'd walked up to Ryan's apartment building, she'd glanced up at his balcony and caught him making out with a redhead in a miniskirt. Marlo had been so startled that she'd dropped the jack-o'-lantern she'd carved onto the pavement, splattering pumpkin pieces across her favorite leggings. Marlo knew she shouldn't have let the Lululemon salesclerk talk her into buying white pants. What a mistake. Twelve hours later, it was still easier to focus on her poor choice in legwear than her horrible track record with men. Hopefully, bleach would get those stains out; otherwise, the leggings were going into the trash, right next to the stack of bridal magazines she had been secretly hoarding.

Now, Marlo wore a navy-blue dress in a stretchy velvet fabric that the bride had chosen. Her long brown hair cascaded down her back, and the black ballet flats she wore were comfortable. The only bothersome part of her ensemble were the chandelier earrings, which were too heavy. Marlo wasn't a bridesmaid—Julia Harper was five years her senior and had so many friends from high school that her wedding party was stacked. Instead, Marlo was in charge of the guest book, where she still felt honored to help. Marlo was Julia's barre fitness instructor at the Cascade Athletic Club, and they'd known each other for years.

Marlo took a long sip of water and stared up at the head table, where Julia and Aaron gazed at each other adoringly, huge smiles on their faces. Aaron's infant nephew, Jack, was in a high chair next to them, attended by one of the many bridesmaids. Marlo sighed without meaning to and looked back at her water glass.

"Don't slouch," said her father, Chuck Jonas, owner and manager of the Cascade Athletic Club. "You know how I feel about slouching."

"Zip it," said Marlo's mother. Laura Jonas had long gray hair that she wore parted down the middle, its color complementing the purple cotton dress she wore. Crystals dangled from her earlobes and hung around her neck. Laura was a big believer in the healing power of crystals to overcome anything, even her dislike of the yacht club. "Marlo is twenty-four years old, and you don't get to boss her around anymore."

"I *am* her boss." Chuck sat ramrod straight. "And it reflects poorly on the club when our Pilates instructor slouches."

"Yes, but I'm also the spin instructor," said Marlo, pulling a lock of her chestnut hair behind her ear. "I hunch over my bike all the time." She didn't intend to be impertinent, but at least one of her parents had raised her to stick up for herself. "I'd have better posture if I weren't so exhausted. Have you given Dahlia her hours back like I asked? I can't keep teaching five classes a day. You're putting me at risk for another injury."

"Don't be ridiculous." Chuck waved his hand in the air like he was brushing the notion aside. In the past few months, he'd doubled Marlo's workload. Unlike the other fitness instructors who earned by the hour, Marlo was on salary and took home the same paycheck no matter how many classes she taught. "The added exercise has been good for you. It combats all the carbs you've been eating since you quit dancing." He pointed at Marlo's bread plate, and she was thankful the other guests couldn't hear his disparaging comment over the loud music.

"I would never have *quit* ballet." Marlo slumped forward for a second before she sat up straight again. "I had a career-ending injury. There's a difference." Marlo winced, remembering how her torn ACL had ruined her first and last season with Seattle's Pacific Northwest Ballet Company. "The double class load at the gym isn't good for me. My physical therapist says I have to be careful with my knee." Marlo stretched her leg out underneath the table and flexed her foot. "Plus, I've been so exhausted that I haven't had any time for myself or my relationship."

"There, there." Laura reached out and patted Marlo's hair. "You know how I felt about Ryan and his unnaturally white smile. The breakup is for the best."

Marlo felt her entire body tense. "Well, sure it is, since it turns out he's a cheater. But that doesn't have anything to do with his appearance."

"I never trust anyone with muscles that large." Laura readjusted the leather cuff with turquoise stones that circled her wrist.

"Ryan did CrossFit, Mom."

"CrossFit," Chuck sneered. "I like Ryan, but you know how I feel about CrossFit."

Marlo massaged her temple. She didn't want to repeat the same old argument with her parents about the changing world of group fitness classes. They were purists. If Jane Fonda or Denise Austin didn't do it in the 1980s, then it wouldn't happen at the Cascade Athletic Club. The only exceptions they made were for the spin studio and barre class. The bikes were the first thing most prospective members asked about, and the barre class used Marlo's skills as a classically trained ballerina. She'd graduated from the University of Washington with a degree in dance, and the year she'd spent dancing professionally had been the high point of her life.

"We wouldn't be in crisis mode," Marlo said in a heavy whisper, "if you'd let the club keep up with the times. Small-group fitness classes are what's popular now, especially with young people willing to pay thirty dollars a class. We shouldn't let boutique fitness studios take all our business."

"We're in crisis mode because the damn port commission is charging us two hundred thousand dollars for our share of the new parking structure," Chuck grumbled. "That's boatloads more than any other business along the marina."

"Well, well, well," said a clear voice. Cheryl Lowrey, co-owner of the Nuthatch Bakery, walked up to the table wearing a seafoam-green pantsuit. Her silvery-black hair was pulled into a loose knot at the back of her neck, and her husband, Nick Wexler, stood right beside her. "It looks like we showed up in time for some juicy port commission gossip." Cheryl double-checked the number card in the table's centerpiece and sat down.

"Hello, Chuck," Nick said in a quiet voice. "Laura. Marlo." He nodded before he sat down next to his wife. Nick and Cheryl's café was sandwiched between Paige's Pages, the local bookshop, and the back-country outfitter store Wanderer's Home on Main Street. Marlo had visited Wanderer's Home a couple of weeks ago to choose Ryan's birthday present. Now Marlo was stuck with a backpacking stove she had no use for whatsoever. The closest Marlo ever came to nature was when she lit the candle in her living room that smelled like a spring meadow.

Marlo glanced behind Cheryl and Nick to see if their obnoxious son, Ben Wexler-Lowrey, was with them. She'd known Ben since kindergarten, but they definitely weren't friends. Especially not since the *incident*. Sophomore year she'd been sitting in the bleachers at a pep rally, in front of Ben and his friend Mike Lu. It was December, which for Marlo meant *Nutcracker* season, and opening night was that evening. As embarrassing as it was, Marlo had had to wear pink curlers to school. Curlers, combined with a sickening amount of hair spray, were what made her straight hair transform into ringlets that held up to dancing onstage as the Sugar Plum Fairy. When Ben popped his bag of Cheetos and exploded dust all over the bleachers, it turned Marlo's whole head orange. She rushed to the PE locker rooms to try to brush it off, but it was too late. Orange dye stuck to her hair spray.

Marlo showered, dried her hair, and borrowed a friend's curling iron to attempt to repair the damage, but her hair wouldn't hold the curl. When she showed up at the theater, Madame Burke gave Marlo's role to her understudy for the night. She said she was sorry to be harsh, but in the real world, a mistake like that would have cost Marlo her job.

Marlo was devastated. She'd spent years earning that spot, and to lose it on opening night crushed her. But she was willing to assume that it had been an accident on Ben's part—until the following Monday, when she stopped by the Nuthatch to order a latte. Ben wrote "Jonass" on her cup, even though he knew her last name was spelled with one *s*. Marlo corrected him, and he pretended to apologize. But the next day when she'd gone back for another latte, he'd written "Jonass" again— only this time he'd added a smiley face. The nerve!

"No Ben tonight?" Marlo tried to keep her tone neutral. Since she didn't see a scraggly mop of hair, a cloud of Cheetos dust, or any sign of cargo shorts, she relaxed. Maybe the empty chairs at the table were for another couple.

Cheryl rearranged a hairpin at the back of her head. The knot fell apart, and she had to twist it back up. "Oh, he'll be here. Ben never turns down the chance for free food."

Marlo faked a smile. "Great," she said.

"Grace couldn't come, because she had a work function," said Cheryl, referring to her daughter.

"What is Ben up to these days?" Laura asked. "Does he still write for the *Seattle Times*?"

"Yup." Nick nodded, a proud smile on his face. Then he looked down at his place setting and fiddled with the napkin ring like he was uncertain what to do with it.

"I've been a fan of Ben's writing ever since he sent that editorial to the *Harper Landing Beacon* when the kids were in middle school," said Laura. "What was it about again?"

"PE credit and why athletes and dancers shouldn't get waivers," said Marlo. "He said the policy was elitist." Her cheeks turned pink as she relived her ire. She'd danced twenty hours a week starting in seventh grade. Of course she'd deserved her PE waiver.

"I thought Ben made good points," said Laura. "Especially now that they offer yoga as a PE option at Harper Landing High."

"Ben bikes to the city each day for work," said Cheryl. "It's thirty-two miles round trip."

"Huh," Chuck grunted, rolling his eyes.

"What's that supposed to mean?" Cheryl asked as she picked up her water glass.

"Nothing." Chuck rubbed the back of his neck. "It's just that I remember coaching Ben in coed soccer back when the kids were little."

"And?" Cheryl raised her eyebrows.

"And nothing," said Laura before Chuck could respond.

Marlo didn't know what her father had been planning to say, but she knew it wouldn't have been positive. Marlo couldn't recall much from her first-grade soccer team, the Angry Hornets, but she did remember Ben turning somersaults when he was supposed to be playing goalie. Chuck was competitive, and it was hard to win when players did gymnastics instead of passing the ball.

"How'd your boyfriend like that camping stove you were carrying the last time I saw you?" Nick asked, mercifully changing the subject.

Marlo felt her stomach drop. "No. I mean, I don't know. I haven't given it to him yet."

"Because she dumped him," Laura blurted out. "Last night after she caught him cheating."

"Cheating?" asked a mellow voice. "That's sordid talk for a wedding."

"My life's not sordid," Marlo said between clenched teeth. There, standing before her, was Ben, wearing slim-fit chinos and a wrinkled button-down shirt. His hair was slicked to the side with gel, like he was stuck in a 1980s movie starring Tom Cruise, and his dark-brown eyes glinted mischievously. Marlo focused on the hair gel because that made it easier to ignore how hunky Ben had become. It wasn't right that he had a razor-sharp jawline and dimples when he smiled. The incongruity made no sense, just like how Ben had developed such broad shoulders without belonging to the gym. Maybe it was all that biking.

"Of course it isn't." Ben smirked and sat down next to his mother. "Good to see you, too, Jonas." Marlo had told him a million times to stop referring to her by her last name, but he never listened.

While Marlo had been dancing at the University of Washington, Ben had been up in Bellingham at Western Washington University studying journalism. He'd always been a newspaper nerd, working on the middle school paper and then editing the Harper Landing High paper and yearbook. Marlo couldn't prove it, but she suspected Ben was behind the Harper Landing Police Scanner Twitter feed, too, which was a fake account that tweeted inane jokes about Harper Landing. "The victim was attacked by a posse of raccoons wearing leather jackets and brass knuckles," a recent tweet warned. Another said, "Medical response. Older gentleman slipped on a banana peel. Sweet Bliss patrons are advised to stop ordering banana splits."

"No plus-one?" Marlo asked meanly. As soon as the words came out of her mouth, she regretted them. Especially since Ryan's seat sat empty beside her.

"My plus-one had other plans tonight." Ben unfurled his napkin and set it on his lap.

"Oh," said Marlo. It was hard for her to picture Ben with a girl-friend. He'd been such a goofball in high school that nobody had wanted to date him. At least, none of Marlo's friends. He had ended up going to prom, though. Marlo thought hard, trying to picture the transfer student from Florida who'd worn her bushy hair in two pigtails with ribbons even though she was eighteen years old.

"Katelyn says hi, by the way." Ben took a piece of bread from the communal basket and slathered on a pat of butter.

"Katelyn with the pigtails?" Marlo asked. "You're still together?"

"And she *still* wears pigtails," Cheryl said in a pained voice.

"I like them," said Ben. "Kate wouldn't be the same without them."

"Sweet," Marlo said a little too brightly.

"I remember when you used to wear pigtails." Laura reached out and twirled a strand of Marlo's brunette tresses around her finger. "You were so cute."

"On a little girl, they're cute," Cheryl muttered. "On a grown woman, they're ridiculous."

"Mom," Ben said. "Don't start."

"She should at least take them out for job interviews so she can stop working at that coffee stand." Cheryl ripped off a piece of bread. "Or is she no longer looking?"

"Can we not talk about this?" Ben took a sip of water and stared so longingly at the empty wineglass that Marlo almost felt sorry for him. She scanned the room and flagged down one of the waiters pouring drinks.

Nick coughed, and at first, Marlo assumed something was caught in his throat, but then she realized he was trying to say something. He spoke so quietly that it was hard to hear him above the wedding-reception noise. "My understanding is that you and Katelyn are only roommates and nothing more," he said before staring at his plate again.

Ben's ears turned red. "That's right," he mumbled. "A plus-one can be a friend."

Marlo raised her eyebrows. Was Ben ashamed of being single? Marlo would rather be free than chained to a scumbag like Ryan.

"Ben shares a house with three other people," said Cheryl, speaking to Chuck and Laura. "Can you imagine? It's practically a commune."

"I lived in a commune near Portland once." Laura smiled dreamily. "It was lovely. My job was to milk the goats each morning so they'd be ready for yoga."

"Please stop telling people that." Chuck grimaced and looked behind him, like he was worried that someone he knew might have overheard his wife reminisce about her youthful adventures in Oregon.

"Would that be goat yoga?" Ben asked, helping himself to a second piece of bread.

"Why yes." Laura nodded, and her crystal earrings jangled. "Every morning the whole farm would do sun salutations in the pasture with the goats to guide us."

"The place reeked of manure." Chuck held up his empty wineglass and snapped his fingers, trying to catch the attention of the wine steward, who still hadn't visited their table.

Marlo wilted with embarrassment. Why did Ben have to ask her mom about the commune? He'd been nosy like that ever since she could remember, like that time in eighth grade when he'd asked their algebra teacher if his wife cut his hair. But before Marlo could change the conversation, Ben started pressing Laura for more details.

"What was the commune's founding philosophy?" Ben asked. "How long did you live there?"

"It was a bunch of vegan hippies." Chuck slapped his palm on the table, and the china rattled. "And they all smelled like goats."

"That's not true." Laura squared her shoulders. "We bathed twice a week in the creek."

"With the goats," said Chuck, wrinkling his nose. "The whole place was falling apart because everyone was too busy petting goats to bother with cleaning out the rain gutters or replacing broken shingles."

"Waiter!" Marlo sprang to her feet and waved at a woman wearing a white shirt and black tie and holding a bottle of wine in each hand. "We haven't been served yet." She hated to sound desperate, especially since she wasn't much of a drinker, but she wanted to stop the argument brewing between her parents. Marlo hated scenes, and being the daughter of Chuck and Laura meant living through them nearly every day.

"So," said Ben, once the waiter had begun circling the table and doling out merlot, "your plus-one was a cheater, huh?"

"Me?" Marlo asked, which she realized was silly since she was the only other single person at the table. "Um . . . yeah. I caught him red handed."

"Good riddance, if you ask me," said Laura. "I never liked Ryan."

"I thought he was great," declared Chuck. "A real man's man. Drove a truck. Bench-pressed one eighty. Ordered his steak rare. Are you sure there's not a rational explanation for what you saw?"

"For Ryan kissing another woman?" Marlo's eyebrows shot up. "No, there's not."

"Maybe she had an eyelash in her eye and he was helping her?" Chuck stuck his nose into the wineglass and sniffed before sipping it.

"I always use my mouth when I assist other people with their vision problems," said Ben with a straight face.

Marlo smiled in spite of herself.

"Benjamin," Cheryl said in a warning tone.

"The thing that made Ryan so perfect for you," Chuck continued, completely ignoring Ben's snarky remark, "was that you two had equal value on the attractiveness scale."

"Huh?" Marlo asked. Her father had said a lot of odd things before, but she'd never heard this particular opinion come out of his mouth.

Chuck swung his arm around Laura's shoulder and squeezed her. "It's like your mother and me. We've been married for thirty-two years, and one of the reasons we've stayed together this long is that we both lucked out in the looks department."

Laura nodded in agreement. "The first time I saw him ride up to the commune on his Harley to buy milk, I knew he was mine." She gazed up at Chuck adoringly and snuggled closer, kissing him right below his left earlobe.

Marlo squeezed her eyes shut and wished she could make her parents disappear. The only thing worse than her parents making a scene by arguing were their public displays of affection that nobody wanted to see. "I don't need my boyfriend to be the 'same level of attractiveness' as me," said Marlo, using her fingers to make air quotes. "But unfaithfulness is a deal breaker."

Laura reached out and patted Marlo's hand. "Honey, I love you, but you're full of it. You've never dated someone uglier than you."

"Whoa." Marlo pulled her hand away. "First of all, calling someone *ugly* is body-shaming, which I am totally against, and two—" She paused, uncertain of how to continue. As she thought of her long line of boyfriends going all the way back to Tommy Ballinger in the eighth grade, she couldn't think of one guy she'd describe as *ugly*.

"If I'm remembering correctly"—Ben smirked—"you and Tommy Ballinger were voted Harper Landing Middle School's cutest couple in the school newspaper."

"There's nothing wrong with dating someone who looks presentable," said Cheryl. She leaned back in her chair as the waiter placed a dinner salad on her plate. "You ought to try it sometime."

"What's that supposed to mean?" Ben asked as he dumped ranch dressing onto his lettuce.

"You always date beneath you." Cheryl shook her head. "It's like you purposely pick the most wack-a-doodle woman you can find. All of your past girlfriends have shared personal vendettas against clean laundry and personal grooming."

"That's unfair," Ben growled. "I look for beauty on the inside, not the outside. Superficial appearances don't matter to me."

Nick chuckled and scratched his beard but didn't say anything.

"Maybe that's why you're still single," said Laura as she picked deli meat off her salad. "You're not dating pretty girls."

"Exactly." Cheryl speared a cucumber with her fork. "Stop settling for the low-hanging fruit."

"You know how I feel about clichés," Ben muttered. "They're lazy."

Cheryl swatted him on the shoulder. "So are most of your old girlfriends. Everyone but the knitting maniac. What was her name, again?"

"Yarn bomber," Ben corrected. "Savannah is a yarn bomber."

"Yarn bomber?" Chuck asked. "Should I know what that is?"

"Someone who knits around tree trunks and lampposts in the middle of the night," Marlo explained.

"That's dumb," said Chuck with a laugh. "Who would do that?"

"Ben's incredibly industrious but homely ex-girlfriend—that's who," said Cheryl.

"Ma!" Ben's eyebrows furrowed together.

Marlo hated hearing women called *homely*. It brought back memories of dance auditions at the University of Washington where she had been judged on looks as well as talent. Marlo knew genetics gave her an advantage, and she felt guilty about it.

"You all are full of it," Marlo declared. "Ben and I are from a new generation, and personal appearances don't matter as much to us. We define beauty differently than you do, and we don't subscribe to body-shaming."

"That's right," said Ben, nodding in agreement. "Looks don't matter to us."

"Prove it, Marlo." Chuck adjusted a monogrammed cuff link.

"How?" she asked.

"From now until New Year's, don't date anyone you'd normally find attractive," said Chuck. "Then come back here, to the yacht club's New Year's Gala, and tell me I'm wrong about appearances mattering. Prove that to me, and you can start up those small-group fitness classes you've been wanting at the gym."

"Great," said Marlo. "It's about time the Cascade Athletic Club modernized. This bet should be easy. I want a boyfriend with a good heart, and it doesn't matter what he looks like."

Laura giggled. "Sweetie pie, I love you, but that's not true."

"And you should choose women who are worthy of you." Cheryl pointed her finger at Ben. "Go for the hot ones."

Ben choked on the water he was drinking and spent the next minute coughing. "Hot ones?" he asked when he could finally breathe again.

"Smart, pretty, successful—you know what I mean," said Cheryl. "Stop dating losers."

"I don't date losers," Ben protested.

"Your last girlfriend made balloon animals for a living." Cheryl twirled her fork in the air for emphasis. "She didn't have a bank account."

"Goldie believed in a cash economy," said Ben, crumpling his napkin. "It was her protest against the capitalistic society we live in that enslaves people to credit."

"Your ex-girlfriend was named Goldie?" Marlo asked. She wasn't one to make fun of weird names, but she'd never met a Goldie before.

"Goldie." Chuck laughed. "That's a good one."

"No," said Cheryl. "It's worse than that. Her name was Goldie Locke."

"It was a stage name," said Ben, staring down at his empty plate.

"It was ridiculous—that's what it was." Cheryl crossed her arms. "You can do better."

"And you could do worse," said Laura in her serene voice. "Don't stop dating handsome men, Marlo. You'll never be happy with someone homely."

"I would never describe a fellow human being as *homely*." Marlo lifted her chin. "But I told you, looks don't matter to me as much as character does. So yes, Dad, I'll take you up on your challenge. From now until New Year's I won't date anyone who's conventionally attractive."

"And you?" Cheryl asked, staring at her son.

Ben shrugged. "I don't let my mom tell me who to date."

"Listen to your mother," said Nick in a soft voice. "It takes courage to ask a woman out who's way out of your league, but it's worth it." He picked up Cheryl's hand and squeezed it.

"Again with the clichés." Ben shook his head. "What is it with you two?"

"Champagne, anyone?" The waiter with the silver platter was back, only this time she carried a dozen flutes of bubbly.

"Sure," said Chuck as he took a glass for himself and Laura. "But we haven't been served our entrée yet."

"I'm sorry," said the waiter as she steadied the tray. "There's a backup in the kitchen."

"No need to apologize when there's free alcohol," said Cheryl, helping herself to a glass.

Marlo stared into the effervescent liquid and felt the turmoil of emotions inside her popping up one by one. Life disappointed her. First ballet, then Ryan; if she didn't make a change soon, she'd be stuck teaching spin classes forever and coming home to an empty apartment. She'd worked hard all her life, and yet she was miserable. Marlo was twenty-four years old, and the most exciting thing she had to look forward to each day was feeding her pet betta, Misty. But she knew, deep in her soul, that she didn't want what her parents had. No way did she wish to spend her life constantly fighting with the person who was supposed to be her soul mate. Plus, her parents were wrong. The world had changed. Yes, she needed a partner who was her equal, but not in appearance.

Marlo took a deep breath and lifted her glass. "I'd like to propose a toast," she said in a clear voice. "Here's to looking past the obvious."

"And?" Cheryl looked meaningfully at her son.

Ben sighed and lifted his champagne glass too. "And here's to dating women who spend three hundred dollars at the salon but who won't spend one buck to buy a newspaper."

Marlo raised her eyebrows in surprise. "You're really doing this?" she asked. "I didn't think you had it in you."

Ben grimaced. "Only until New Year's." He gestured to his parents with his thumb. "And to show them that traditional definitions of beauty and success are meaningless."

"Well, I'm doing this to prove a point too." Marlo nodded. "And to get my way at work." She reached across the table to touch her glass to Ben's. "Here's to being right."

"I'll drink to that," he replied. They clinked their glasses together so hard that some of the champagne sloshed onto the tablecloth. Ben laughed, and Marlo decided she wasn't charmed by his dimples at all.

CHAPTER TWO

Ben guzzled coffee and stared at his computer screen. It was Sunday afternoon, and he was at work, monitoring the comments on an article he'd written about bike lanes. Ben was responsible for covering the news in Harper Landing and the surrounding communities north of Seattle, and the Facebook comments about his articles were often heated.

The dialogue about Ben's most recent article didn't disappoint. As an avid bicyclist himself, he fully supported expanding bike lanes. It took him an hour and a half to bike in to work each day, and the transition from the Interurban Trail to city streets was the most dangerous place along his commute. Ben wore a bright-orange safety vest with embedded flashing lights in addition to his helmet, but he'd endured several near misses, and none of them had been his fault. Usually, it was parents in SUVs distracted by their kids complaining in the back seat or businesspeople opening their car doors without looking behind them. Still, as dangerous as his commute was, biking to work was better than being stuck in traffic for an hour, praying that his ancient Kia would hold together.

Most of the Facebook commenters were in support of increased safety. Many were also concerned by the financials of making that happen. But there were also trolls, whose expletive-laced comments cited government conspiracies and flat-earth logic to argue that any change to the status quo would destroy the world. Those were Ben's favorite commenters to follow because they were so stupid, and he often used them as inspiration for his faux Twitter account, @HarpLanPDScan. Some of his best tweets came from when he selected a troll comment from the newspaper's Facebook page, mixed in a few woodland creatures, and added the Harper Landing hashtag.

"Here we go." Ben zeroed in on a particularly nasty comment about unsheltered people. "What a jerk." He pulled out his phone and logged into Twitter. "Bike lane obstructed by squirrels. Caller reports that squirrels are ruining #HarperLanding." He followed it up with an adorable GIF of squirrels eating nuts. Ben knew that most of his followers saw his Twitter feed as a joke, but really he used it to express his outrage against all the harmful online comments he processed at work. As an unbiased reporter committed to neutrality, Ben couldn't unleash his personal opinions in print, but he could express them as satire through his anonymous Twitter feed.

A few minutes later another troll posted something hurtful about cyclists, and Ben whipped out his phone again. "Possum blames goldendoodle for confrontation in Brackett Woods. Goldendoodle bow-wow-vows revenge. #HarperLanding." He was pleased to see that his first tweet had already received two likes but annoyed that one of them was from Goldie. Ben hovered his thumb over the block button but didn't have the guts to go through with it. Despite his passionate defense of his balloon-animal-creating ex-girlfriend last night, Goldie was unpredictable, and he wouldn't give her any reason to come at him with a balloon sword. He never should have told her about his Twitter account. It was fine that Savannah and Katelyn knew about it. They were two of his most frequent retweeters, but not in an obsessed-stalker kind of way like Goldie was. Ben didn't believe in ending relationships on bad terms. But maintaining a friendship with his exes had become complicated.

"Hey, Ben, I'm assigned to review a new Greek restaurant in Ballard— want to come with me?" A short woman with frizzy blonde hair stood in front of Ben, jingling her car keys. Her baggy jeans ended midcalf and showed off the wool socks she wore with her sandals. "I can give you a ride home afterward so you don't have to bike home in the rain."

"Hi, Savannah." Ben turned his phone over and reached for his mouse, opening multiple tabs on his computer screen so he could look busier than he actually was. As much as he'd have liked to avoid a soggy ride home in the dark, he did not, under any circumstances, want to go to a restaurant with Savannah ever again, even if the newspaper paid for their dinner. It wasn't worth the yarn drama. "I wish I could, but I have loads to do."

"No you don't." She pointed to her watch. "It's time to clock out. You know what management said about not working overtime. There's no budget for it."

Ben clenched his jaw. "Right," he muttered.

"Don't worry," Savannah said, throwing her arm around his shoulders. Her sweatshirt reeked of body odor. "We're just going as friends. I've got a new boyfriend, remember?"

Ben wished he could close his nostrils. Maybe he could give Savannah some more deodorant soap this Christmas. "Um . . . ," he began, stalling for time. "The thing is . . ."

"I could use your help." Savannah squeezed Ben's shoulder and then picked up his wallet and phone, which were next to his keyboard. "I've got an idea for my next yarn installation that I need your opinion on." She tossed him his bike vest and shoved his helmet into his arms. "Come on. Let's go. Our reservation is in half an hour."

Ben sighed, already defeated. He told himself that the free meal and ride home in the rain would be worth it, but the truth was, he couldn't hurt Savannah's feelings by saying he didn't want to go. Savannah had been kind to him since the first moment they'd met, when she'd been assigned as his mentor during the new-employee orientation three years ago. If it weren't for her, he'd still be a cub reporter, fighting for assignments instead of covering his hometown. Ben was a lot of things, but disloyal wasn't one of them.

"Great." Ben reached underneath his desk and picked up his bike shoes. "I love falafel." He followed Savannah out the building and briefly parted ways with her as she went to get her car while he retrieved his bike from where it was triple locked on Denny Way. When he saw Savannah's Toyota Corolla pull up to the curb, with the bike rack attached to the back, he knew he'd made the right decision to dine with her tonight. That bike rack was just for him. She'd found it via the classifieds when they'd first started dating a year and a half ago and kept it installed even after they'd broken up five months later, committed to remaining friends. Ben hooked his bike to the back of the Toyota and climbed into the passenger seat.

The interior of the sedan smelled like wet wool. Or maybe it was acrylic; Ben wasn't sure. He always got his yarns mixed up, despite Savannah's incessant explanations of the fiber arts. The back of the car was packed with brightly colored scarves that Ben knew she used to wrap up tree trunks and stitch together on the spot. A plastic container on the seat held knitting needles and crochet hooks and a pile of knitted circles with ribbons sticking out.

"Are those faces?" Ben asked, doing a double take.

"Yes! They *are* faces. That's the new installation I wanted to tell you about." Savannah pulled into traffic so quickly that Ben's seat belt bit into his shoulder. "I'm bombing Mill Creek with yarn faces next weekend to protest their cuts to the community art center. What do you think? Will you write about it for the paper?"

Ben rubbed the back of his neck. "Savannah, you know what my editor told me about yarn-bombing articles."

Savannah rapidly changed lanes without using her blinker. "I know, but it's been at least three months since you submitted the last one. Maybe he's changed his mind?"

"I've already written four articles about your yarn-bombing exploits, and two of them have been printed. I agree with my editor. One yarn-bombing story a year is all our readers can handle. But I'd be happy to tweet a picture for you under my main Twitter account."

Savannah sighed. "That's nice of you to offer, but your Twitter only has three hundred followers."

"That's three hundred and four followers. And it takes a while for reporters to build up a Twitter presence."

"And another story about yarn bombing might be just what you need to take your account to the next level."

Ben picked at the cleats on his bike shoes. "Half of my followers are knitters. That's probably why the growth algorithm is stacked against me. I need Seattleites and people in Snohomish County following my account, not yarn addicts."

"There's nothing wrong with being a yarn addict." Savannah slammed on the brakes too hard at an intersection, and the car lurched. "Xander weaves blankets from his sheep's wool."

"And I'm really happy for you. That's great that your new boyfriend raises sheep."

Savannah smiled and giggled girlishly. "It is, isn't it?" She looked at him sideways and bit her lip guiltily. "I mean, not to discount what you and I had, which was great at the time, but—"

"It's so much better to be with someone who shares your interests."

"Exactly. Xander's opened my eyes up to the world of sheep farming too. I mean, I know he's a hobby farmer and not making a living on his property in Snohomish, but his herd is big enough to keep me knitting all year."

"That sounds like a situation to dye for."

"That better not have been a pun, Mister." Savannah poked him in the shoulder. "You know puns are my pet peeve."

Ben winced. "And you know how I feel about clichés. How's your grandpa doing?" he asked, changing the subject. Savannah's grandfather was dying of colon cancer.

"Not well." Savannah pressed her lips together in a firm line. "His colostomy bag keeps getting infected, and my grandma has to take care of it." She shuddered and shook her head like she could shake off sadness. "Anyhow, back to the plans for my next yarn installation." Savannah launched into an hour-long explanation that continued right up until they were eating dinner at the restaurant. She didn't bother asking Ben anything about himself until later that evening when they were finishing the last bites of their meals. "So," she said, picking apart her dolma. "What's new with you? Did you do anything fun this weekend?"

"Besides learning about your plans for yarn domination?" Ben dipped pita into tzatziki sauce. "I went to a wedding last night and got stuck at a table with my high school nemesis."

"Ooh!" Savannah leaned forward. "Do tell."

"It started in kindergarten." Ben wiped his sticky fingers on a napkin. "I was in the lowest reading group, the Sleepy Sloths, and Marlo was in the Leaping Lemurs." He shuddered, remembering the humiliation.

"What were the Leaping Lemurs?"

"The highest reading group," said Ben. "The teacher didn't say it, but everyone knew. I had other friends in Leaping Lemurs, and it wasn't a big deal; we still played together. But Marlo lorded it over me. She sat next to me in our table group of six kids. We were the Antarctica table."

"Who named these things? Psychopaths?" Savannah asked.

"Our teacher, Ms. Hanline," said Ben. "Anyhow, Ms. Hanline wouldn't let our table group go out to recess each morning unless all six of us had our work completed. For the other kids at the table, it usually wasn't a big deal." Ben took a deep breath to steady himself before continuing, "But for me . . ." He couldn't believe that nineteen years later, this still hurt so much to talk about. Dyslexia wasn't something he was ashamed of, but it was a part of himself that he held close. "I wasn't reading yet," Ben explained, unable to share his secret. Technically, workplace discrimination was illegal, but that didn't mean he wouldn't be discriminated against because of his learning disability, especially in an industry that revolved around words. He needed to protect himself.

When Ben was a kindergartener, he would stare at the Sunday comics in the newspaper, laboriously sounding out words and trying to figure out the pictures. The alphabet was a code he had been determined to crack, especially since his sister, Grace, had made fun of him for not knowing how to read yet. Ben knew that words had power, and he was eager to harness them. But it wasn't until fifth grade that his dyslexia was finally diagnosed, and it took another two years of after-school tutoring for him to catch up to grade level.

By sixth grade, when he was eleven years old, Ben challenged himself to read the front page of the Sunday paper each week, mainly to prove to Grace how smart he was. They spent every Sunday in the back room of the Nuthatch Bakery, listening to the timers and taking trays out of the oven. Grace worked on homework—she was five years older than him and always busy. Ben gobbled up cinnamon rolls and carefully decoded words one by one, starting with the headline and reading all the way down to the fold. Grace insisted that he couldn't possibly understand what he was reading, and sometimes she was right, but Ben never admitted it. Instead, as soon as they got home, he'd go to his room and listen to the news on the radio. Hearing the top stories described aloud filled in the comprehension details he'd missed while reading them.

By middle school, reading had become easy for Ben, although he'd never be fast. Handwriting was a problem, too, because of his dysgraphia, but that was what computers were for. On Sundays in middle school, he'd read the editorial section—not in the *Seattle Times*, but in the *Harper Landing Beacon*, which published a long list of letters to the editor each week. It was there that Ben first saw his name in print, one Sunday morning while eating muffins at the café. "PE Waiver Program

Elitist and Unnecessary, by Benjamin Wexler-Lowrey." Seeing his name in print was a high he chased throughout the rest of high school. It propelled him into a journalism major at Western Washington University, even though his parents worried whether he'd be able to earn enough money to support himself. Ben had added a minor in business management to make them happy and had written one thousand words a day for the *Western Front*, the school's newspaper.

Now, at twenty-four years old, reporting for the *Seattle Times* was his proudest accomplishment, even though it garnered a meager paycheck. Over the past decade, the newspaper had suffered deep cuts, including layoffs and positions that were left unfilled. The future was uncertain, but Ben loved reporting on Harper Landing and Snohomish County.

Savannah wiped gyro juice off her fingertips with a napkin. "So if you weren't reading well in kindergarten, it must have been hard for you to get your work done, huh?"

"Yes." Ben nodded. "And since Marlo sat right next to me, she'd lean over my shoulder and rush me. Sometimes she'd even write on my paper for me, and Ms. Hanline would accuse me of cheating. The situation was horrible."

"Marlo sounds like a know-it-all."

"Yes." Ben crumpled up his napkin and left it next to his fork. "She is. In eighth grade, the school paper assigned me to interview her about dancing in a local production of *The Nutcracker*, and she refused to answer questions about it, like she was too important to be bothered by something so trivial." He shook his head, remembering the sting. "Her dad is even worse. A total blowhard who owns the Cascade Athletic Club. You couldn't pay me to step foot into that place. It's a bunch of rich snobs."

"Sounds like a place that should be yarn bombed," said Savannah, with an evil glint in her eyes.

Ben laughed. "I know a Twitter account that would tweet some pictures about that."

Forty-five minutes later Savannah dropped Ben off at the house he shared in Harper Landing with three roommates. It was a brick home built in the 1930s, complete with a decommissioned oil tank buried in the backyard. The roof sagged, and one of the gutters had fallen completely off, but the price was right. Ben's rent was $900 a month, which was all he could afford on his meager salary. Ben manually opened the garage door to the one-car spot and parked his bike between Simon's pottery wheel and Katelyn's stand-up paddleboard. After making sure the garage door was securely locked, he headed inside.

Mike Lu, Ben's best friend since day care, stood at the kitchen counter, wiping up a mess from the rice cooker. Mike worked at Paige's Pages, his mother's bookshop on Main Street, and at Wanderer's Home, his dad's backpacking store, but his dream was to become a professional musician. His band played gigs on the side. "You hungry?" Mike asked as he put down the dishcloth. "My dad sent me home with some smoked halibut, and I made rice to go with it."

"Nah, thanks anyway." Ben walked through the kitchen holding his load of biking gear. "Savannah took me out to dinner in Ballard."

Mike glared at him. "You're kidding me, right? I thought you two were over a long time ago."

"We are." Ben dumped his stuff onto a kitchen chair. "We didn't go *out*, out. She had a restaurant review to write for the paper."

"Oh." Mike scooped dinner onto his plate. "Well, that's a relief." He sat down next to the chair where Ben's things were. "Between her, balloon girl, and . . ." Mike paused. "Other people we won't mention, you don't have the best track record with women."

"Don't you start too. I already got lectured by my mom last night."

Mike chuckled. "You should have been at *my* table." He leaned back in his chair with a self-satisfied smile. "It was filled with bridesmaids."

Ben slumped down in a chair and folded his arms across his chest. "You had it worlds better. I was stuck with Marlo Jonas all night."

"Marlo Jonas!" shrieked a high-pitched voice. "I thought we vowed never to utter that name in this house." Katelyn stomped into the room with her customary clogs. Her pigtails were wound up into buns. Since she was a barista at a drive-through espresso stand, her hoodie and leggings reeked of coffee beans. "There'd better be a good explanation for this outrage." Katelyn shoved Ben's biking gear off its chair and onto the floor and sat.

Ben reached down to retrieve his helmet and inspected it for damage. "Easy with my biking gear, Kate. This equipment saves my life."

"Sorry," she said, with a shrug. "But you know how Marlo pushes my buttons. I'll never forgive her for what she wrote in my senior yearbook."

"All she said was *nice hair*." Mike shoved chopsticks into his mouth and kept talking with his mouth full of food. "That hardly warrants a personal vendetta."

Katelyn's eyes narrowed into tiny slits. "For a smart guy, you're pretty stupid. Marlo was making fun of my signature look."

As much as he loved to hear Katelyn rant against Marlo, the combination of smoked halibut, ground espresso beans, and the tzatziki sauce he'd spilled on his pants was making him queasy. Ben collected his shoes, vest, and helmet and stood. "It's been a long day," he said. "I think I'll go shower and read."

"G'night," Mike said, popping another bite of halibut into his mouth.

Ben walked down the stairs into the musty daylight basement, where his bedroom was. Three of the basement walls were built into the hillside, but the fourth had a row of windows that faced outside. The bonus room was in the darkest part of the downstairs and set up with Mike's and Simon's band equipment. Simon was their landlord and fourth housemate. He was an engineer at Boeing who liked to prove how cool he was by playing bass and dating as many women as he could find on Good Catch, the new dating app that was increasing in popularity. Created by an ex–Microsoft employee, the program matched people based on a scientific algorithm that calculated compatibility on key data points from the application questionnaire. Ben didn't like the sound of Good Catch, because it reminded him of baseball, and he'd always been horrible at organized sports. Plus, he preferred to meet people organically at school and work. That was how he'd met his previous girlfriends. Although admittedly, a prescreening questionnaire might have saved him some trouble where Goldie was concerned. Maybe it was time to give Good Catch a try?

Ben entered his bedroom and shut the door behind him. He closed the flannel drapes against the night sky and twisted the knob of the electric Cadet heater on the wall. The daylight basement kept his room cool in the summer and freezing cold the rest of the year. The heater worked fast, quickly bringing the damp space up to a cozy temperature. Ben lay down on his bed and pulled out his phone. Since he'd never used Good Catch before, he had to download it first.

Five minutes later, Ben struggled to select his profile picture. There was his headshot for the *Seattle Times*, but he didn't own the photo rights to it, and as a journalist, Ben was sensitive about copyright violations. Most of the pictures on his phone showed baked goods at the Nuthatch Bakery that he used to help support the café's Instagram and Facebook accounts. His dad was too busy baking to bother with things like online marketing, and his mom insisted Facebook was too political, but Ben recognized the importance of the café having a quality presence on social media, so he posted on their behalf.

As for pictures of people, Ben's phone had pics of Simon at his pottery show, Katelyn paddleboarding on Puget Sound, and Mike playing the guitar last summer at the Harper Landing Fourth of July celebration. He also had pictures of Grace and their parents at her University of Washington graduation ceremony when she'd received her PhD in chemistry. But the only pictures of Ben were selfies on his bike, and it was hard to tell what he looked like wearing a helmet and sunglasses.

Help, he texted Katelyn, instead of bothering to walk upstairs to her room. Do you have a good picture of me on your phone?

Sure, she replied immediately. Lots. What do you need it for?

Ben hadn't officially signed up for the dating app yet, and he already felt ridiculous. Good Catch, he replied. Simon finally talked me into it.

That's awesome! Katelyn added a smiley face emoji. Then she deluged his phone with half a dozen pictures. I like this one the best, she added, sending a profile of him standing in front of Mount Rainier. He wore his black raincoat, and his dark-brown hair was swept casually to the side. It was from a hike they had gone on this summer for Mike's birthday.

Thx, Ben responded. I appreciate it.

Now there was no excuse not to go through with it. The photos Katelyn had sent were all profile-picture worthy, but she'd been right—the raincoat one was best. Ben liked that it showed him smiling. He uploaded it to Good Catch and worked on the next step, which was to write a six-word description of himself. *That's easy,* Ben thought and quickly typed, "Broke journalist who can't say no." Then he remembered that the point of this experiment was to try to date women who were, as his dad had put it, "out of his league." Ben scrunched up his face and deleted his first answer, determined to try again. "Industrious journalist seeks smart, talented woman," Ben wrote. He clicked the link to save his answer and moved on to the next screen.

Now the app wanted him to check all the boxes that described him. Ben glanced over the attribute list and felt his confidence deflate. He wasn't *athletic, financially comfortable, well traveled,* or *outdoorsy.* He was five feet eleven, so he couldn't tick the box for *taller than six feet.* Ben couldn't prepare anything beyond baked goods, so he didn't select *good in the kitchen.* He did mark *likes kids* and *enjoys reading,* though. Plus, he added *environmentally conscious* since he always recycled. It pained him to check the box for *allergic to cats*, but that was his fate. Ben clicked the button and proceeded to the next set of questions, which asked about his education level and salary. Then, with a deep breath, he typed in his credit card information and clicked enter. Ben watched as the screen went blank a few seconds before an animated fish swam onto the screen and "Come on in, the water's fine" popped up in a text bubble.

But Ben wasn't ready to dive into Good Catch just yet. He threw his phone onto his quilt and grabbed a clean pair of boxers, his pajama pants, and a robe before heading down the hallway to the shower. The Cadet heater had warmed his bedroom, but the rest of the downstairs felt ice cold. At least the shower had plenty of hot water. Ben let the steaming spray pour over him and knead away the tight muscles from sitting at his desk all day as well as from his sixteen-mile bike ride to work that morning. He thought about the story he'd been assigned to write this week, about the renovations being made to the Harper Landing Senior Center, and looked forward to writing something that would make his hometown proud. By the time he toweled off in front of the foggy mirror, Ben had almost forgotten about Good Catch. Then, like a ripple spreading across a pond, it pushed back into his memory. Curious, and in a more relaxed state of mind, Ben quickly dressed and walked back to his room.

There, in the center of his bed, his phone buzzed with notifications. When Ben picked it up to see who was contacting him, he saw the notifications were from the dating app. Six women had already "hooked" his picture—and all of them were gorgeous.

CHAPTER THREE

Marlo toweled off her sweaty forehead and waved goodbye to the students leaving her ten o'clock spin class. The room buzzed from the blades of a dozen fans circulating the air. Ribbons attached to the air-conditioning vents fluttered in the breeze, but despite the expensive cooling system, the room was humid. When Marlo taught spin class, she felt like she was trapped in a cave, accented only by fluorescent lights and the glowing monitor behind her showing everyone's heart-rate stats. "See you next time," she said, nodding to people as they left. Marlo kept a close eye on who did and did not disinfect their bikes. As soon as the last student departed, she grabbed the spray bottle and started cleaning.

Although she hadn't gone "all out" while teaching class, Marlo dripped with sweat. She felt it run down her back in rivulets and get stuck in her sports bra. Her leggings were designed with special wick-away-moisture fabric, but even they were damp. Marlo looked at the clock and calculated how much time she had to clean the bikes and change before teaching her next class. Maybe if she hurried, she could sneak in a shower.

Still, as stinky and tired as she was, Marlo was grateful to be on her feet, moving her body and working, instead of laid up in bed. Three years ago she'd been at McCaw Hall, dancing onstage with Pacific Northwest Ballet, when she'd heard a *pop*, and then the worst pain in her life had brought her crashing to the floor. All she could do was hold her knee in place and beg for help. Tears rushed down her cheeks, and the world went white. The pain from her torn ACL was so intense that it blinded her. The ligaments holding her knee bones in place had snapped.

At first, her doctors hoped that with six to twelve months of physical therapy after her surgery, she'd be able to return to the stage. She had an allograft from a deceased donor, which meant that a patellar tendon was used as a graft for new ligament to form. But unfortunately, Marlo developed an infection, and instead of her body accepting the graft, it rejected it. It took a special team of surgeons to reconstruct Marlo's knee a second time, using tissue from her other knee, and then multiple rounds of heavy antibiotics to keep her well.

Marlo's twenty-second birthday was a blur of pain medication and tears. Her contract with the Pacific Northwest Ballet Company was canceled pursuant to the injury clause, and there was no hope that ballet would ever be part of her life again, at least not as a performer. The worst part was needing to move back in with Chuck and Laura during her recovery. Her parents' endless cycle of arguments and makeups was drama she didn't need. It was the desire to move into her own apartment that propelled Marlo to physical therapy each day, even though it meant listening to her father's endless pep talks that "everything would be fine if she worked harder" as he drove her to her appointments. By the time she'd turned twenty-three, she was in her own apartment, working as a fitness instructor at the Cascade Athletic Club, and dating Ryan. Now, only two of those things were still true.

Marlo threw the towel she used to clean bikes into the laundry basket and turned off the lights in the spin studio. As she walked down the hallway into the main lobby of the club, she gazed around the room. The two-story lobby had custom murals of the Cascade Mountains, painted by a local artist, as well as clusters of sofas and coffee tables to create cozy seating areas. At eleven o'clock, the crowds were light.

Most of the guests present were sixty-five or older, using discounted SilverSneakers passes. The Cascade Athletic Club was an important local hangout for them, along with the Harper Landing Senior Center. Marlo greeted members she knew as she hurried to the smoothie bar.

"Your usual?" Dahlia asked, picking up the blender. Her dark eyelashes were exceptionally long, even though she wasn't wearing any makeup. Twenty-six years old and naturally beautiful, Dahlia made the gray leggings she wore with her apron and Cascade Athletic Club sweatshirt look like high fashion. That was partly due to her height, since she was five feet eleven, but long black braids, full lips, and high cheekbones helped too.

"Yes please," said Marlo. "A smoothie is just what I need."

"One Oscar's Delight coming up." Dahlia opened a tub of spinach and scooped out leaves with tongs. She taught arthritis water aerobics and SilverSneakers strength-training classes. Dahlia used to be a spin instructor, too, until Chuck had cut her hours. Since then, Dahlia had supplemented her income by picking up shifts behind the smoothie counter.

Marlo sat on a barstool and kneaded her quadriceps with her knuckles. "I should sneak off and take a shower, but I think I'll rest here a minute."

Dahlia looked at her with concern. "Is your knee bothering you?"

Marlo shook her head. "No, but those five thirty a.m. classes are killing me. I'm not an early bird like you."

Dahlia ripped open a bag of frozen strawberries. "I like the early-morning shift at the bar the best because that's when I get the biggest tips. All those Microsoft and Amazon people working out before they leave for Seattle." She clamped on the lid of the blender. "Hang on a sec." The whir of the Vitamix made it impossible to converse for a minute. When the smoothie was emerald green and silky smooth, Dahlia poured it into a glass and popped in a paper straw. "So it's been five days since you dumped Ryan. How are you doing?"

Marlo poked her straw up and down in her drink and sighed. "Okay, I guess. I just feel so stupid to not have recognized what a jerk he was, and I also feel like it was my fault that he cheated."

"Your fault?" Dahlia tightened her apron belt around her navy-blue sweatshirt. "Don't be ridiculous."

"Maybe if I had been more available, Ryan wouldn't have cheated on me." Marlo slid her elbow onto the counter and rested her head on her hand. "I've spoken to my dad about rebalancing the workload for the fitness instructors, but he said it's not financially possible at the moment." She sat up straight again. "But I told him it *would* be feasible if we added those small-group fitness classes I want, because they would bring in extra income."

"And?" Dahlia asked in a hopeful tone. She'd never mentioned it, but Marlo knew that the cut to her hours hurt. The smoothie shifts didn't pay as much as teaching a spin class.

"My dad and I made a bet. I have from now until New Year's Eve to find the perfect boyfriend, but he can't be someone my parents would consider to be at the same level of attractiveness as me. If I can do that—if I can find someone who's wonderful on the inside—then my dad's promised to let me launch the small-group fitness classes and reduce my spin hours."

"That's great," said Dahlia. "But who gets to judge beauty on this one? Your dad? A sixty-year-old cisgender white guy?"

Marlo wrinkled her nose. "That's a problem. Part of the reason I agreed to this was to prove to my parents that body-shaming was *not* okay. I catch them making snide comments about how people look all the time. 'His teeth are too white,' or 'Her muscles are too large.'"

"Not cool."

"I know, right? My plan is to use a dating app to select guys without looking at their pictures, but I'm not sure which app to use."

"How about Good Catch?" Dahlia suggested. "I've used it for a few months and really like it. If only Mr. Bookstore was on it." She leaned against the counter and gazed up at the mural on the wall, a faraway look in her eyes. "I keep hoping he creates an account. But in the meantime, I've been texting a really cool guy the past few days."

Marlo grinned. "I still can't believe you have a crush on Mike Lu. I've known him since preschool."

"And yet you won't set us up." Dahlia pouted.

"Yeah, because we're not friends." Marlo frowned. "He's best buds with my sworn childhood enemy. This one time, in tenth grade—"

Dahlia held her palm up. "Stop. Do not tell me about the Cheetos again. You bring it up every time I mention Mr. Bookstore."

"Okay, I won't." Marlo rolled her eyes. "But did I tell you about the fourth-grade recorder concert?"

"Oh dear." Dahlia wiped the counter with a wet cloth. "No, you didn't, but I'm not sure I—"

"During our fourth-grade recorder concert," Marlo interrupted. "I was performing a solo ballet routine that I'd spent months perfecting. Ben dropped his recorder right in the middle of 'Ode to Joy' and finished the song by burping into the microphone." She made a fist and pounded it on the countertop. "Can you believe it? The music teacher pulled Ben offstage, but it was too late. I was humiliated."

"It was fourth grade," said Dahlia. "That was a long time ago."

"It was all people talked about for the rest of the year!" Marlo exclaimed. "Sometimes kids would burp when I walked past them."

Dahlia belched and pounded her chest. "Excuse me."

"Very funny." Marlo slurped her smoothie. "But back to your love life—why don't you go into Paige's Pages and ask Mike out already?"

"I've tried." Dahlia's shoulders sagged. "But every time I go in there, he's either helping a customer or in the back room doing stock or else his mom is around. I can't ask a guy out in front of his mother."

"Write your number down on a slip of paper, and hand it to him," Marlo suggested.

"I wish I was bold like you."

"You've got to be bold to get what you want," Marlo said, repeating a sentence she'd heard her dad say a thousand times as she was growing up. She didn't like quoting Chuck, but it was true. Boldness had helped her pursue her career in ballet. Boldness had pushed her through rehabbing her injury. Boldness had prompted her to ask Ryan out when they'd first met at physical therapy over a year ago. Okay, maybe that last example wasn't a good one, she realized. "Uh-oh." Marlo looked at the time. "I'd better go. Thanks for the smoothie."

"I'll add it to your tab," Dahlia said, walking over to the cash register.

Marlo drained the last drop of her drink and rushed back to the women's locker room to change into clean clothes before her eleven-thirty barre class. A shower would have to wait, but at least she could put on fresh leggings and a clean bra and tank top. Five minutes later she felt considerably fresher and was standing in front of the mirror fixing her ponytail when Brittany Barrow walked up to the sink to wash her hands.

Brittany was one of Marlo's most devoted barre students, coming to class six days a week and sometimes more. In her late thirties with bleached-blonde hair and a perpetual tan from unknown sources, Brittany owned the advertising agency that mailed out the *Harper Landing Coupon Pack* and *Harper Landing Delights*, a faux magazine that was full of sponsored articles. She had two kids: a freshman daughter at Harper Landing High and a seventh-grade son at the local middle school.

"Hi, Brittany," said Marlo. "Fancy seeing you here."

"I'm doing a double." Brittany dried off her hands on a paper towel. "Your mom's yoga class was my warm-up."

"Good for you." Marlo smiled. "I wish all my students were that devoted. See you in a bit." She turned to walk away, and Brittany followed her out.

"Was that a Green Machine smoothie you were drinking just now, or was it an Oscar's Delight?" Brittany asked.

"An Oscar's Delight," said Marlo. "I'm not a fan of kale."

"Really?" Brittany raised her eyebrows, but her forehead didn't move. "I eat kale every day."

"That's great. It has lots of vitamins." Marlo quickened her pace. Her barre class started in ten minutes, and she liked to be there to greet students as they arrived. When they reached the studio, Laura was still there, stacking up the yoga blocks. "Hi, Mom." Marlo hurried over to help.

"Hi, sweetie," said Laura, patting Marlo on the back. "Sorry I'm still in your way."

"No problem." Marlo stacked the last block and then set up a yoga mat at the front of the studio. She turned on the overhead lights so that the room would be brighter, hooked her phone's Bluetooth to the sound system, and started her playlist.

"Can I get you anything?" Laura asked on her way out. "Do you have water?"

"Right here." Marlo lifted her bottle. "Thanks anyway." As soon as her mom left, Marlo circulated, chatting with students. She was on a first-name basis with most of them and took extra time to introduce herself to new people. When she reached Brittany, she held back, not wanting to interrupt the conversation Brittany was having with Melanie Knowles, the volunteer admin of the Harper Landing Moms Facebook group.

"We have a date this Friday," Brittany was saying. "We met on Good Catch."

"And you still haven't told him how old you are?" Melanie pulled a scrunchie off her wrist and used it to secure her curly brown hair.

"Not yet." Brittany put her ankle on the barre and stretched her hamstring. "My profile says I'm twenty-six."

Melanie snickered and then immediately stopped. "How are you going to explain your fifteen-year-old daughter to him?"

Marlo wanted to know the answer to that question, too, but she didn't mean to be nosy, so she kept moving to give the women privacy. Besides, it was time to start class. Minuet in G Major by Bach was playing, the same song that Madame Burke had always used for ballet warm-ups at the Red Slipper. Marlo strode up to the front of the studio and faced her students, standing with perfect posture. Her spine felt lifted from above. "Are you ready to move today?" A huge smile was on her face. She might have been a long way from McCaw Hall, but at least she was standing next to a barre. "Let's begin in sixth position. Feet parallel, facing the mirror, and core sucked in."

Sixty sweaty minutes later Marlo was still thinking about what Brittany and Melanie had been talking about before barre had started. First Dahlia had told her about Good Catch, and then Brittany had mentioned it. Maybe that was the dating app she should try first. Marlo hurried to the locker room, showered, and changed into her third pair of leggings for the day. Then she walked through the club to the very back, where the Pilates studio was located. The tiny room had a variety of apparatuses including a reformer, a Wunda Chair, and a Cadillac. This was where Marlo taught her private Pilates clients, but she also used it as her office. A tiny refrigerator sat next to her desk.

Marlo took out a can of sparkling water and a salad she'd made the night before. She popped open the beverage and took a few sips before looking at her phone. The first step was to download the Good Catch app. No, Marlo suddenly realized, the first step was to delete Ryan's phone number from her contact list. She should have done that Friday night, but it had been too raw. Once Ryan's number and pictures were off her phone, Marlo felt freer. The Good Catch app loaded, and Marlo clicked through one response after another without any hesitation.

Her profile was easy. Marlo used her headshot from the Cascade Athletic Club staff directory. A professional photographer had taken it, and the lighting was perfect. Her brown hair was silky smooth, and her blue eyes gazed straight into the camera. Next up was a six-word profile description. "Looking for kind, honest, interesting man," Marlo wrote. *This is simple,* she thought to herself. She was whizzing through it. When she got to the part where the questionnaire asked her to describe herself, Marlo checked off boxes quickly and without hesitation. *Dislikes sports,* she marked, but she also added *athletic, enjoys reading, likes kids, goal driven,* and *independent.* The next part of the questionnaire asked her to describe her ideal mate. *Loyal,* Marlo marked, as well as *honest, trustworthy,* and *caring.* She skipped the boxes about personal finances because those didn't matter to her. But she did click the one that said *passionate about his career.*

Filling out the Good Catch application took so much time that Marlo only had a few seconds left to enter her credit card information and hit send before her Pilates client arrived. Not until later that afternoon when her third client left was Marlo able to open up the app and check her notifications. *This is it,* she thought to herself as she walked over to the desk. She sank into her chair and stretched her bad leg out in front of her. Maybe her perfect match was waiting for her. As soon as she looked at her Good Catch dashboard, she saw dozens of men who had "hooked" her profile. But before she clicked on any of them, she wanted to test the waters herself by "casting a net." Marlo set her parameters for age, interests, character descriptions, and location—but blocked out the profile pictures—and waited. A Dungeness crab crawled across the screen while it loaded. Then the screen lit up with a list of possibilities. When Marlo saw the first name on the list, she dropped her phone.

"You've got to be kidding me," she exclaimed to the empty room. Marlo scrambled forward to retrieve her phone from where it had fallen on the floor. Luckily, the screen protector had saved it from being scratched. She looked at the list one more time and swore. Right there at the top of the list, with a golden starfish next to the name, was

Benjamin Wexler-Lowrey. "Well," Marlo mumbled, "I might as well see what he says about himself." She clicked the link and scanned Ben's description. Why did it say he couldn't cook? Ben had worked at the Nuthatch Bakery throughout high school and every summer when he'd come home from college. He was the only person Marlo knew who could make sourdough bread from scratch. And that part on his profile that said he wasn't athletic? Sure, Ben was a mess on the soccer field, but didn't his mom say he biked to work each day? Marlo shuddered while imagining how difficult it must be to bike from Harper Landing to Seattle and back. She wasn't brave enough to try it, even though she clocked thirty miles a day on the spin bike.

But no way was she pointing out Ben's attributes. The only reason she'd homed in on any of these details was to prove how inaccurate his profile was and how silly it was of Good Catch to suggest it to her. It didn't speak well of the entire program. Hopefully, the other matches weren't this bad. Still, Marlo spent more time than was necessary poking around Ben's profile. She didn't know that he enjoyed reading. He'd always been in a different English class than her in middle school and high school. Marlo had taken advanced English, and Ben had been in regular. They were both allergic to cats, but big deal. That didn't make them soul mates.

Now that Marlo had dived this deep into Ben's profile, she might as well click on his picture, she figured. A quick thumb tap later, and Marlo was staring into Ben's soulful dark eyes. His hair was longish around the ears and windblown. There was a huge smile on his face that showed off his dimples and straight jawline. In the background, Marlo saw the icy outline of Mount Rainier. It looked like he was standing in Paradise, the flowery meadows in front of the mountain that were popular with day hikers. Marlo had only been there once when her mom had brought her on a weekend yoga retreat when she was little.

Again, Marlo thought to herself, *there's proof that Ben's athletic.* He was hiking around Mount Rainier for fun. So why hadn't he marked that on his profile description? For a journalist, that was poor reporting. Marlo's index finger hovered over the "Hook" and "Release" buttons. Was there a "Block" button? She certainly didn't want Ben snooping around her profile in the same way she had explored his. Marlo hit "Release" for now and made a mental note to investigate the privacy features later.

Now feeling discouraged with the whole app in general, Marlo didn't have much hope when she returned to her net to click on suggestion number two. It was someone named Simon Vaughn, and he lived in Harper Landing. Marlo had lived in Harper Landing her entire life, except for when she had studied at the University of Washington, but that didn't mean she knew everyone who lived here. New people moved to Harper Landing all the time, especially as the increasing housing prices in Seattle kept pushing renters into the suburbs.

Marlo clicked on Simon's profile and read his six-word description. "Senior software engineer with poetic soul." *Wow,* thought Marlo. A senior software engineer. Simon had probably worked hard for that senior status, unlike Ryan, who had been at the T-Mobile store for five years and still wasn't assistant manager. Marlo stretched out her calf muscle and kept reading. Simon was a few years older than her, a homeowner, and an avid potter who specialized in mugs. He played bass in a garage band called the Monte Cristos and volunteered at the Christmas toy shop that the Harper Landing Food Bank organized for needy children.

Simon sounded great. Marlo chewed on her bottom lip nervously as she revealed his profile picture. It was almost like she could hear the sound effects of trumpets whining "*Wa, wa, waah*" in the background. The face she saw looking back at her neither attracted her nor repulsed her. Simon was balding, with orange-red hair around the sides of his perfectly round head. His cheeks bore a pinkish tone, like he sunburned easily. The most noticeable thing about him was a feathered earring, which dangled from one ear. Marlo wondered if he wore that earring in public and if he'd be open to removing it when they were seen together.

Oh no, Marlo realized. She was doing exactly what she'd told her father she never did. She was judging someone based on his appearance, and that was totally unacceptable. If Simon was happy with the way he looked, that was all that mattered. Marlo stared at the picture again and looked past the hair. The hazel eyes gazing back at her revealed a poetic soul. It was obvious to her now, and she could definitely be attracted to that. Here was a guy to hook. Marlo clicked on the button and waited.

Nothing happened. No notification. No nibble back. Nothing. Marlo sighed and leaned back in her chair. Well, that had been anti-climactic. Her eyes drifted up to the clock on the wall, and she saw that it was 4:40. It could be that Simon was still at work, she realized. After all, he was a senior engineer. Switching over to her internet browser, she googled his name and pulled up his LinkedIn profile, which said he worked for Boeing.

Okay, well, there were many fish in the sea. Marlo went back to her net and clicked on the third suggested profile, which was another name she didn't recognize but that sounded promising: Hunter Darrington. Good Catch said he lived in Port Inez, which was on the other side of Puget Sound but easily accessible thanks to the Harper Landing–Port Inez ferry. Marlo clicked on Hunter's profile without looking at his picture so she could form an objective opinion. He was twenty-nine years old and a local business owner, owning not one but three drive-through espresso stands called Hunter's Fuel. One was in Port Inez, one was in Port Orchard, and the third was in Harper Landing. Marlo was familiar with the Harper Landing location but had never visited it. Hunter said he was a "truth-seeking adventurer and dog lover." That sounded good to Marlo. After dating Ryan, honesty was paramount. She had nothing against dogs, either, having always wanted to adopt one. Marlo clicked on Hunter's picture with high hopes.

The first thing she noticed about him was his hair. There was just so much of it. Hunter's mousy-brown hair was almost as long as hers, and he parted it straight down the middle. His beard was a different color because it seemed to be graying faster than the hair growing on top of his head. But it was his handlebar mustache that really stuck out. It was three inches long on either side as if he had been preparing for Movember—the November mustache fad—all year. How much wax was on that thing?

No, no, no, Marlo told herself. Again with the body-shaming. Marlo was better than this, and she would prove that to not only herself but her father. There was nothing wrong with the way Hunter looked; he just followed a style aesthetic that was different from the men she had dated before. Plus, the way his eyebrows grew together into one furry unibrow was natural. If you thought about it, plucking stray eyebrow hairs was bizarre. All that pain for what? Meeting the style expectations of people like her father? Marlo took a closer look at Hunter's picture. Despite his masculine-sounding name, he didn't look like a "man's man." Chuck would probably hate him. Marlo clicked on the hook button and grinned.

A knock at the door interrupted her before she could explore the app further. "Come in," Marlo called, swiping out of Good Catch.

"It's me," said Dahlia. She'd changed out of her navy Cascade Athletic Club sweatshirt and now wore a fuzzy cream-colored sweater, tight jeans, and knee-high boots. "I've decided to follow your advice and be bold."

"Really?"

Dahlia nodded. "I'm going to the bookshop tonight to ask Mike out. Will you come with me?"

"Sure," said Marlo, who wasn't looking forward to going home to her empty apartment. "I'll do some Christmas shopping while we're there."

"Great." Dahlia took a deep breath and smiled. "I hope I won't regret this."

"You won't." Marlo unlocked the drawer where she kept her purse. "Ready," she said a moment later.

It was only a ten-minute walk. They used that time for Dahlia to practice what she would say to Mike. "Hi, Mike," Dahlia said in a monotone voice. "Would you like to go out this Saturday?"

"That's great," said Marlo. "Now try it again without sounding like a robot."

Dahlia took a deep breath and tried again. "Hi, Mike," she squeaked. "Would you like to go out this Saturday?"

"That's slightly better," said Marlo. They kept practicing as they walked up Main Street. The November night was chilly, and they were both glad to enter the warmth of Paige's Pages. Soft jazz music played in the background, and the heater made the whole shop cozy. A handful of customers roamed around, exploring the new releases and the used section at the back of the shop. Paige stood behind the cash register, cracking a roll of quarters against the counter to break it open and refill her till.

"He's not here," Dahlia whispered hoarsely. "What am I going to do?"

"Maybe he's working at his father's store tonight," Marlo suggested. Wanderer's Home was two doors down.

"Good thinking." Dahlia grabbed Marlo's elbow. "Let's go."

But it was too late. Paige had already seen them. "Marlo!" she called, slamming the register shut. "Good to see you."

Marlo smiled at Paige and spoke to Dahlia through clenched teeth. "You go," she said. "I'll stay here and distract his mom."

"Thanks." Dahlia squeezed Marlo's arm and took off, right as Paige was approaching them.

"How are you doing?" Paige asked. "Is there anything I can help you find?" Her eyes drifted over to the self-help section, and Marlo noticed.

"Um . . . I'm here for Christmas shopping."

"Thirty days left before Christmas," Paige said with a nod. "Who are you shopping for?"

"My friend Dahlia," Marlo said, stumbling upon the idea. "She just left. You would love her. She's smart, thoughtful, caring, and she loves to cook."

"Does she like cookbooks?" Paige tapped her chin. "There's a brand-new one from Emerald City Books that released last week. It focuses on Pacific Northwest cuisine."

"Let's see it," said Marlo as she followed Paige across the store.

By the time she exited the shop, purchases in hand, she was positive that Dahlia would have had the time to go into Wanderer's Home and ask Mike out. But what she found on the sidewalk stopped her in surprise. There, standing in front of the Nuthatch Bakery, were Dahlia and Ben, both of them with a goofy grin on their face. Correction—Dahlia's grin was goofy; Ben's smile was divine. His head was tilted to the side, and his dimples peeked out as he gave Dahlia the full force of his attention. Standing in front of his parents' café, he looked more relaxed than he had at the wedding. His hair was tousled, as if he'd taken off his bike helmet but hadn't succumbed to hat hair. Marlo tightened her grip on the paper bag holding the cookbook and willed her heart to stop pounding so hard.

"Marlo," Dahlia cried. "Look who I ran into. This great guy I've been texting the past few days on Good Catch."

Marlo felt like her feet had sunk into concrete. It took her full concentration to move them forward and walk up to Ben. "Hi," she said.

Ben's face froze when he saw her, until the smile he wore melted, like a dripping Popsicle. Marlo watched with regret as his dimples disappeared.

"Marlo," said Dahlia. "I'd like you to meet Ben. Ben, this is my friend Marlo."

"We've met," said Marlo, not stepping any closer. Why did he have to be so handsome? She'd not felt anything when she'd seen Simon's and Hunter's pictures half an hour ago, but now that she stood in front of Ben, she felt an undeniable zing of attraction. Luckily, the loathing tamped that down.

"Marlo and I go way back," Ben said in a neutral tone of voice.

"This is *Ben*," Marlo said with emphasis.

"*Ben*, Ben?" Dahlia's perfectly arched eyebrows shot up. "From the recorder concert?"

"The recorder concert?" Ben echoed. "Huh?"

"Never mind." Marlo squared her shoulders and put on her stage smile. "So you two met on Good Catch? Cool," she said in a chipper voice.

"Yeah," Ben nodded. "We did."

"So, um, hi again, Ben," said Dahlia with a glazed look in her eyes. "Would you like to go out this Saturday?"

Ben's eyes traveled from Marlo to Dahlia. "Sure," he said. "I'd love to."

"Great," said Marlo, still wearing her fake smile. "That's just great."

CHAPTER FOUR

Ben was less than a week into his dating experiment, and he already felt shallow. When Dahlia had asked him out a couple of days ago, of course he'd said yes. What else was he supposed to do? He couldn't very well say, "Sure, but are you okay with the fact that I have a date on Friday with another gorgeous woman I met on Good Catch?" That would have been awkward, especially since Marlo was watching, standing in front of the bookshop like an ice princess. Her hair was up like normal, slicked back in a ballet bun that accentuated her long neck. Marlo was the only person Ben knew who could appear graceful even when bundled up in a puffer jacket and Ugg boots. She carried herself with a regal posture like she owned the sidewalk. It was infuriating how alluring she was, but Ben prided himself on being immune to all things Marlo Jonas.

Now, for the first time in his life, Ben had two dates lined up for one weekend. It was like he was Simon, only without the BMW. Ben's ancient Kia Rio had been one of the deciding factors in his suggesting to Brittany that they meet at the restaurant instead of him picking her up. That was why he now stood in front of the Parisian Café on the corner of Main Street and Second, bracing himself against the icy wind whipping up from Puget Sound as he waited for her to arrive. He thought about stepping into the lobby to warm up but didn't want Brittany to drive by the restaurant and worry that he'd stood her up.

Ben's pulse spiked at the thought of finally meeting Brittany in person after their flirty messages via the Good Catch app this past week. He still couldn't believe that someone like her was interested in him. For one thing, there was her profile picture, which made her look like Emma Roberts. Blonde hair, brown eyes, and sun-kissed skin—plus that sultry pout. What was Brittany doing living in Harper Landing when she could be modeling in New York? The other pictures Brittany had texted him were equally jaw dropping, especially the one of her in a bikini at Lake Chelan. It was a good thing Katelyn had sent him lots of pictures of himself that he could share back. Otherwise, all he'd have had to exchange would have been bagel pics from the Nuthatch Bakery.

Ben shivered in the misty wind and rubbed his hands together to warm up. He was too cold to pull his sleeve back and look at his watch, but he guesstimated that Brittany was ten minutes late at this point. A dark thought occurred to him. Hopefully she wasn't standing him up. After all, it would make total sense if she did, especially since he'd been so brutally honest about his salary level. Brittany was only two years older than him, but she made four times as much money. Ben had googled her and verified everything she'd told him about her successful advertising business. To think, all those times he'd thrown away the *Harper Landing Coupon Pack*, labeling it as junk mail, it had been Brittany getting rich off her business savvy.

"Ben?" A silky voice from behind caught his attention. Ben turned around and saw a leggy blonde standing underneath a black umbrella. She wore a trench coat, black stockings, and razor-sharp stilettos. Ben wolf-whistled before he realized what he was doing and felt like an idiot, but the woman laughed. "I'll take that as a yes." She tiptoed up to him and kissed his cheek.

"You must be Brittany," he said in a voice that was an octave too high. Ben cleared his throat and tried again. "I mean, you must be Brittany," he said, taking her umbrella for her. "It's a pleasure to meet you."

"The pleasure is mine, I assure you." Brittany licked her thumb. "Oops," she said, wiping red lipstick off his cheek. "It looks like I got you."

Ben pushed back the hood of his raincoat and grinned. "It looks like you did. Shall we?" He opened the door of the restaurant for her and watched appreciatively as she sashayed inside.

As soon as they entered the cluttered lobby, Brittany turned up her nose. Ben was confused by Brittany's reaction, because the Parisian Café had been her suggestion. Sure, the restaurant was in the middle of remodeling work, but it was still one of the nicest places in town. "Don't worry," he said. "Lots of buildings on Main Street are being refurbished right now. But the food here should be—" Ben hesitated. He'd never been a fan of the cooking of Dave Parson, the restaurant owner and chef. The only dependable things at the Parisian Café were the baguettes, and that was because they were from the Nuthatch Bakery. "The food here should be the same as always," he said diplomatically.

"Of course." Brittany's nostrils flared as if she smelled something stinky. Her eyes were locked on the hostess, a high schooler with dyed blue hair that thinned into feathery wisps as it reached her waist.

Ben thought the girl looked familiar, but he couldn't quite place her. It wasn't until she spoke that he realized it was Lily Parson, Dave's daughter.

"Bonsoir, Madame Barrow," Lily said as she offered them two menus. "Bienvenue au Parisian Café."

"Bonsoir," Brittany said in a perfect French accent.

"Do you two know each other?" Ben asked. He wouldn't have been surprised if they did. Harper Landing was small enough that it wasn't unusual to run into people you knew.

"Oui, oui," said Lily. "I know her daughter well."

"Thank you, Lily, but we'd love to be seated now, if you have our table ready." Brittany ripped the menus out of Lily's hand and shoved one at Ben.

That was odd, thought Ben. Brittany hadn't mentioned having a daughter in her Good Catch profile. He tried to be understanding. It was probably difficult for a single mom to date when so many men would discriminate against her if she had kids. But what had Lily meant about knowing Brittany's daughter well? Ben's journalist instincts tingled. He decided to ferret out more information through normal conversation.

Lily led them to a table in the corner of the room next to the window that looked out at the ferry. Yet the dark November evening meant that there was nothing to see. Ben sat down and put the linen napkin in his lap. Too late, he wondered if he should have pulled out Brittany's chair for her. He'd never done that with his previous girlfriends, but then again, Katelyn, Savannah, and Goldie had never worn little black dresses with slits up the side. Ben's gaze drifted over Brittany's tanned shoulders and toned arms. He admired the freckles that adorned her skin like glitter. It felt strange to sit at a table with a woman who was so well put together. None of the other diners stared at them wondering why his date was knitting or twirling her pigtail or loudly arguing with the waiter about the price of soda and how ice cubes were theft. Ben opened his menu and relaxed.

"Well, that was awkward," said Brittany, not opening her menu.

"What do you mean?" Ben asked, looking at her across his menu. He was curious about how she would explain her undisclosed daughter.

"You've probably already guessed that I have a daughter." Brittany folded and then unfolded her hands. "That hostess and her big mouth."

"Oh, that." Ben closed his menu. "I said in my profile that I like kids, and I meant it." He left it at that and waited to hear what she'd say.

"I'm protective. That's all." Brittany tapped her long manicured fingernails on the tablecloth. "There are just so many jerks out there, you know? And being a single mother is hard, especially with my ex making life difficult at every turn." She reached out her hands like she was choking someone. "Anyhow, I didn't mention Porsche—that's my daughter—because do people really need to know about her unless the relationship is serious?" Brittany shook her head. "No, they don't. It's a need-to-know situation. Anyhow . . ." She flipped open the menu. "What are you going to order? The chicken cordon bleu is to die for."

"Actually, according to a rumor going around town, they serve chicken cordon bleu from Costco," said Ben. "The chef doctors it up with a cream sauce."

"No way," said Brittany. "What liar told you that? The owner is one of my clients, and Dave is a genius in the kitchen."

"My mom told me," said Ben. He was grateful that the waiter had arrived with the fresh baguettes.

"No thank you," said Brittany, waving the breadbasket away. "Too many carbs."

"Are you sure?" the waiter asked. "They're from the Nuthatch Bakery, fresh from the oven this morning."

"The Nuthatch Bakery?" Brittany shook her head. "I'm doubly sure. That place is a dump."

Ben froze, too stunned to speak. He knew those baguettes were delicious. Plus, he didn't want the waiter to go back to Dave and report that customers were complaining about the bread's quality. "Wait!" he said as the waiter started to walk away. "I'd like a baguette. They smell wonderful."

"Suit yourself," said Brittany, pushing over the container of butter. A flirty smile crossed her face. "Silly me," she simpered. "You're probably fine with carbs. Didn't you say you biked thirty miles a day?"

"Sometimes more, if you want to be technical about it." Ben ripped open a foil packet of butter and slathered it on the chewy baguette. "I bike to work at the *Seattle Times*, and I often ride to assignments as well."

Brittany leaned over the table and squeezed one of Ben's biceps. "So how did your arms get so buff?"

Lifting fifty-pound bags of flour for my parents at the Nuthatch Bakery,
Ben wanted to say but didn't. He still helped out at the bakery when
needed. "Yard work helps," he said instead. "My landlord isn't interested
in home maintenance, so I end up mowing the grass and things like
that. I repaired the deck for him last summer."

"My, my," Brittany said as her fingertips lingered on his arm.
"You're so handy."

"Not really. I can fix things—that's all. My dad's the handy one. He
built our house when I was little."

"Really?"

Ben nodded. "It has some quirks, but it's home. Or it was home for
eighteen years. I don't live there now."

"That's right." Brittany rubbed the tip of her finger around her
water glass. "You mentioned your landlord."

"So," Ben said, "tell me about your business. How did you get
started in advertising?" An hour later, Ben knew everything about the
Harper Landing Coupon Pack and *Harper Landing Delights*, including
the fact that Brittany relied on unpaid intern labor to write the articles
for her faux magazine. "You don't pay them anything?" he asked in
shock.

"Nope." Brittany shook her head. "It's brilliant. I hire journalism
students from Harper Landing Community College to be my interns,
and they do my work for college credit. It makes my clients think I have
a full staff of writers working for me, and all I have to do is fill out a
form from the community college."

"I always noticed that the writing level in *Harper Landing Delights*
was high," said Ben. "Now I know why." He frowned, but Brittany
didn't notice.

"The magazine is great because I only work with the best businesses
in Harper Landing." Brittany took a long sip of the expensive glass of
wine she'd ordered before continuing to blather on. "Sweet Bliss is a

client, of course. Julia Harper owns half of the town, and we are like this." She held up two fingers crossed together.

"Really?" Ben asked, trying to keep his tone neutral. "I must have missed you at her wedding last weekend."

Brittany's expression froze for a second before she recovered. "I was so sorry to have missed it, but I had other plans." She plunged forward, prattling on about all the important people she knew, listing them off one by one. "And one of my best clients is the Cascade Athletic Club. They take out a two-page spread in every issue of *Harper Landing Delights* but never issue a coupon in the *Harper Landing Coupon Pack*, for obvious reasons."

"Bargain hunters are too lowbrow for them?"

Brittany nodded. "Exactly. Cheapskates can go to the YMCA."

"The YMCA is pretty expensive unless you qualify for the supplemented low-income rate." Ben took the last bite of the salad he'd ordered. It was the most affordable thing on the menu, but he still wasn't full. Maybe the waiter would offer to bring him more bread.

"How would you know that?" Brittany asked. "Did you write an article about it or something?"

It was the first time that evening that Brittany had asked him anything about himself, unless the comment about his biceps counted.

"I went to the Y for day care growing up," Ben explained. It seemed like the perfect segue to ask Brittany about her daughter. "What do you do for day care for Porsche?"

"Oh . . . um . . ." Brittany picked at the expensive cut of salmon she'd ordered but hadn't finished. "It helps knowing high schoolers like Lily," she said, pointing at the lobby with her knife.

That explained how Lily knew Porsche well—from babysitting her. "High school babysitters are a great option," said Ben. "Unless it's your older sister watching you all the time."

"What's that supposed to mean?"

"My sister, Grace, loved to boss me around, that's all. Once she was old enough to take care of me, I stopped going to the YMCA for day care." That was only part of the story. After his dyslexia diagnosis in fifth grade, he'd begun private tutoring. It was so expensive that his parents had no longer been able to afford day care. But Ben wasn't about to tell Brittany that. He was done with this conversation *and* the evening. Brittany and her selfishness bored him; plus, his journalistic instincts told him she was lying. About what, he wasn't entirely sure, but something smelled off. "So I take it you don't work with the Nuthatch Bakery?" he asked, trying to fill the last few minutes of the meal with conversation before she mentioned his arm muscles again. "I've never seen a coupon from them in your pack."

Brittany folded her arms across her chest and shook her head. "No way. That bakery is a pit. Have you been in there? The whole place is shabby. And what's with the bird decor? It's tacky."

"Shabby *chic*," Ben said, unable to hold himself back. "My roommate said she thought the bird decorations were cute."

"You have a female roommate?" Brittany glared at him in dismay.

"I have three *housemates*, and one of them is a woman." Ben caught the waiter's eye, hoping he'd bring back the breadbasket. Instead, the waiter offered them the dessert menu.

"Chocolate soufflé is our specialty," he said. "But it does take an additional thirty minutes to prepare."

"No thank you," said Ben, wanting the date to be over as quickly as possible.

"I would love the soufflé," said Brittany, not bothering to look at the menu.

"In that case, I'd like another glass of water, please." Ben would have ordered coffee, but he wasn't sure he could afford it. The only good thing he had to say about dating Goldie was that she was always conscientious about the bill. Ben offered to pay for all his dates, because he was old fashioned that way, but Goldie had always insisted on going Dutch.

"So," said Brittany, leaning into the table and giving Ben a perfect view of her cleavage. "Did I tell you about my vacation to Europe this summer?"

An hour later, Ben was $200 poorer and still hungry, but at least he was walking Brittany to her car. A bitter wind blew off Puget Sound and cut through Ben's thin raincoat. He rarely wore his winter coat, because it was too hot for biking. Once they rounded the corner into the alleyway where Brittany's Porsche Boxster was parked, buildings blocked the wind, and it was warmer. "Nice car," said Ben, privately wondering if Brittany's daughter minded sharing her name with an automobile.

"You should see the back seat," said Brittany in a sultry voice. She grabbed Ben's raincoat and pulled him toward her, planting her lips on his mouth before he had a chance to breathe. Her tongue tasted like chocolate mixed with salmon and red wine. Ben fought the urge to gag.

"Um . . . I have an early day at work tomorrow," he said, disentangling himself from her clutches.

"Not so fast." Brittany snaked her arm around his waist with one hand and pulled out her phone with the other. "Let's snap a selfie."

"What?" Ben blinked, right as the camera's flash blinded him.

"One more, just to be sure." Brittany pressed her cheek against his broad chest and snuggled close. Ben looked at her phone with a mixture of dread and dazed confusion and then pulled away.

"Call me?" Brittany asked in a pleading tone.

"I'll be in touch," said Ben as he hurried down the alleyway.

When he arrived home ten minutes later, it was past eleven o'clock, and the only one there was Katelyn, who was sitting on the couch with a giant bowl of popcorn watching *Tiny House Nation* on Netflix. Her long frizzy hair was french braided into two long plaits, and she was wrapped up in the afghan Savannah had knit for Ben's birthday last spring. The upstairs was toasty because the Cadet heater was on full blast. "You're home," Katelyn said. "Just in time for the tiny-home reveal."

"It's always time for the reveal with you," said Ben as he plopped onto the couch next to her. "You fast-forward through most of the show so you can get to the payoff."

Katelyn's thumb hovered over the pause button. "True. But think of how much time I save." She tossed some popcorn in her mouth and handed him the bowl. "Here, take this from me before I ruin my digestion."

Ben stared into the half-empty bowl. "Oh no, Kate," he said, knowing in an instant that her sensitive digestive system was already ruined. "Tell me you didn't eat all of this yourself."

Katelyn nodded guilty. "I did."

Ben shook his head in dismay. Katelyn's picky stomach was a regular topic of conversation around the house, especially since the plumber had needed to be called not once, not twice, but three times after she'd clogged the toilet. As a landlord, Simon was pretty chill, but after that third plumbing bill, he'd taken a can of paint and written "courtesy flush" on the bathroom wall. Only, as Goldie had pointed out after visiting the house for dinner one night, he'd painted it *behind* the toilet, which wasn't very helpful when a woman needed the reminder.

"If anyone asks, I made this popcorn," said Ben.

"Thanks," said Katelyn, right before she burped. "Maybe if I time things right, I can go on the ferry. I have a shift at the Port Inez stand tomorrow afternoon."

"I hope Hunter agreed to pay you extra for that." Ben shoveled popcorn into his mouth as fast as he could. It was seasoned perfectly. "The ferry toll's going to cost you thirty-three dollars."

Katelyn shrugged. "It didn't come up. Hunter asked me, and I couldn't say no."

"Why not?"

"You know why not." Katelyn sank back into the couch. "Every time I look at him, I forget how to talk. He's *that* good looking."

"So? You're beautiful, too, and you're the best employee he's got. You always show up for work on time, your cash register always balances perfectly at the end of your shift, and customers love you. He should be giving you a raise, not asking you to pick up shifts on the other side of Puget Sound."

"I know, I know." Katelyn pulled the blanket tighter around her shoulders. "I just wish he'd notice me, for once, instead of treating me like all of his other employees."

"You *are* one of his employees, but you don't have to be." Ben licked his finger and wiped up buttery salt from the bottom of the bowl. "Why don't you take Simon up on his offer of a small business loan so you can open up your own espresso stand?"

"I could never." Katelyn shook her head. "You know I failed algebra."

"That has nothing to do with running a business. You're great at the math that counts for running an espresso stand. As for the bookkeeping, you could contract that out."

"But I'd have to apply for a license, and deal with health inspectors, and find a location, and then figure out business taxes." There was a panicky edge to Katelyn's voice. "I can't deal with all that." She reached the remote out to unpause the TV but stopped herself. "How was your date? I forgot to ask."

"Miserable." Ben relayed the night's events and didn't leave anything out, including Brittany's slobbery good night kiss when he'd walked her to her car. He wished he could forget that part. But really, it was her criticism of his parents' bakery that bothered him the most. "Can you believe she said the Nuthatch Bakery was shabby?"

"That's totally unfair, because it's not shabby," said Katelyn, who seemed equally outraged. "That place is so clean you could eat off the floors. So what if the curtains are faded? That's part of its charm. And the bird memorabilia is adorable, especially the birdsong that chirps when you open the front door."

"It's a robin."

"See? That's so cool. I love it, and I love your parents, too, even if your mom *is* always bugging me about finishing college and getting a new job."

"You're so close. Eighteen more units, and you'll be done."

"Eighteen units would take forever. Can we please not talk about this?"

"You're right. I'm sorry. Let's see this tiny house get revealed."

Katelyn's strategy of fast-forwarding through most of the programming meant that by one o'clock, Ben had watched enough tiny-home reveals to make him wonder why people who pursued that lifestyle didn't save themselves the trouble and buy an RV. They were about to start the next show when Mike and Simon walked in, coming home from their band gig. "How was the crowd tonight?" Ben asked.

Mike carried his guitar case back to his bedroom, but Simon left his right by the front door, where one of them would eventually trip on it. "They loved us," said Simon, his cheeks flushed pink. Tonight he wore a guitar pick on a chain dangling from one ear as well as his too-tight leather jacket over his cargo shorts. Simon always wore shorts, even if it was freezing. He reached into his pocket and pulled out slips of paper. "I got three numbers tonight, and all of them were from foxy ladies."

"Please don't call women that," said Katelyn, rolling her eyes. "You're not Jimi Hendrix."

"Ben?" Mike called from the back bedroom. "What did you do?"

"Huh?" Ben sat up straight on the couch, even though he was exhausted. He had no idea what Mike was talking about.

Mike strode back into the living room holding up his phone. "Why is Goldie texting me this picture?"

Ben couldn't see the photo clearly at first, but when he did, his eyes practically popped out of his head. It was a picture of Brittany and him from that evening. Her head was nestled against his chest, and her arm squeezed him in an intimate embrace as she puckered her lips for her camera. "How did Goldie get her hands on that?" Ben exclaimed. "And why is she texting you about it and not me?"

"Is your phone on?" Mike asked. "Goldie said she'd been trying to reach you."

Katelyn took Mike's phone out of Ben's hand and stared at the picture. "So this is Ms. Slobberface, huh?"

"Now who's using demeaning names for women?" Simon asked, wagging his finger.

Ben tried to bring his phone to life, but the battery was dead. "I still don't understand where Goldie found this picture," he said, walking over to the charging dock in the kitchen. "Even I don't have it."

"Probably because she's a stalker." Katelyn stood up from the couch and dropped the afghan to the floor. "Goldie's watching your every move."

"You mean she has a Google alert set up for me or something?" Ben asked.

"No," said Katelyn, pointing through the living room window. "I mean she's outside our house right now peering through the drapes."

"You've got to be kidding me!" Simon leaped from the recliner and ran over to Katelyn, standing in front of her. "I always knew that chick was a nut."

"You sure can pick 'em," said Mike.

"What's that supposed to mean?" Katelyn asked.

"Nothing," said Mike, skulking away.

Ben sighed and reached for his coat. "I'll handle this," he said, walking toward the front door.

"Don't let her inside," said Simon. "As your landlord, I'm telling you that Goldie is not allowed inside these premises. Use me as an excuse."

"Gotcha." Ben nodded appreciatively. He double-checked that the porch light was on before opening the front door and stepping outside.

Goldie stood on the wooden steps, illuminated by the fluorescent light. Her curly blonde hair was cut close to her head, and she wore an orange coat with balloons peeking out of one of the pockets. Six different shades of cat fur covered her clothes. Goldie wasn't quite an animal hoarder, but she adored kittens and thought that the push to spay and neuter animals was driven by a capitalized veterinary system designed to rip people off. Goldie owned so many cats that her apartment smelled like a litter box, and she carried the scent with her wherever she went. "Hi, Ben," she said, a huge smile on her face. "I didn't know you were home."

"It's the middle of the night. Of course I'm home. What are you doing here?" Ben zipped up his coat and stuffed his hands in his pockets.

"Oh, you know me—I keep odd hours. Plus, I figured you guys would be awake. Can I come in?"

Ben wiggled his fingers inside his pockets. "Sorry, but Simon said we're not allowed to have guests this late, and he owns the place so . . ."

"Typical landed gentry," Goldie said with a frown. "Did you get my messages?"

"No. My phone died. What's up?"

Goldie took a balloon out of her pocket and twisted it around her finger. "Nothing, I just saw that you had a new girlfriend, is all. As your friend, I'm happy for you." She smiled brightly, and the orange lipstick she wore looked like she'd scribbled it on herself with a highlighter. "I wanted to tell you that in person, is all. As your friend."

Ben wasn't sure what to say but thought fast. If he admitted that he never wanted to see Brittany again, that would give Goldie false hope. But he didn't want to lie either. "Thanks," he said. "I appreciate that, coming from a friend."

"That's right." Goldie twirled the balloon in the air. "We're friends, right? That's why I thought I should tell you about how Porsches are overpriced Volkswagens, and if you look at it from a cost-advantage standpoint, then—"

"What?" Ben pulled a tissue out of his pocket and wiped his nose. The cat hair was getting to him.

"Your girlfriend's Porsche." Goldie stuffed the balloon back into her pocket. "She drives a Porsche, right?"

Ben sneezed. "Um . . . yeah," he said, wiping his nose. "But how do you know that?" Goldie was eccentric, but Ben had never pegged her as crazy-stalker eccentric until now.

"I was working at a late-night birthday party at Sweet Bliss tonight," Goldie explained. "It was for a group of eleven-year-olds having an all-nighter." She chuckled and shook her head. "I don't think those chaperones will get much sleep. Anyhow, I was walking to my car when I saw you and your girlfriend say good night. That's all. And as soon as I saw her Porsche, it made me think of this article I read in the *Guardian*, which—"

"That sounds fascinating," Ben said, interrupting her. "But could you email it to me? It's late, and I'm exhausted."

Goldie bit her bottom lip so hard it became white. "Sure," she said when she finally released her lip. "I'll email it to you again. I guess you didn't get it the first few times since your phone was dead."

"Thanks." Ben blew his nose on the tissue. "Drive home safe." He darted back inside before she had the chance to say goodbye. The living room was so dark that Ben stumbled over Simon's guitar and almost crashed to the ground. He caught himself on the couch right before he fell.

"Hey," said Simon, coming out of the kitchen. "Careful with my stuff, man. That's a Fender Mustang."

Katelyn was two steps behind Simon, holding a glass of water. "You've got to break up with her, Ben."

"Who?" Ben pulled himself to his feet. "Brittany?"

Katelyn shook her head and pointed at the front door. "No, dummy. Goldie."

"I *did* break up with her. Three months ago," Ben protested.

"You need to break up your friendship with her," said Katelyn. "Some people aren't built to be friends with their exes, and Goldie's one of them."

"I can't be heartless like that," said Ben. "What am I supposed to tell her? 'Go away—I don't want to see you anymore'?"

"Yes." Katelyn nodded. "That's exactly what you're supposed to tell her."

Ben sneezed again and searched his pocket for another tissue. "Or maybe I could blame it on her cats," he said.

CHAPTER FIVE

Marlo opened the bag of Epsom salts and poured half of it in the tub. She knew that was excessive, but her sore muscles hurt so much that she was desperate. She sank into the warm water, feeling the heat soothe her aching bones. It wasn't right that her body should be broken down like this at such a young age, but as a dancer, she was used to it. Pain was a price Marlo had been willing to pay for ballet, but not now. Not for teaching fitness classes at her parents' club. She leaned back against the porcelain and closed her eyes. Why couldn't her father see what this grueling schedule was doing to her? It wasn't fair, but Marlo felt trapped. She opened her eyes and looked out at her luxurious accommodations. The sunken bathtub in her master bath was gigantic, even though the tile was outdated. Next to her was the glass shower with five separate jets. The spa-like bathroom had been a deciding feature when her parents had purchased this condo as an investment property ten years ago. Marlo lived in it rent-free so that her parents could claim owner occupancy for tax reasons she was unclear about.

Marlo didn't just rely on her parents for employment; she relied on them for everything—job, housing, health insurance, and even the money it cost to pay for her fitness certificates. Studying to be a Pilates instructor wasn't cheap.

It wasn't like she could go get a job with better hours at a different gym. That would be impossible. For one thing, she'd never be able to work less and earn as much money as her parents paid her now. For another, Marlo wouldn't want to teach at any place besides the Cascade Athletic Club, which was like her second home.

Actually, that isn't true, Marlo thought ruefully as she massaged her arm with a loofah. There was another location in Harper Landing that she would not only adore teaching at but that also felt like home—her old ballet studio, the Red Slipper. But Madame Burke had passed away when Marlo was in college, and the new renter had turned it into an antiques store.

Marlo dipped her head underwater for a few seconds and surfaced to wash her hair. There was no use ruminating on any of this. Her best path forward was to convince her father to start up the small-group fitness classes. "Stand up straight," Madame Burke used to tell her. "Put on a smile, and remember to breathe, because the show must go on." Marlo sat upright in the bathtub and vowed to make Chuck listen to her. Small-group classes would make money for the gym and help reduce her workload. That was why she'd moved so fast on Good Catch and accepted a date with Hunter. Normally she would have taken her time, considering her breakup with Ryan happened a week ago. But instead of giving herself time to heal, she was meeting Hunter later this afternoon.

One thing about Hunter that Marlo already appreciated was his beagle, Buster, that she'd seen in multiple pictures. Hunter definitely put off a "love me, love my dog" vibe that Marlo respected. She didn't quite feel the same way about her fish, Misty, but she still understood where Hunter was coming from. Plus, it was cute that Hunter had made Buster the mascot of his espresso-stand chain. The next time she drove past Harper Landing's Hunter's Fuel location, she'd know who the smiling dog holding a mug was.

Marlo drained the bathtub and stepped out onto the cushy mat. She toweled off her long limbs and hung her head upside down while she used the blow-dryer so that her straight tresses would have more volume. Marlo picked out her skinniest pair of jeans, high-heeled boots, and a red cashmere sweater that would fit underneath her raincoat. When she was all dressed, she walked out into her living room and up to the front window that looked out at Puget Sound. It was a clear day, and the sun shone brightly, despite the frigid weather. The Olympic Mountains rose before her, blanketed with snow, and the Harper Landing–Port Inez ferry was just departing. That meant Marlo had half an hour to walk down to the ferry dock and board as a pedestrian before the next one left. She was due to meet Hunter in Port Inez in an hour.

Marlo pulled the drapes closed so that the sun wouldn't bleach her couches. Their rose-print velvet fabric was luxurious to the touch but not very durable. Ryan had spilled beer on one of the cushions, and there was still a bad stain. The rest of Marlo's apartment was spotlessly clean. She was rarely home and almost never had friends over. It was the life of an introvert—only Marlo wasn't sure if she was an introvert. Her happiest time in life was when she'd been in the Pacific Northwest Ballet Company, surrounded by people at all times—even when she'd gone home to the messy house she had shared with fellow company members in Seattle. Life had energized her. Now life exhausted her. Spending time in her lonely apartment left her feeling drained. It had been so much easier to go out with Ryan and his friends, to do the things he wanted to do, like she was a rag doll being carried along for the ride. The prospect of figuring out her own entertainment was daunting.

When Hunter had texted her this morning and suggested meeting up in Port Inez that afternoon, Marlo had said yes, even though it would have been easier for her if he had come here, to Harper Landing. Marlo grabbed her coat and gloves, slung her purse across her shoulder, and locked her front door behind her, trying to ignore the nerves she felt fluttering around her insides. She'd never dated someone she'd met online before, and something about meeting Hunter in Port Inez instead of Harper Landing made it scarier. In Harper Landing she would have had the hometown advantage. But at least a benefit of meeting in Port Inez was that if the date was a spectacular failure, there would be fewer people she knew to witness it.

The line to drive onto the ferry was over an hour long, but since Marlo was on foot, she paid her fare and walked right on. Vehicles loaded the bottom of the craft, while the upper decks were devoted to lounge areas and a small café. Marlo walked through the lobby to the topographical map of Puget Sound on the wall that had entranced her ever since she was little. She held out her left hand like her mother had taught her. The Olympic Peninsula, where the Olympic National Park was and where Kurt Cobain had grown up in Aberdeen, was the left part of her hand. Seattle was at the bottom of her thumb joint. Harper Landing was on her thumb knuckle, and the ferry would bring her across the waters of the sound over to the Olympic Peninsula, where Port Inez waited on the other side. Marlo looked at the map one more time and then hurried over to the windows to watch the ferry depart. The ferry's horn bellowed, and the ship moved forward, unnoticeably at first but then picking up a steady pace.

Marlo gazed at the water, searching for harbor seals and California sea lions, but this time of the year meant her chances of spotting one weren't good.

Her phone buzzed, and Marlo pulled it out of her coat pocket. It was another notification from Good Catch. Hopefully it wasn't Hunter canceling their date now that she was fully committed. But no, it was a message telling her that she had a match. Simon Vaughn had hooked her picture back and sent her a message.

Marlo looked up from her phone and scanned the room like someone might catch her. She felt weird answering Simon's text while she was on her way to meet Hunter. But she wasn't on an official date yet—plus, exclusivity had never been mentioned. Besides, she was curious to see what Simon had to say. She tapped on the link.

You're a former ballerina? Simon had texted. I'll get to the pointe. The arts fascinate me. How long have you danced?

Wow, thought Marlo. *Punny*. At least he'd tried, though. A lot of the unsolicited messages she'd received on Good Catch had been so gross that she'd finally figured out how to use the block feature.

I started dancing when I was in preschool, Marlo texted back. So twenty years until I needed to quit.

I Googled your name. Saw the notice on PNBC website about you leaving the company due to an injury. I'm sorry. Simon added a sad face for good measure, and it made Marlo feel understood, like this person she'd never met before was really listening to her.

It was my ACL, she responded. You're an engineer? As soon as she hit send, she second-guessed herself. Simon was a senior engineer. She should have been more specific.

For Boeing, Simon texted back. I write the code to make user interface more flexible from system to system.

That sounds . . . Marlo struggled to come up with an adjective besides *boring*. Complicated, she wrote.

But the arts are my passion, Simon continued. When I'm not jamming with my band, I'm at the pottery studio, or performing live theater.

Theater? Marlo was surprised. She didn't remember that mentioned on Simon's profile.

I was in Snoopy Come Home last year in the Harper Landing Players. Did you see it? he texted.

Marlo was ashamed to admit that she'd never attended any of the local community theater's productions. In high school and college she'd always been too busy with ballet, and as an adult, it hadn't occurred to her. When she'd dated Ryan, he used to take her to the movies sometimes, but only for the big-budget action films he'd wanted to see.

I've always wanted to go see a Harper Landing Players production, Marlo texted. It's on my list of things to do.

How about next Saturday? Simon asked. I've got tickets for Waiting for Godot.

That would be lovely, Marlo wrote, just as the ferry announced that they were arriving in Port Inez. Text me the details later. She added a smiley face and silenced her phone. Her chat with Simon had kept her so busy that she'd forgotten how nervous she was about meeting Hunter. But now the ferry was docking, and she hadn't visited the restroom or touched up her lipstick.

Tossing her phone in her pocket, Marlo hurried to the nearest restroom. As soon as she entered it, she pinched her nose. The trash can was empty, and the sinks were clean, but the room reeked. Marlo used the toilet as quickly as possible and washed her hands. She had only a couple of minutes left before the ferry docked, so she needed to be fast. Marlo was reaching into her purse for her hairbrush when she heard someone moan from the stall behind her.

Marlo looked back and saw two Doc Marten boots peeking out from under one of the stalls. "Are you okay in there?" she asked.

"I need more toilet paper," a voice whimpered.

"Hang on." Marlo raced to the stall she'd just visited and spun the roll. Once she had a massive mound of tissue, she passed it underneath the wall to the woman in the green Doc Martens.

"Thanks," said the voice.

"No problem." Marlo ditched the idea of touching up her lipstick, because she needed fresh air. She slung her purse over her shoulder, hung on to the strap, and marched out of the restroom, through the ferry's cabin, and out onto the dock to meet Hunter.

He was right where he said he'd be, standing at the passenger terminal, with his beagle, Buster, at his feet. Hunter's long brown hair was in a ponytail, and his handlebar mustache had been twirled up with wax, as if he'd groomed himself in front of his profile picture. Hunter wore a red plaid jacket that matched the bandana around Buster's neck. Buster sat obediently with Hunter, unleashed yet calm despite the crowds. He looked at Marlo with rheumy eyes, his fur a spotted mix of gray, black, and brown.

The butterflies in Marlo's stomach grew bigger and scarier. They beat so hard she thought they'd fly up her throat and strangle her. It was the same feeling she'd gotten before every ballet performance. *Stage fright*, Madame Burke had called it, only worse. But years of Madame Burke's training had taught Marlo how to handle stage fright. She sucked in her core, elongated her neck, and plastered on a pleasant smile. "Perfect composure," Madame Burke used to say. "The audience must never know how anxious you feel."

"Hey," Hunter grunted when he saw her. "You must be Marlo." He drew out the last syllable of her name so it sounded extralong. Hunter's voice was deep, like he could be a radio announcer. He held out his hand to shake.

"Nice to meet you." Marlo removed her gloves and put her hand in his. So far, she was impressed by his manners.

"This is Buster." Hunter reached down and stroked the beagle's fur. "Say hello, fellow."

Buster shifted his weight and lifted up one paw. While she was kneeling to greet Buster, Marlo noticed two Doc Marten boots approaching them.

"Hunter," called a cheerful voice. "What are you doing here? I told you I didn't mind biking to the stand."

Marlo stood up and saw two bushy pigtails she recognized. Katelyn Grouse stood on the ramp, wearing a bulky coat and her green Doc Martens. She walked her bicycle beside her.

"Katelyn?" Marlo asked. "It's good to see you. It's been a while."

"Marlo Jonas," Katelyn said in a pinched voice. She twisted her hands back and forth on her handlebars. "What are you doing here?"

"She's here with me." Hunter leaned against the railing that looked out over the sound. "We're on a date. Sorry, Kate. I can't give you a ride to the stand. But you'd better hurry—your shift starts soon."

"I know it does," said Katelyn. "I'm never late." She unclipped her bicycle helmet from where it swung on her handlebar and crammed it on her head. "See ya," she mumbled before biking away.

"Is Katelyn one of your baristas?" Marlo asked as she watched the green Doc Martens pedal off, up the hill.

"Yup." Hunter nodded. "Come on. I hope you're hungry. I have a picnic planned at the beach."

"That sounds like fun." Marlo put her gloves back on, thankful that she'd dressed warmly. A picnic on the beach did *not* sound like fun. Not when it was forty-eight degrees out and windy. But it did sound romantic. The most romantic thing Ryan had ever done for her was buy her a pink kettlebell for her birthday. Since Marlo didn't like kettlebells, she wasn't sure that counted. She never lifted weights heavier than eight pounds.

Hunter led Marlo to a custom Ford truck with the Hunter's Fuel logo painted on the side. A much younger version of Buster stared back at her, holding a coffee mug. "I love your branding," she said as she waited for Hunter to unlock the passenger door.

"Thanks," said Hunter, opening up the door. "Katelyn designed it."

"Really?" Marlo climbed up into the truck seat and buckled her seat belt. "I didn't know she was so talented."

"Um . . ." Hunter pinched his mustache. "Sorry, but that's Buster's seat."

"What?"

"You'll have to sit in the middle." Hunter leaned down and picked up the beagle, who moaned in pain. "He's got arthritis and needs to stretch out," Hunter explained.

"Oh. Of course." Marlo unclicked her seat belt and slid over, stacking her purse on her lap.

The cab of the truck smelled like coffee grounds and fur. Buster's hair was everywhere, like the inside of the cab was his personal lair. Marlo didn't mind, though, especially since Buster stretched out next to her and rested his snout on her thigh, like her leg was a pillow. She tentatively petted the dog's back, and he sighed.

"He's got arthritis," repeated Hunter as he buckled his seat belt and turned on the ignition. "That's why he can't jump up into the truck on his own anymore. Keep massaging his back, and he'll be your friend forever."

Marlo, who understood pain, gently kneaded her fingers down Buster's vertebrae and smiled as the dog moaned with pleasure. "He's so sweet," she said. "Does he always make sounds like this?"

"Not always," said Hunter in his low-timbre voice. "I think the cold gets to him."

They lapsed into a silence that made the truck feel empty. Marlo kept waiting for Hunter to say something, to ask her about herself or how she knew Katelyn, perhaps, but he didn't. The silence dragged on until she felt compelled to fill it herself. "Did you grow up in Port Inez?" she asked.

"Yup." He nodded.

"And you own three coffee stands?"

"That's right."

"What made you decide to open one in Harper Landing when the other two are on this side of the water?"

Hunter shrugged. "I dunno. It seemed like a good idea at the time."

"Oh." Marlo rested her hand on Buster's back and stopped petting him, since the beagle was now snoring. "How long have you had Buster?"

"Since he was a pup." Hunter turned on the blinker and waited for oncoming traffic to clear before turning left down a forested road. Douglas firs, hemlocks, and cedars grew on each side. Big-leaf maples intermixed with the evergreens and shaded the forest a brilliant red, blanketing the ground with fallen leaves. Marlo was unfamiliar with Port Inez geography and had no idea where they were. Driving out to the middle of nowhere with a stranger wasn't a wise idea, she realized, but it was too late now. At least Katelyn knew who she was with, which was a good thing, because Marlo hadn't told anyone else where she was going. There was so much about online dating that she needed to learn, such as steps to ensure her personal safety.

"I know Katelyn from high school," she said to have something to say. "She went to prom with one of my friends." Marlo's cheeks turned pink when she said the word *friend*. There were lots of words she used to describe Ben Wexler-Lowrey, but *friend* wasn't usually one of them.

"Katelyn's a good worker." Hunter shifted gears and slowed the truck to a crawl down a one-way dirt road. "She's reliable."

"And she has a great memory," said Marlo, tensing her muscles. The truck lurched from side to side, and since she was sitting in the middle, there wasn't anything for her to hold on to. She glued her feet to the ground to brace herself so she wouldn't lean into Hunter. Buster shifted across the upholstery but kept sleeping.

"Here we are." Hunter stopped the truck and put the gear into park. They were at the edge of the forest, where the trees met a rocky shore. Puget Sound stretched out before them—only instead of seeing Harper Landing, Marlo saw Seattle.

"Oh my," said Marlo as her jaw dropped. "Is that the Space Needle?"

"Yup." Hunter pointed at a tiny sliver on the horizon with twinkling lights. "Right there." He reached behind the seat and pulled out a blanket and a canvas grocery bag. "Are you hungry?"

Marlo nodded. "I'm always hungry."

"Good." Hunter smiled and opened up his door to climb out of the truck. "Why don't you come out on my side so Buster won't wake up? The poor fellow has had a long day." Hunter reached out his hand to help her.

"Thanks." Marlo put her hand in his and climbed out of the truck.

"Oh, I almost forgot." Hunter pulled a down parka from the back of the cab. "I brought this in case you were cold."

"How thoughtful of you," said Marlo as she snuggled into it. The coat smelled like beagle and espresso, but its warmth was a welcome release. She smiled brightly, and this time her smile was genuine. "Let's eat." Marlo followed Hunter down to the rocky shore of the beach. The tide was in, and there wasn't a sandy area to spread the blanket down, but there were massive pieces of driftwood, fallen trees that had been weathered by the elements, wedged into the ground. Hunter laid the blanket over one of these logs, and Marlo perched herself on it precariously, bracing her feet on granite so she wouldn't fall off.

"I hope you like sausage," Hunter said as he reached into the grocery sack.

"Yes," Marlo replied, uncertain what to say. She looked to the left and right of her. There was nothing but forest and water as far as she could see.

"Good, because I brought salami." Hunter opened up a brown-paper package that revealed thinly sliced meat. "There's cheese to go with it," he mumbled, reaching back into the bag.

"This looks delicious." Marlo removed her gloves and picked up a slice of salami with her fingertips. "Do you come here a lot?"

Hunter nodded. "It's a good place to be alone."

They lapsed into silence again, and Marlo struggled to think of ways to fill it. So far, Hunter didn't seem to be much of a conversationalist. "I'm not a big outdoors person," she confessed. "My apartment has a balcony, and sometimes I sit out there in the summer. Oh, and I often walk to work."

"Cool." Hunter stuffed another bite of cheese into his mouth.

"I take it you like the outdoors?" Marlo prompted.

"Uh-huh." Hunter nodded.

"Do you hike, or camp, or fish?" Marlo was tempted to ask about hunting but didn't want him to think she was making fun of his name.

"Sometimes." Hunter shrugged. "I do whatever it takes to find crime scenes."

"What?" Marlo sat up straight.

"I said in my profile that I was a truth seeker," Hunter drawled. "True crime is my passion." He pointed out at the sound. "The first time I came here, I thought it would be a great place to dump a dead body, and I was right."

A little bit of sausage got caught in Marlo's throat, and she struggled to cough it up. "You were?" she asked as soon as she could speak.

"Yup." Hunter fingered the edges of his mustache. "Turns out that in the 1950s, a woman's body was found here, floating in the driftwood, and the coroner's report said it had been here for at least three weeks before anyone found it." He shrugged. "It was so decomposed they didn't even know it was female at first."

Shivers ran down Marlo's spine. "You know," she said, unzipping her purse to pull out her phone. "I just realized I needed to text my brother and remind him to feed my fish." Marlo swiped her screen and waited for it to come to life. "He's a cop," she said, improvising on the spot. If she was going to invent a fake brother, he might as well sound intimidating. "Before that, he was an army ranger." Marlo stared at her phone and watched in horror as it showed no bars.

"This far into the forest you won't be able to get reception," said Hunter. "Just like that poor Jane Doe who was strangled to death with jumper cables. Nobody could hear her cry."

"And you know this how?" Goose bumps broke out across Marlo's skin.

"I volunteer with the Doe Network."

"The Doe Network?"

Hunter nodded, a fierce look in his eyes. "Volunteers from around the world who solve cold cases in their spare time. Genealogists, weapons experts, historians, and trackers—that's me and Buster." Hunter jabbed himself in the chest with his thumb.

An animal howled behind them, and the mournful sound made Marlo quake. "What was that?" she asked, looking over her shoulder at Hunter's truck.

"That would be Buster waking up from his nap." Hunter rose and walked back to the Ford. He came back a minute later holding Buster in his arms. "I wouldn't worry about your fish if I were you," said Hunter as he sat on the log next to her. "Most people overfeed them." Hunter took the last few pieces of salami and hand-fed them to his dog. "Just a little nibble, old fellow. You know too much fat isn't good for you."

"Yeah, um . . . the thing is, I forgot to feed Misty—that's my fish—yesterday too. And the day before that," Marlo added, scrambling to find an excuse for getting out of there fast. As noble as Hunter's intentions might have been to solve cold cases, something about him gave her the creeps. "Pet care is really important to me," she added. "I think I'd better go home and take care of her, since I can't get ahold of my brother."

"Pet care is important to you?" Hunter furrowed his brow and held Buster close. "But you forgot to feed your fish for three days straight?" Both man and beagle looked at her accusingly. "How could you be so careless?"

Marlo felt herself start to sweat, despite the frigid weather. "I'm reading a book about betta fish, but I acknowledge that I have a lot to learn." She collected the trash and stuffed it into the grocery bag. "I'm sorry to have to end our afternoon early."

"I'm not." Hunter cradled Buster and stood up. "I think I'm done here too." He frowned and marched back up to the truck.

Marlo shook out the blanket and folded it as fast as she could. Taking one last look at the foreboding landscape, she hurried up to the vehicle and hoped that she'd never get this close to a crime scene again.

CHAPTER SIX

Ben dived headfirst into the back seat of his Kia, searching for coins. There was still hope that he would be able to scrape together some extra money for his date with Dahlia. Brittany's expensive taste at the Parisian Café last night had left him broke. That was the main reason he'd suggested meeting Dahlia at Sweet Bliss for dessert this evening at eight o'clock instead of going out for dinner. Ben's fingers reached into the crevices of the threadbare upholstery, digging into the used car's mysterious past, but all he found was a ticket stub to the Harper Landing Players' production of *Snoopy, Come Home*. Ben climbed out of the car and slammed the door shut. He looked across Main Street at the ATM, knowing that he had no choice. If he hurried, he could take out cash before he met up with Dahlia in ten minutes instead of using his credit card. The problem was, he'd run his bank account dangerously low.

Ben waited for traffic to clear and then jaywalked across the street. He slid his debit card into the machine, typed in his PIN, and tried to ignore the sick feeling in his stomach when he saw his checking account balance. He worked fifty hours a week at the *Seattle Times* and could barely afford frozen yogurt. But Ben knew he was lucky to have a job in journalism at all, especially at a paper like the *Seattle Times*, which paid better than other publications.

Ben slid the eighty dollars cash that needed to last him the rest of the week into his wallet and walked up Main Street toward Sweet Bliss. Maybe his parents could give him some shifts at the bakery. Business usually picked up before Thanksgiving when people ordered cookies and pies. Ben could roll out a piecrust that was so symmetrical even his father was impressed. It was weird, because even though Ben's dysgraphia made it difficult for him to write legibly, when it came to big shapes—such as making piecrust circles, braiding bread, or forming baguettes—Ben did great. His mom said he had an artistic nature.

Ben slowed his pace as he approached Sweet Bliss so he wouldn't be too early. The frozen yogurt shop was a Harper Landing favorite, although it wasn't as crowded in November as in summer. Sweet Bliss's owner, Julia Harper, had come back from Italy with a vision several years ago and had taken the abandoned ice cream shop she'd inherited from her father and turned it into a modern establishment that the health-conscious residents of Harper Landing loved. Now Julia was on her honeymoon with her new husband, Aaron Baxter, and Ben wasn't sure when they were getting back. He couldn't remember if their return date had been mentioned at their wedding last week at the Harper Landing Yacht Club.

When Ben reached the entrance to Sweet Bliss, he peered through the window to make sure that Dahlia wasn't already inside.

"I'm over here," said a friendly voice.

Ben spun around and saw Dahlia, wearing a parka, skinny jeans, and earmuffs. Her braids were tied back in a ponytail, and the hint of makeup she wore made her long lashes stand out.

"Sorry I'm late," said Ben, feeling rattled.

"You're not late. We're both right on time." Dahlia smiled and opened the door to Sweet Bliss, making the tiny bell attached to the top jingle merrily. "After you." She ushered him inside.

"Thanks." Ben walked into the brightly lit frozen yogurt shop and breathed in the heavenly aroma of freshly baked brownies and waffle cones. The ceiling was covered in sponge-painted clouds, and cherubs smiled sweetly on the walls. The back of the shop displayed a row of self-service dispensers, and to the right was the buffet of toppings. NOW SERVING BIG FOOT PALEO GRANOLA read the sign behind one of the dishes.

"I love this place," said Dahlia as she walked across the black-and-white-checkered floor to select a paper cup. "But I have to watch myself. I spend a lot of time standing at work and not as much time exercising as I used to."

"I think you're gorgeous," Ben said truthfully. He was never sure what to say when women made comments about their weight like that. It felt like a trap. Ben served himself multiple ounces of Tahitian Paradise and then added scoops of crumbled brownie on top. When he reached the register, he opened his wallet and waited for Dahlia's cup so he could pay for that too.

"I don't mind paying for my own." Dahlia unzipped her purse.

"That's okay." Ben handed the cashier a twenty-dollar bill. "My treat."

"Thanks." Dahlia picked up two spoons and a few napkins. "I'll go get us a table."

Ben joined her a minute later at the place she'd chosen by the window overlooking Main Street. He took off his jacket and hung it on his chair. Dahlia had done the same, and now that she had taken off her parka, he could better appreciate her hourglass figure. The tight black sweater she wore accentuated every curve. "I hope you don't mind meeting for dessert instead of dinner," he said, digging his spoon into the vanilla. "I worked all day, and this is my only break. Later this evening I have a story to cover in Mill Creek." Savannah had made him promise to come support her yarn bombing. Whether the *Seattle Times* would print his report on the event was unclear.

"That's right." Dahlia paused midbite. "You're a reporter. I'll look for your byline. My work gets several copies of the *Seattle Times* delivered each day."

"What do you do for a living?" Ben asked, searching his memory for what Dahlia had written in her profile. He thought she'd said something about working with senior citizens but couldn't remember.

"I teach fitness classes at Cascade Athletic Club." Dahlia blotted her lips with a napkin. "And I also work at the smoothie bar." She tapped her spoon against her frozen yogurt cup. "Coming to Sweet Bliss is a treat for me. I'm always too broke to spring for FroYo."

Because of course the Jonas family doesn't pay living wages, Ben thought to himself. He was annoyed, especially after seeing Chuck at the wedding last weekend. "I'm surprised that a fancy club like that doesn't pay better," he said.

"It's fancy—that's for sure." Dahlia nodded in agreement. "There are tennis and racquetball courts, a saltwater pool, and steam saunas in each locker room. But no, it doesn't pay well."

"I don't understand that, because the Jonas family is rich."

Dahlia shrugged. "Yes, and no. I don't know the details, but my understanding is they've had financial problems lately because of the new parking structure at the port they need to help fund. Chuck and Laura have to come up with a bunch of cash, fast."

"That should be easy for them, with membership prices set so high."

Dahlia fiddled with one of her braids, twisting it around her manicured fingertip. "You'd think that, right? But half their members are senior citizens coming to the gym for almost free on the SilverSneakers program. The government reimbursement rate isn't enough to make up for the lost revenue."

Ben raised his eyebrows. "It sounds like that program won't last long at the club."

"Actually, it has." Dahlia stirred the flavors in her frozen yogurt cup. "My hours teaching spin have been cut, but my class time with the SilverSneakers crowd is sacred. Mr. Jonas is committed to keeping our senior members happy, because that's the mission of the club—to serve the community by promoting health and wellness."

Ben, who had been inside the Cascade Athletic Club only once in twenty-four years for his soccer team's end-of-the-season pool party in first grade, was shocked. He'd never thought of the club as a mission project for the community. To him, it was a bastion of wealth and privilege. "You're serious?" he asked in a skeptical tone. "You think the Jonas family runs Cascade Athletic Club like it's a community service project?"

Dahlia nodded her head. "I know it. Think about how much money that property would make if they sold it for waterfront condos. The Jonas family would make millions. That would be the easy way out. But instead, they've held on to that land for over twenty years, building it into what it is today—a place where people get fit while spending time with their friends. If I was retired, it would definitely be part of my daily routine." Dahlia put her spoon down and fluttered her lashes at him. "But enough about me. I want to learn about you. Tell me about being a reporter. When did you learn that you wanted to be a journalist?"

"In fifth grade." Ben stared into his almost empty bowl. These few minutes with Dahlia were already light-years ahead of the disaster with Brittany, who'd never once asked him about himself. He needed to slow down, or this date would be over way too soon. "I wrote a report on harbor seals, and Mrs. Fiege, my teacher, read it to the whole class because she said it was the best one." He flushed, remembering Mrs. Fiege's praise. He could picture her standing at the front of their classroom (this was before she had been diagnosed with multiple sclerosis) holding up his paper and reading it out loud in her clear voice. "There was one student," Mrs. Fiege had said, "who wrote with such voice that I was not only informed about harbor seals—I was entertained." When she had read Ben's opening paragraph and he had realized that she was talking about *his* report, tears had sprung up in his eyes, and he'd had to fake sneeze so his friends wouldn't realize he was crying. It was the first time he'd ever been the best at anything school related. The work he'd started with his after-school dyslexia tutoring was paying off. He'd dictated what he'd wanted to say to his tutor, and she'd scribed it into the computer for him. The words had been inside him all along, and he had finally been learning how to release them.

"That's sweet." Dahlia stretched her leg underneath the table and rubbed her shin against Ben's. "She sounds like a wonderful teacher."

"She was." Ben wasn't sure if Dahlia's leg flirting was intentional. Just in case, he kept his leg right where it was, pressed against Dahlia's. "A few years later Mrs. Fiege had to take early retirement for her health, but she's still active in the community. She leaves comments on the *Seattle Times* Facebook page, on all of my articles." He grinned, thinking about how fierce she was. "You should see her argue with trolls." A buzzing sound emanated from Ben's raincoat pocket. "Sorry," he said. "That might be work." He retrieved his phone and glanced at the screen.

I'm a mess, the text from Katelyn said. Please call me.

I'm on a date at Sweet Bliss, he texted back. Is this an emergency?

"Work?" Dahlia asked.

"No, sorry." Ben put the phone facedown next to his Froyo cup. "I thought it might be about my assignment tonight." Ben's phone vibrated on the table as another text came in. "Shoot," he said. "Sorry about that." He turned over his phone and saw another message from Katelyn.

A date with Ms. Slobberface?

No, Ben replied. I'll call you later. But before he turned off his notifications, another text from Katelyn flashed across the screen.

Hunter's on a date with Marlo Jonas right now! Katelyn added multiple lines of broken-heart emojis plus some crying faces.

"Is there a problem?" Dahlia moved her leg away.

"Um . . . no, sorry. Roommate drama." Ben's thumbs tapped the screen. I'll call you as soon as I can, he texted Katelyn. Ben stuffed his phone back in his pocket. "I'm sorry. I don't mean to be rude. I should have turned off the notifications before I arrived, except I'm waiting to hear the location for the story I'm writing tonight."

"What's it about?" Dahlia asked.

"The roommate drama?" Ben froze, unsure how to explain that he was texting his ex-girlfriend in the middle of a date.

"No, your work assignment." Dahlia tilted her head to the side. "Unless the roommate drama's more interesting."

"A yarn bombing," Ben blurted out. "To protest cuts to the community center in Mill Creek."

"You mean those crazy people who knit sweaters on trees?" Dahlia raised her perfectly arched eyebrows.

"Yes." Ben nodded. "I've been writing about one of the most notorious yarn bombers in Snohomish County. I can't tell you who it is," he said, trying to sound mysterious, "because I won't reveal my source."

Dahlia chuckled. "Don't worry," she said. "I'm not interested. Yarn bombing sounds like a waste of time and money."

"It's art combined with a public statement," Ben protested. He thought Savannah went overboard in her fiber-arts-related activities, but he admired her passion.

Dahlia pressed her lips together and raised her eyebrows even higher, like she was trying to stop herself from expressing what was really on her mind. "It takes all kinds," she finally said before eating the last bite of her Froyo.

"Yarn bombers express themselves in a way that captures people's attention and forces them to not look away." Ben slipped his hand into his coat pocket, itching to check his messages. He still needed to verify the address for Savannah's adventure in Mill Creek. But now he couldn't check his phone again without being rude. Plus, he worried about Katelyn. Seeing Hunter on a date with Marlo would have crushed her. Katelyn might be halfway into a bag of oatmeal cookies by now, and Katelyn was not, under any circumstances, supposed to eat oatmeal. But Ben knew he shouldn't be letting worries about his ex-girlfriends invade his thoughts when he was on a date with someone new, especially someone as wonderful as Dahlia. "Tell me more about yourself," he said. "What do you like to do in your free time?"

"I spend a lot of time with my family," said Dahlia. "My sister and her husband are both nurses at the hospital. She's in labor and delivery, and he works in the ER. Their son is three, and I take care of him whenever I can so he doesn't have to go to day care."

"My day care experience was great," said Ben, instantly taking offense. "That's where I met my best friend, Mike Lu."

"Mike Lu?" Dahlia's cheeks turned pink.

"Yeah." Ben crumpled his napkin. "Do you know him?"

Dahlia shook her head. "I've seen him in the bookstore a few times, that's it."

"We both went to the YMCA for day care until our siblings were old enough to watch us. The Y's program was great. I don't know what it's like now, but has your sister looked into it?"

Dahlia frowned and nodded. "Yes. It's still a wonderful program, but it's too expensive. We share a house together, but even saving on rent like that, she and her husband don't earn enough to pay their college loans and day care. That's why they work opposite shifts, and I pitch in when I can."

"That's generous of you." Ben wanted to know how much the YMCA's day care cost these days but was afraid to ask. Something told him it would be too much for a journalist's salary. That was a problem, because Ben wanted to be a father . . . once he met the right woman. "My sister, Grace, would never help me out like that," he said.

Dahlia adjusted the silver bracelets she wore on her wrist. "What does Grace do for a living?"

"She's a chemist for a manufacturing plant that builds airplane parts for Boeing. Grace lives in an apartment on Main Street, but we hardly ever see her."

"Why not?"

"I don't know." Ben shrugged. "She's too busy, I guess. Whenever our folks need help at the bakery, they call me, not her. I'm the one with the flexible hours." *And the person who needs the extra money,* he thought to himself.

"What bakery do they run?"

"The Nuthatch on Main Street."

Dahlia's eyes sparkled. "I love that place! It's so quaint, and they make the best cheddar-and-chive muffins."

"Those are popular." Ben folded his hands on the table and leaned forward, relieved that she didn't call it a dump like Brittany had. "Have you been in there recently?"

"Does last week count?" Dahlia leaned forward, too, so that their hands were inches apart.

"Absolutely." Ben grinned. "Would you mind telling me what you think of the inside? Someone recently told me they thought it was shabby, and I wanted to get another opinion. Because if it *is* shabby, then—"

"Shabby chic," said Dahlia, interrupting him. "Yes, some of the fabrics are faded, and the wooden tables are scuffed, but that's part of the charm. All those bird decorations are cute. The rustic-farmhouse look is on purpose, right?"

"On purpose," Ben repeated. "Right." Kind of . . . more like his parents had been so busy running the day-to-day operations of a successful business that they hadn't found time to redecorate in fifteen years. Things that used to be brand new were now artfully distressed.

"My nephew loves the Nuthatch Bakery," said Dahlia. "Whenever we go, he orders the chocolate-chocolate."

"Hot cocoa and a Nutella sandwich." Ben smacked his lips. "My favorite."

Dahlia giggled. "Don't tell my sister, because she'd kill me. Lucas isn't supposed to eat sugar except on special occasions."

Ben laughed as they exchanged a conspiratorial grin. "You told me about work and your family, but you didn't tell me about what you liked to do for fun," he said. "So?"

Dahlia straightened her shoulders and looked up at the cherubs holding gilded harps painted on the wall. "I like to sing," she said matter-of-factly. "I'm in the choir at church, and I take voice lessons on the side whenever I can scrape up the money."

"That's wonderful. Are you a high singer or a low singer?"

"You mean an alto or a soprano?" Dahlia arched one eyebrow at him. "I'm an alto, but I can sing contralto parts too."

"Have you ever sung in a band?" Ben asked. "My friends Mike and Simon have a jazz group called the Monte Cristos, and they've been thinking about adding a singer."

"Mike Lu from day care?"

Ben nodded. "The same."

"I didn't know Mr. Bookstore—I mean Mike—was in a band." Dahlia's jaw dropped, and then she closed her mouth and blotted her lips with a napkin. "That would be amazing—I mean if he'd consider giving me an audition." She spoke in a rush. "Where do they perform?"

"The Western Cedar and some other places. Last summer they played at the Harper Landing Fourth of July celebration in the evening before the fireworks started."

"I was home with Lucas that night," said Dahlia. "It was a busy night at the hospital, and both his parents had to work." She scraped the side of her Froyo cup with the spoon. "And I've never been to the Western Cedar because it's so expensive."

"Same." Ben nodded, ashamed of admitting to his financial situation but also wanting to be honest. "But Simon gave me a gift card for my birthday that I haven't used yet. Would you like to go this Friday to hear them play?"

"I'd—" Dahlia started to reply, but then her gaze shifted from Ben to the front of the shop. "Do you know that woman?" Dahlia asked.

Ben whipped his head around to look over his shoulder, afraid of what he might find. A forlorn figure stood on the outside of the glass window, illuminated by the streetlight. Her face was pressed up against the glass along with one palm, and she stared right at them, trying to get Ben's attention. At first, he thought it might be Goldie spying on another one of his dates, but when he saw two long pigtails sagging in the November mist, he knew it was Katelyn. Her mascara had smudged so badly it left tracks down her cheeks like she was a rabid raccoon, and her bicycle had been thrown on the ground beside her. "Ben!" she mouthed through the glass. "Help!"

"I'm so sorry." Ben picked up his empty Froyo cup but then put it back on the table, not wanting the date to officially end yet. "That's my roommate. I'd better check on her."

"Okay." Dahlia leaned back in her chair and crossed her arms.

"I'll be right back." Ben crumpled his napkin. "I promise." He left his coat where it hung on his chair and rushed across the restaurant, flinging the front door open in such a hurry that the bells jingled insanely. He found Katelyn sobbing, her helmet dangling from her wrist and the sleeve of her coat ripped to shreds. A cut on her chin dribbled blood down her neck. "Katelyn!" Ben exclaimed. "What happened?" He offered her his napkin to stop the bleeding, but then pulled it away, worried that it might be germy.

"I . . . fell . . . down," Katelyn gasped out between sobs. "I . . . was . . . crying . . . so . . . hard . . . I . . . didn't . . . see . . . where . . . I . . . was . . . going."

"Oh boy." Ben took her helmet from her and looked at her cut. "Is it okay if I hug you?" he asked.

Katelyn nodded and threw her head on his shoulder, keeping her injured arm close to her torso. "I don't think anything's broken," she managed to get out. "But my arm really hurts."

"We need to take your coat off so we can look at it." Ben held Katelyn steady as she started to cry harder. "What if your wrist is fractured?"

"I just want to go home," Katelyn moaned. "Please take me home."

"Is there a problem here?" Dahlia asked in an annoyed tone. She had put on her parka and zipped it up. But when she saw that Katelyn was crying, her tone softened. "Oh no. Are you hurt?"

"My roommate's had a biking accident." Ben awkwardly reached down with one hand to pick up Katelyn's bike while keeping a close hold on her with the other. "I need to drive her home. I'm sorry to have to leave like this."

"No, that's okay." Dahlia helped Ben pick up the bike. "Hang on, I'll go get your coat."

"Thanks." Ben waited while Dahlia headed back inside to collect his raincoat.

"I'm sorry to ruin your date," Katelyn said between gulps for air. "I didn't mean to."

"It's okay, Kate." Ben stroked her hair. "Everyone has accidents." He thought it was a good sign that she was able to talk but was still worried she might have broken something. "I think we should take you to urgent care."

"No!" Katelyn flinched. "I can't. My insurance is so crappy I can't afford that. It would take me years to pay off."

Ben sighed, knowing she was probably right. "Okay, well, we'll get you home and take a look at your arm and figure out what to do. If there's any chance it might be broken, you'll need to see the doctor."

Katelyn nodded. "I don't think it's broken," she said. "Just banged up."

"Here you go." Dahlia came back outside holding Ben's coat. "Let me help you get the bike to the car."

"Thank you," said Katelyn. She sniffed hard. "I'm sorry to interrupt your date. Ben is a really good guy."

"I can tell that," said Dahlia as they slowly walked down the hill toward his car.

Ben was grateful that it was dark so that Dahlia couldn't see the deplorable state of his dilapidated Kia. He hadn't washed it in over six months, and the left-side passenger door was a different paint color. Luckily, the streetlight made that difficult to see. Ben helped Katelyn climb inside and then walked up to where Dahlia was propping up the bike and holding his jacket. "This has been . . ." Ben, normally fluent with words, struggled to finish his sentence. "I'm sorry," he finally said. "I really like you, and I didn't want our date to end like this."

"Yes." Dahlia handed him his coat.

"Yeah." Ben's shoulders slumped. "Okay." He grabbed the bike's handlebars, feeling defeated.

"Yes, I'll go with you to the Western Cedar next Friday." Dahlia let go of the bike and smiled. "And tell Mike that I'd be thrilled to audition for his band if he'd let me."

"I'll do that." Ben smiled. He thought about kissing her, but the bike was between them, and Katelyn was in pain. "Thanks again for all the help."

"No problem." Dahlia leaned forward and pecked him on the cheek. "You're cute," she said with a wink. "See you on Friday."

Too stunned to speak, Ben watched in awe as she hiked up the street, her long black braids swaying behind her. But then he remembered Katelyn's injury, and he hooked her bike to the rack on his trunk as quickly as possible. By the time he climbed inside, Katelyn had already taken off her coat and peeled back her sleeve and was inspecting her arm. There was a gash across her skin, but it wasn't as bad as the one on her chin, which she was holding a tissue against to stop the bleeding. "How does it look?" Katelyn asked through clenched teeth.

"It's hard to say." Ben turned on the map light and frowned. "Can you move your elbow?"

"I think so." Katelyn extended her arm and flinched.

Ben felt like flinching with her. His gut told him that Katelyn should see a doctor, but he agreed with her that the medical bill would ruin her financially. "Let's go home, give you some ibuprofen, and wrap your arm in ice," he suggested.

"Okay." Katelyn leaned back against the seat and closed her eyes. She didn't say one more word all the way home.

Katelyn's silence made Ben nervous because she wasn't usually so quiet. Either she was in more pain than she admitted to, or she might have hit her head when she'd fallen. He knew she needed rest, but he wanted to keep her alert. "The next time Hunter asks you to take a shift in Port Inez, you're telling him no," he said. "Now you've got the ferry bill and a possible injury, all because of that commute."

"It's not Hunter's fault," Katelyn whimpered. "Besides, you have no right to talk about crazy commutes considering you bike to Seattle each day."

"That's different."

"How is it different?"

"Because it is," Ben insisted. "My job has the potential to go someplace. I'm building a career. But working at someone else's espresso stand is a dead end, and you're better than that."

"Shut up, Ben." Katelyn squeezed her eyes shut. "Not everyone wants to save the world like you do. Besides, who's to say that what I do isn't important too? Coffee makes people feel better." She opened her eyes and sneered at him. "The news makes people feel worse."

Ben held back his retort because he knew Katelyn was in pain. He was grateful when they parked in front of their house a couple of minutes later. Simon and Mike were in the driveway, loading musical equipment into Mike's van. Ben pulled the keys out of the ignition of his Kia and hurried around the car to open Katelyn's door for her, then helped her climb out onto the dead front lawn.

"What's the matter?" Simon called, stuffing his Fender guitar into the van in a hurry. "Why is Katelyn holding her arm like that?"

"I fell off my bike," Katelyn replied in a weak voice. "Do we have Advil?"

"Her arm needs ice," said Ben. He braced Katelyn as she made her way up the path to the front door. "Lots of it."

"I'll go get some," said Mike as he headed inside.

Simon trotted across the driveway and onto the grass, where Katelyn was slowly making her way up the lawn. "Can you move it? Is it broken?" he asked, his voice filled with concern. "Why aren't you going to the doctor?"

"They're too expensive," Ben explained as he helped Katelyn up the porch steps. "We're going to try the ice and hope for the best." But as soon as they stepped into the porch light, he reevaluated that decision. Katelyn's arm had turned yellow and was swelling up like one of Goldie's balloons.

"Like hell you are," Simon snapped. He reached into his pocket and pulled out his keys. One click of the key fob, and his BMW's lights blinked as the doors unlocked. "I'm taking her to the doctor, and I'm paying for it, so nobody can stop me."

"I wouldn't think of it," Ben said with gratitude. A minute later, he watched Simon and Katelyn drive away to urgent care and felt flooded with emotions. He couldn't afford to go out to dinner two nights in a row. He couldn't pay the day care fees for his future children. He couldn't whip out his wallet and have one of his best friend's injuries healed. Ben knew deep in his soul that America needed journalists like him. But the industry was suffering financially, and he was paying a heavy price for pursuing his dream. Was it worth it?

CHAPTER SEVEN

Marlo sat in the Cascade Athletic Club conference room, waiting for her parents to arrive for their weekly meeting, and scrolled through Twitter to pass the time. She fought the urge to laugh when she saw the @HarpLanPDScan's latest tweet: "Friendly spiders #yarnbomb Mill Creek protesting cuts to the art funding. Charlotte's bail set at 1 lb. of bacon." *Bingo,* she thought to herself. Here was further proof that Ben was behind the faux police Twitter account. He'd loved *Charlotte's Web* ever since Ms. Hanline had read it aloud to them in kindergarten and they'd had a popcorn party to celebrate the conclusion of the book. The following October Ben had dressed up as Charlotte for Halloween. Another reason Marlo was certain Ben was behind that Twitter account was that he had just written about the yarn bombing for the *Seattle Times* yesterday. Budget-Slashing Mill Creek Council Faces Backlash, the headline had read, accompanied by a picture of dozens of knitted faces in various hues wound onto stakes mounted at the entrance to the town.

As a general rule, Marlo never read Ben's articles unless they were interesting, because she didn't want to pay attention to someone that annoying. The problem was, Ben's articles were always interesting, which meant that Marlo had read practically all of them. He was the only *Seattle Times* reporter who covered Harper Landing news, and she wanted to be informed about her local community. Plus, when he wrote about the other cities in Snohomish County, he made difficult topics easier to understand. Derelict boats polluting the Snohomish River wasn't something that directly affected Marlo, for example, but she knew they were a problem because she read Ben's articles. Not that she looked for Ben's byline, of course. The only reason she knew that he published articles on Monday, Tuesday, Wednesday, and Friday was that she had a good memory.

"Shoot, you're early," said Chuck as he barreled into the room. He dropped a folder on the conference room table. "I just got off the erg machine and haven't had time to stretch." He grabbed his left ankle, folded his leg, and stretched out his quadriceps. Sweat dripped down the gray cotton T-shirt he wore and pooled around the headband holding back his silvery hair. "Where's your mother?"

"I'm sure she'll arrive ten minutes late like always." Marlo turned her phone facedown so she wouldn't be distracted and opened up the file. "These are the latest numbers, I assume?"

Chuck nodded and switched over to stretching his other quad. "Yup. Membership is up, but revenue is down."

Marlo scanned the data, looking for an explanation. "You mean our SilverSneakers membership is up, but our regular-rate membership is declining."

"Is that what it says?" Chuck dropped his foot to the ground and leaned forward to stretch his hamstrings. His mother had passed away in her sixties, and since her death, he'd made supporting their senior clients a top priority.

Marlo understood that, but she also valued the importance of gathering a younger clientele. "Don't play dumb, Dad. We've talked about this before. You know we need to focus on recruiting millennials."

"I don't want to discriminate," said Chuck. "Our seniors are valued members of the gym."

"I'm not debating that." Marlo laid down the paperwork. "I love our senior clients, too, but they're signing up based on word-of-mouth recommendations from their friends. Plus, the senior center is about to be remodeled, so Cascade Athletic Club is becoming their new place to hang out. But we need more members paying full-price fees, and that means targeting a younger demographic, which is why I'm pushing for small-group fitness classes."

"You can have them if you win our bet. Have you dated out of your comfort zone yet?"

"Yes." Marlo frowned. "I have."

"And how was it?" Chuck raised his bushy eyebrows and looked at her with a smirk on his face.

"Uncomfortable," Marlo admitted. "But not because of his looks. The perfect guy might still be waiting for me."

"A perfectly ugly guy?"

"Dad!"

Chuck laughed. "You'll never be happy with someone who's not as attractive as you."

"Back to our budget." Marlo pointed to the numbers. "We need to do something fast, or we'll be operating in the red."

"Things would be fine if it weren't for that port commission levy," Chuck grumbled.

"What did I miss?" Laura asked, breezing into the room smelling of lemongrass. Her long gray hair was pulled into a bun, and she wore a tight purple tank top and formfitting yoga pants. Rose quartz crystals dangled from her necklace. She held a tray of three smoothies, which she passed out to her husband and daughter.

"Thanks," said Marlo before taking a sip of her emerald-green smoothie. "We were discussing the need to attract younger clients."

"No, we weren't," said Chuck as he sat down at the table and grabbed his drink. "Marlo and I were talking about how to increase revenue, and that doesn't mean courting the millennial generation who blows all of their money on avocado toast and cappuccinos."

"What?" Marlo slapped her palm on the table. "That's a ridiculous stereotype, and you know it."

"Avocado toast would be such a delicious addition to our smoothie bar," said Laura in a dreamy voice. She twirled the paper straw in her cup. "Maybe we could offer gluten-free bread as an option."

"We don't have a toaster." Chuck folded his arms across his chest. "I don't see how that would work."

"We could buy a toaster," said Marlo.

"That might require permits," said Chuck. "We don't have a permit for a full kitchen."

"I'd look up the permit situation." Marlo, too, fidgeted with her straw. "Look, I know you don't like change, but Mom's idea is an easy example of how we could make money if we incorporated new trends."

Chuck shook his head. "The SilverSneakers crowd doesn't want to eat avocado toast. Trust me."

"What about smoked salmon?" Laura suggested.

"Too smelly," said Chuck.

"You're only saying that because I suggested it," Laura argued.

"No," Chuck said with a frown. "I'm saying it because I'm right. Nobody wants to play racquetball and smell fish as they walk through the lobby."

"I didn't say pickled herring." Laura jabbed her straw into her smoothie hard enough that the liquid plopped through the plastic opening. "I said salmon. Which you know doesn't smell nearly as bad. I mean—"

"Okay. Okay." Marlo held up her hands like she'd done hundreds of times before to stop her parents' bickering. "Let's regroup." She didn't have any business experience, but she did know a thing or two about keeping prima ballerinas happy. "Dad wants to continue catering to our senior clientele. Mom wants to offer new items at the smoothie bar that might tempt people to spend more money. That's what we're talking about. Right?"

"Yes," Chuck grunted, scratching his jaw.

"I'm just saying that smoked—"

"Mom!" Marlo snapped, louder than intended.

"Yes," said Laura, rolling her eyes. "That's what we're talking about."

"Okay, then." Marlo looked at the numbers. "The senior center is closing for remodeling soon, which means that all of our SilverSneakers members who used to work out at the ten and eleven slots and then head over there for lunch won't be able to do that anymore, correct?"

"Yes, I suppose so." Chuck nodded. "But we don't have the equipment to serve lunch."

"But we do already serve smoothies and coffee," said Marlo. "And Mom's idea about toast is a good one. I'll contact the city to make sure our permit works. Then, it would be easy to purchase a toaster—or a toaster oven—and then we could serve a smoothie-and-toast combo."

"Or a hummus platter," Laura suggested. "With olives."

"A tapas bar," Chuck mumbled. "Like that time we went to Spain." He looked into Laura's eyes and licked his lips. "Do you remember?"

"Of course I remember." Laura fiddled with the shoulder of her tank top. "I had on that—"

"Little black dress with the spaghetti straps," Chuck said, finishing her sentence. "And I ordered that sangria you said was too strong."

"Because it *was* too strong," Laura said, giggling.

"Okay, stop." Marlo held up her hands for the second time that meeting. "I sense that we're getting off topic."

"And we went to the track where Hemingway bet on horses." Chuck reached for Laura's hand, and she slid her fingers up his wrist.

"You're so sweaty," Laura said in a sultry voice. "I love it when you sweat."

"Why don't you come over here and taste me?" Chuck asked. "I'm salty."

"We're buying a toaster oven," Marlo declared. "And I'm leaving." She picked up her phone and smoothie and hurried out of the conference room, right as her parents began making out. She closed the door behind her and made a mental note to ask the cleaning crew to give extra attention to the conference table later.

Marlo marched downstairs and through to the back of the club, where the Pilates studio was located. She unlocked the door, sat down at her desk, and switched on her computer. Despite the awkwardness, the meeting with her parents had resulted in two meaningful action items: looking up permitting and exploring a new tapas menu. Providing the SilverSneakers crowd with an attractive lunch option when the senior center closed for remodeling was a good idea. But Marlo needed more details to devise a plan. How much did lunch cost at the senior center? What did they serve, and what were the portions like? She typed "Harper Landing Senior Center" into her search engine and pulled up the website.

At first glance, the website was slick. A beautiful painting of the Harper Landing–Port Inez ferry sailing into the sunset graced the front page, along with links about membership, activities, dining, and rental opportunities. But when Marlo clicked on the dining link, it said "Under Construction." She clicked on the other links and got the same message. What was going on? Marlo scrolled to the bottom of the home page and saw a date from ten years ago. Nobody had bothered to update the website in ages.

Marlo looked at her watch. She still had an hour and a half before her first Pilates client came that afternoon. If she hurried, she could walk to the senior center over her lunch break, find out more information, and be back in time for her appointment. Marlo grabbed her down coat, stashed her phone in the pocket, and flew out the door. Her walk to the senior center was brisk, the cold air from the sound blowing across her face and turning her cheeks pink. The Olympic Mountains glinted blue on the horizon, heavily capped with snow. During the summer, walking in the port district was relaxing. Marlo loved seeing the sailboats and yachts moored in the marina and searching for harbor seals swimming in the water. But in November, the walk was a challenge, especially in her thin leggings. Marlo pulled up her hood and wished she had remembered her gloves.

Thankfully, the senior center was close, and Marlo arrived five minutes later. The one-story edifice dated to the 1950s and was a large concrete rectangle plopped down on some of the most beautiful beachfront property in the entire Seattle metro area. The roof sagged, and the siding crumbled. Marlo wasn't sure why the city didn't tear it down and start from scratch, as it was long overdue for a remodel, but that decision wasn't hers to make. She opened the front door and walked into the lobby, grateful for the warmth that greeted her as soon as she crossed the threshold. Marlo pushed back her hood and rubbed her hands together while she waited for the lady at the front desk to notice she was there. She looked familiar, but Marlo couldn't quite place her. Maybe she'd seen her at Julia's wedding? Marlo was unsure until the woman looked up and smiled.

"Why, hello there," she said, putting down the book she was reading. "You're the girl from the guest book."

"Jack's grandma," Marlo blurted, unable to remember the woman's name. "Hi. I'm Marlo Jonas."

"Martha Reynolds, nice to meet you." The woman stood up and held out her hand. She had tight gray curls and wore a tracksuit with fall leaves embroidered across the velour. "I'm Julia's next-door neighbor, and yes, baby Jack is my grandson."

Marlo shook Martha's hand, quickly remembering the details Martha had left out. Her son, Jared, had died earlier that year and left his brother-in-law, Aaron Baxter, as Jack's guardian. "Where's your husband?" Marlo asked, recalling that Julia had mentioned something about Alzheimer's.

"Frank's inside at the sing-along for memory-care patients. He looks forward to it every week." Martha looked down at her hands. "Well, he asks me about it every day, at least. He has trouble remembering that music class only happens on Tuesday." She shivered slightly and looked back up, wearing a forced smile. "What can I do for you?"

"I wanted to find out information about when the center is closing for remodeling and other details like how much lunch costs and what people like to eat."

"Oh?" Martha lifted her eyebrows. "Why?"

"I work at Cascade Athletic Club," Marlo explained. "My parents own it, actually. We want to offer a small-bites menu once the senior center closes so our SilverSneakers clients have an affordable place to eat lunch."

"That sounds like an excellent idea." Martha scurried around the table. "I've always wanted to belong to the club, but I can't with Frank. You have childcare, not eldercare, right?"

Marlo nodded. "I'm sorry. That sounds like it would be a helpful service, but it's not something we currently offer."

"Currently offer?" Martha perked up. "Are you thinking about it for the future?"

"Um . . . we're actively looking at ways to cater to our senior clientele while at the same time making sure we create an atmosphere that all ages can enjoy." Marlo unzipped her coat and took it off.

"Why don't you hang your coat up in the closet there, and I'll show you around the dining room?" Martha offered.

A minute later, Martha was giving Marlo the full tour. The inside of the dining room was covered in wood panels and boasted a full wall of windows facing the beach. The linoleum floor was worn in places yet still sparkled in the florescent light. There were tables for eight, like at the yacht club, and folding chairs. At the center of each table sat salt and pepper shakers, a stack of paper napkins, and bottles of ketchup and tartar sauce. Since it was noontime, half of the tables were full, and conversation buzzed all around them. Marlo recognized many of the SilverSneakers members from the club, still wearing their exercise clothes. But it was a table over in the corner that caught Marlo's attention. A gentleman in his fifties was eating lunch with Ben.

"When does the remodeling work begin?" Marlo asked, not taking her eyes off Ben. He wore a navy-blue polo shirt that showed off his arms and gray slacks with leather sneakers. A black raincoat was draped over his chair, and his bike helmet lay on the floor. How could Ben survive the November chill without an insulated coat? He must have been freezing.

"Two weeks from now," said Martha. "It's the end of an era, that's for sure. I remember them building this place when I was little."

Marlo's gaze lingered on Ben as he wrote something down in a notebook. His phone lay on the table next to him. Ben looked like he was deep in concentration, but every once in a while he'd look up at the man he was eating lunch with, say something, and laugh.

"I *said*," Martha declared in a louder-than-normal voice, "would you like to see the lunch menu?"

"What?" Marlo jerked her attention away from Ben and gave it to Martha. "Sorry. Yes, I would love to see the lunch menu."

Martha's eyes sparkled merrily. "I take it you know that gentleman?" she asked, with a bemused smile.

"The man in the blazer and tie? No, I don't."

"What about the young one in the polo shirt with the biceps that could crush walnuts?"

"Ben?" Marlo asked, not sure she'd heard Martha correctly. "I wouldn't say his biceps could crush walnuts."

"Oh. So you've noticed his biceps, have you?" Martha smirked as she grabbed Marlo by her elbow. "I see you're not wearing a wedding ring."

"I'm only twenty-four."

"No boyfriend?"

"My ex was a cheater."

Martha clucked her tongue. "What a shame. A pretty woman like you, with a heart for community, definitely deserves someone better."

They stood at the lunch counter now, standing in front of a menu printed in giant easy-to-read letters. "Let's order you a meal so you can sample what the food tastes like."

"Oh, I don't want to impose," said Marlo. "And I didn't bring my wallet with me."

"Wallet?" barked a man behind the counter. His beard was as white as his apron. "Wallets don't matter here. We don't turn anyone away. Lunch is on me, and you can pay it forward when you're able to help someone else in need."

"Meet Luke Holter," said Martha. "He's a handyman who's worked for over forty years in Harper Landing but still finds time to volunteer at the senior center twice a week."

"This was my mother's favorite place," said Luke. "You're one of Lottie Burke's girls, aren't ya? I recognize you from your ballet posters."

Unexpected tears sprang to Marlo's eyes at the mention of Madame Burke. "Yes," she said. "That's right. Did you know her?"

"She was my sister," Luke said gruffly.

"She was a wonderful teacher." Marlo scanned Luke's features for some resemblance to his sister and saw it at once. They had the same prominent cheekbones. "Madame Burke changed my life."

"Yours and so many more." Luke cleared his throat. "So? What'll it be?"

Marlo looked across the stainless steel trays on the buffet line in search of something healthy. "I'll have the grilled chicken and vegetables, please, with just a little bit of mashed potatoes."

"Thanks, Luke," said Martha.

"Yes," Marlo said. "Thank you. I'll be sure to pay it forward. How much do lunches here cost?"

"Five bucks." Luke scooped up the rest of Marlo's meal. "And a slice of pie is an extra dollar. Would you like some? We've got rhubarb."

"No thanks," said Marlo, who hated rhubarb.

"And the coffee is free," said Martha.

"How nice." Marlo's heart sank. There was no way the club could compete with these prices.

"We'll sit you down over here." Martha guided Marlo over to an empty table near the wall, close to the table where Ben and the man in the blazer sat.

"Oh, I don't know—" Marlo started to say, but it was too late; Martha was already pulling out a chair.

"I'll go get you some coffee and be right back. Do you take cream or sugar?"

"Cream, please." From the corner of her eye, Marlo saw Ben look at her in surprise. She felt sweat break out across the back of her neck as she watched Martha walk away. How had this happened? She was eating lunch alone, one table away from Ben Wexler-Lowrey, in the middle of the Harper Landing Senior Center. When she'd woken up this morning and read her calendar, this had definitely not been on the agenda.

Marlo picked up her knife and fork to slice her chicken breast with care. The portion was small and blackened with grill lines. When she bit into it, the first thing she tasted was salt. She took a bite of green beans next, and they were equally salty. Like they'd come from a can. Well, that partially explained how the senior center kept prices down. Probably most of this food was frozen or canned. Processed food was cheaper than the fresh ingredients they used at the smoothie bar, but it wasn't as healthy. The SilverSneakers might be willing to pay extra for a better-quality product.

"Here you go," said Martha, setting a mug of coffee beside Marlo's plate. "I need to go back to the front desk, but let me know if you need anything else."

"Thank you so much for your help," Marlo said with a smile. "I appreciate it."

"My pleasure," said Martha. But instead of walking back to the front lobby, she walked over to the man in the blazer and tapped him on the shoulder. "Excuse me, Ralph, but I have a question about the filing system. Could you please help?"

Marlo watched in horror as the man left with Martha. Now she was sitting by herself at a table next to Ben, who was also eating alone.

"The only way this could be more awkward is if our parents were here," said Ben loudly.

"Yeah," Marlo mumbled, feeling her cheeks turn pink.

"I know what I'm doing here, but what brings you to the senior center, Jonas?" He held up a bite of fried food. "The fish and chips?"

"Kind of." Marlo bit her bottom lip and plotted her escape. The sooner she finished her meal, the sooner she could leave. But that would be hard to do shouting to Ben across the tables. She picked up her plate. "Mind if I join you?"

"I'm in the middle of interviewing the director about an article I'm writing for the *Times*."

"Oh." Marlo set her plate back down and cursed herself for asking.

"But I'd love to join you," said Ben as he brought his own plate over. "If I linger here too long by myself, my old-lady magnet turns on, and I get swarmed."

"What?" Marlo laughed in spite of herself.

"Sure. Look around the room. Y chromosomes are in short supply."

Marlo followed his suggestion and took stock of the dining room. Ben was right. Men were definitely sparse. "Have you eaten here before?" Marlo asked.

Ben nodded. "I've written several articles about the senior center, and every time I do, they insist I eat lunch. But you didn't answer my question, Jonas. What are *you* doing here?"

"I'm trying to figure out if Cascade Athletic Club's smoothie bar could offer a meal comparable to the lunch here once the senior center closes for remodeling, but I'm not sure we could come up with something this affordable."

"A five-bucks lunch is hard to beat." Ben dipped a french fry in ketchup. "Even if it's fifty percent sodium."

"Plus, this is a hot lunch, and we don't serve hot meals." Marlo forked a bite of chicken. "I still don't understand how they can make the meals this cheap. This chicken breast was probably one or two dollars, plus half a can of vegetables, a potato or two, gravy, and the coffee. That must be at least three dollars and eighty cents' worth of goods. That means their profit is only one dollar, which wouldn't cover their overhead."

"Wait." Ben dropped a french fry on his plate. "How do you know all that?"

"How much food costs? Why wouldn't I know? I go grocery shopping."

"You do?"

The conversation was getting weird, as far as Marlo was concerned. "Of course I do. I have to cook, don't I? I live alone, and preparing for one person can cost a lot of money if you're not careful."

"I always assumed you lived on takeout."

Marlo snort-laughed and then coughed into her napkin to try to make it look like something was just caught in her throat. "I like eating out at restaurants, and sometimes I do get takeout, but as a dancer—" Marlo paused, feeling her heart pound in her chest as soon as she said those words that were no longer true. "When I was a dancer," she began again, "I had to be careful that I was eating the right balance of protein, carbohydrates, and fats. I'm not a fancy cook, but I can prepare simple meals. My dad taught me. My mom, too, although she mainly does vegetarian dishes."

Marlo wanted to ask Ben about his skills in the kitchen—and most specifically why he'd said on his Good Catch profile that he didn't know how to cook when she knew that wasn't true. But she couldn't call him out on that without admitting to stalking his profile. So she went at it obliquely. "You're probably much better at cooking than I am," she probed. "Especially when it comes to baking."

"Baking isn't cooking." Ben shrugged.

"Of course it is," Marlo argued. "It involves following a recipe, mixing ingredients, and using an oven, doesn't it?"

Ben sighed. "I suppose. I can make sandwich bread and the fillings to go in them. That's it."

"What about the Nuthatch Bakery's smoked-salmon chowder? Can you make that? It's one of my favorites."

"Yeah. I can make it if I have to. It's not that hard." Ben sipped his coffee and set it down slowly. "Do you think my parents' restaurant is shabby? You can be honest."

"Shabby? Of course not. It's quaint. I love how the restroom has that fake bird nest with all of the extra toilet paper in it. And the whole place is always so clean." Marlo wrapped her fingertips around her mug. "Did someone insult the Nuthatch?"

"Well, yeah," said Ben. "I guess they did. But I didn't know if it was the truth or not, and so I wanted an objective opinion."

"I *love* the Nuthatch Bakery," Marlo said with feeling. "It's one of my favorite places in all of Harper Landing."

"Thanks." Ben stared into Marlo's eyes in a way that made her stomach flutter. "I appreciate that. And look," he said, pointing at her lunch. "About the food. The reason it's so cheap is that it's subsidized by the federal food assistance program. Not only does the center receive commodity food from the government, but they also have volunteers on site who can help low-income seniors sign up for SNAP benefits, like an EBT card that helps pay for groceries."

Marlo looked out across the dining room at the packed tables and wondered how many of her SilverSneakers guests needed help with food. The idea of tapping them for revenue no longer seemed appealing. She let out a long sigh.

"What's the matter?" Ben asked.

"It's the club." Marlo pulled back a long strand of brown hair that had escaped from her ponytail and tucked it behind her ear. "We're committed to providing a welcoming space for our SilverSneakers members, but that means we're losing money by not catering to the younger demographic that pays a higher fee."

"That's why you were arguing with your dad at the wedding about starting up the small-group fitness classes?" Ben asked.

Marlo nodded. "Yes. I think they would help, because they'd involve an extra fee. In the meantime, I thought we could make money by changing things up at the smoothie bar. But now I feel stupid because I realize that our SilverSneakers members might not be able to afford our snacks."

"Well, not all of your SilverSneakers members are food insecure. There's probably a wide range. I bet you have plenty of rich members too."

Marlo nodded. "I assume so. It's not like I profile them or anything. Although maybe I should, because if I knew more about our membership base, it might help." Marlo put her elbows on the table and rested her forehead in her hands for a few seconds before she sat up straight again. "I don't know anything about business," she said dejectedly. "I'm learning it on my feet as I go, and my parents aren't much help at all." She couldn't believe that she was confessing this to Ben, but since he was also the child of local business owners, it felt safe to talk to him.

"The first step might be a survey," Ben suggested. "Do you have an email list?"

"Yes." Marlo nodded. "We use it to send out the monthly newsletter."

"Try sending out a survey that lets you find out more information about your clients. What's their income bracket? What are the age demographics? What services do they most want at the gym? Would they like to eat lunch at the club? That sort of thing."

"How would I get them to fill it out?"

"That's easy." Ben took another sip of his coffee. "Say you'll pick a name from all the responses, and the winner will get a free smoothie or a personal training session. People love to win stuff."

"That's brilliant." Marlo smiled. "Thanks." She couldn't believe Ben was being so helpful. It was the first productive conversation she'd had about solving problems at the club in months. "How did you learn so much about business?" she asked. "Did your parents teach you?"

"Yeah." Ben nodded. "A little bit. I also minored in business administration in college." His phone buzzed, and he turned it over. "Shoot. My deadline's approaching. I need to go. You'll have to tell me about your date with Hunter Darrington later," Ben said with a twinkle in his eye.

"How do you know about that?" Marlo asked, feeling her cheeks turn red again.

Ben took one more fry off his plate and popped it into his mouth. "Katelyn told me."

"He's a psycho killer. Or a psycho-killer aficionado. I don't know; it was hard to tell."

"Hunter's a strange one, all right."

Marlo pointed at him. "And do *not* put that in your @HarpLanPDScan feed."

Ben stared at her with his mouth wide open for a moment before collecting himself. "I don't know what you're talking about."

Marlo folded her arms across her chest and tilted her head to the side. "Oh?"

Ben leaned forward into the table. "I'm flattered that you think I'm clever enough to be the voice behind such whimsy, but I swear it isn't me." He flashed his dimples in a wide grin and sprang up from his chair. "See you around, Jonas."

CHAPTER EIGHT

Ben measured flour on the scale to add the perfect amount to the sourdough starter that the Nuthatch Bakery would use in its popular waffles the following morning. As soon as he finished his Friday-night shift, he was meeting Dahlia at the Western Cedar for dinner and drinks. Ben normally used his time away from the paper to unwind and catch up on laundry, but he'd picked up hours at the bakery to replenish his bank account. Once the food scale balanced at the right weight, Ben scraped the rye flour into the starter and folded it into the mix. He put a clean towel over the bowl and set it on the counter next to the oven, where it would double in size by morning.

Ben tried to focus on baking so he would stop thinking about Marlo, but it was impossible. Three days after eating lunch at the senior center together, their conversation was still on his mind. Marlo had been so easy to talk to—and humble, too, like when she'd shared why her family's business was struggling and that she didn't know how to help. The real shocker was learning that she cooked. It was hard for Ben to picture Marlo with her slicked-back hair, low-cut shirt, and skintight leggings roaming the aisles of the grocery store to pick out onions, but it turned out that Marlo was more human than he had thought.

Dahlia was beautiful, too, Ben reminded himself, and it was Dahlia he was meeting at the Western Cedar in an hour, not Marlo. He just needed to finish his duties first. That meant deboning a chicken, slicing up celery and Granny Smith apples, and mixing up the chicken salad for sandwiches for the lunch crowd tomorrow. Oh, and he had to assemble the dough for the pumpkin-spice scones that his father, Nick, would bake fresh at three o'clock in the morning. A natural introvert, Nick preferred working at the bakery when nobody else was there and then leaving early to go to bed promptly after dinner.

"Good," said his mother, entering the kitchen from the front of the bakery. Her hair was wound into a loose knot at the back of her head, and her apron smelled like cinnamon and frosting. "You're still here."

"Of course I'm here," said Ben as he lifted two roast chickens out of a massive dutch oven and set them on a cutting board. "I'm on the clock for another thirty minutes, and I have a bunch of work to do."

"Too much work," said Cheryl, shaking her head. "November used to be a quieter month for us, but we're busier than ever. That's what I wanted to talk to you about. Your dad thinks we should hire more staff, and I agree."

"Dad wants to hire more people?" Ben pulled chicken off the bone with two forks. "I'm shocked."

"Nick does like his solitude." Cheryl washed her hands as she spoke. "But even he can see that we're swamped." She took celery out of the refrigerator and selected a sharp knife to slice the stalks. "We're thinking of hiring a full-time manager to take some of the burden off of running this place."

"But you're the manager," Ben said. "And you already have two assistants."

"That's the point." Cheryl chopped with expert precision. "I'm not ready to retire yet, but I don't want to keep working sixty hours a week like I've done for the past three decades. I'm ready to cut back."

"That makes sense to me," said Ben as he lifted the first chicken carcass. "Where's the stockpot? I'll get this simmering."

"You can toss the carcass." Cheryl hunched her shoulders guiltily. "We're using canned chicken broth at the moment because we don't have enough time to cook from scratch anymore."

Ben was stunned. "You want me to throw out a perfectly good chicken carcass?" He held up the backbone. "But you can make bone broth with this."

"Who will monitor it?" Cheryl looked around the empty kitchen. "We're short staffed."

Ben sighed. "I see your point." He wrapped up the carcass in plastic and put it back in the refrigerator so he could take it home himself. "It sounds like Dad is right. You guys need more employees, and a general manager would be a great place to start."

"That's why I wanted to talk to you." Cheryl pushed sliced celery into a stainless steel mixing bowl from her cutting board. "The manager job will pay well." She wiped her hands on her apron and walked over to a small desk, where she picked up a clipboard off a stack of papers. "Here's the job announcement we're considering posting, with the salary allotment." She held the clipboard under her son's nose since his hands were juicy.

When Ben saw the figure his parents were offering their new manager, he felt his stomach flop. It was $15,000 more than he made at the *Seattle Times*. "How many hours a week is that for?" he asked.

"Forty." Cheryl put the clipboard away. "We're offering a set schedule with no overtime."

Ben, who already knew where his mother was heading with this conversation, chose his words carefully. "Ma," he began. "You know I love picking up shifts here and there to earn extra money, but I'm a journalist. Working full time at the bakery isn't for me."

"But it could be," Cheryl said with a hopeful smile. "It's taken years, but your father and I have built a thriving business that can support a family." She waved a stalk of celery in the air. "All of this could be yours someday."

"I love the Nuthatch Bakery," said Ben. "You know I do. But journalism is my passion."

"Journalism can't support a family in this economy. Not with Harper Landing real estate skyrocketing like it's been doing. How will you be able to afford to live here?"

Ben's shoulders slumped. "I don't know," he said, shaking his head. "I hope I don't have to move." He shrugged. "But there are more important things than owning a house."

"That's Goldie talking." Cheryl ripped off another stalk of celery. "She's filled your head with unrealistic nonsense. Paying rent is throwing money down a rathole."

"Paying rent is what I can afford." Ben wiped the grease off his fingers. "And *you* taught me to live within my means."

"True," Cheryl grumbled. "But it pains me to see you here working on a Friday night to scrape up extra cash when you should be out meeting my future daughter-in-law."

"As a matter of fact," said Ben, stirring mayonnaise into the chicken-and-celery mixture, "I have a date tonight with a beautiful woman."

"You do?" Cheryl grabbed a Granny Smith apple and tossed it from one hand to another.

"I do indeed." Ben ground fresh pepper into the chicken salad. "I'm meeting her at the Western Cedar to hear Mike and Simon's band play."

Cheryl winced. "That'll drive her away."

"The Monte Cristos are great!"

"If you like jazz." Cheryl peeled the apple skin into one long coil.

"Jazz and blues," Ben corrected.

"I never trust music with an uneven rhythm." Cheryl set down the peeler and picked up a paring knife. "Well, what time are you meeting this gorgeous woman?"

"Seven thirty." Ben looked up at the clock. "Shoot. I won't have time to drive home and shower." He looked at the chicken juice all over his wrists. "I smell like a delicatessen."

Cheryl took the mixing bowl away from him. "Go upstairs and use Grace's shower. She won't mind."

"But I don't have a clean shirt."

Cheryl looked at Ben's disheveled brown hair. "A shower and shampoo will be better than nothing." She waved him away with her hands. "Go on. I'll finish up."

"No, I will." Ben took back possession of the mixing bowl. "You're paying me for a reason. I need the money, and you need the break." He pointed to the chair at the desk. "Go put your feet up while I put this away." When Cheryl didn't budge, Ben smiled in a way that he knew would flash both dimples. His mom was a sucker for his dimples.

"Oh, all right," she said, trudging off. "But don't forget the tarragon."

Ten minutes later, Ben raced up the back steps to the upstairs apartment that Grace rented from Julia Harper. She had turned the two-bedroom home into a jungle of houseplants. There was even a strange-looking cactus hanging by the front door that looked half-dead from the cold. As Ben poised his finger to press the doorbell, he had second thoughts. He hated relying on his older sister for anything, even a hot shower. But one whiff of his armpits told him that he needed all the help he could get. He rang the doorbell and waited.

Grace opened the door thirty seconds later wearing gray sweatpants and a University of Washington hoodie. Her dark-brown hair was in a messy bun, and she wore the thick black glasses that their mom said made her look like Groucho Marx. "Oh," said Grace as she pushed up her glasses by their bridge. "It's you. What's up?"

"I need a favor," Ben said in a rush. "Can I take a shower? I've got a date in twenty minutes, and I don't have time to drive home and change."

"Wow. Great planning."

Ben had known this was a bad idea. Grace always had to be superior about everything. "Never mind." He turned to go.

"Wait." Grace grabbed his sleeve. "You can use my shower." She offered him the bag of SkinnyPop popcorn she was holding. "I suppose you're hungry too?"

"Famished." Ben dived his hand down and picked up a handful. "Thanks, Grace. I'll be superfast." He raced down the hall.

"There are towels in the cabinet above the toilet," Grace called after him.

"Whoa," Ben exclaimed when he opened the door to the bathroom and saw that every surface area was covered with pots. "I don't think you have enough succulents."

"I can stop buying houseplants anytime I want to," she said, sneaking up behind him. "Here's a clean shirt."

Ben held up the gray polo shirt she offered. It had the logo of her company on it—Custom Aeronautic Plastics—along with a tiny drawing of an airplane window seal that they manufactured. He checked the label, men's medium, which would fit. "Thanks," he said. "This smells better than what I'm wearing." Ben didn't ask why Grace had a man's shirt on hand, because they never talked about their respective love lives. In fact, they never talked at all, unless it was about their parents or the bakery or how much stress Grace was under at work.

"You're lucky you caught me," Grace said as she walked away and collected a glass of red wine from the coffee table. "I came home ten minutes ago. It's been an *excruciating* week at work." She flopped on the couch and unpaused the TV. Ben heard the opening jingle from *Golden Girls* in the background. He knew all the episodes by heart because of Grace. It had been her favorite show to watch in high school. She'd said it kept her company while studying for the SAT.

Ben flew through his shower and emerged a few minutes later smelling like orchid-mist bodywash and moonlit-lavender shampoo. He wasn't sure the combination mixed well, but it beat chicken juice. "Mom and Dad want to hire a general manager for the bakery," he said as he towel-dried his hair.

"That's a good idea." Grace didn't look up from the television, where the four *Golden Girls* were eating cheesecake.

"They think it should be me."

Grace turned and looked at him. "That's a horrible idea." She paused the show.

"I know." Ben nodded, but he was secretly annoyed that his sister agreed with him. Was it because Grace didn't think he was up for the job? "I'm a journalist," Ben said, to clarify why he thought the manager idea was a bad one.

"And not everyone wants to own a bakery." Grace fiddled with the drawstrings of her hoodie. "Or have a husband and a family. I mean, there are lots of ways to live your life that are perfectly fine and look nothing like the way our parents lived theirs."

"That's right." Ben folded the towel and went back to the bathroom, where he hung it on the rod. He came back into the living room, sat on the wood floor, and tied his shoes.

"What Mom and Dad have is special," Grace continued, crumpling the popcorn bag as she spoke. "They've been together since high school, and it was love at first sight. And they're still together! That's statistically implausible." She pushed up her glasses with her index finger. "Most people don't have that kind of luck, but Mom thinks everyone should be lucky like them, and it's not fair."

"Wow. It sounds like I'm not the only person Mom's been advising recently." Ben double knotted his laces.

"She should stick to baking, that's what she should do," Grace grumbled. "Who named her Mother of the Year?"

Ben was torn. He was scheduled to meet Dahlia in three minutes, and the Western Cedar was two blocks away. If he hurried, he could make it on time. But he also sensed that Grace was hurting, and he hated to leave her there eating popcorn for dinner and slurping red wine. "Is there anything you want to talk about?" he asked.

"With my little brother?" Grace curled her lip. "No."

"Okay, then," Ben said as he put on his raincoat. "Thanks for the shower."

"No problem." Grace looked back at the TV.

Ben rushed out the door, down the stairs, and outside to the sidewalk below. As annoying as Grace was, what she'd said about their parents made sense. Nick and Cheryl's love story was unique. The way Cheryl had described it, she had been sitting in homeroom one day in tenth grade and had looked over at the new guy sitting next to her, and that had been it. Love at first sight. Ben thought witnessing something like that in person would be cool—two people glomming together with instantaneous attraction.

Ben hustled two blocks down Main Street, hung a left, and continued on until he reached the Western Cedar. Despite his quick pace, he was five minutes late, and when he reached the restaurant, he saw no sign of Dahlia. Ben opened the door of the lobby and peeked inside, hoping she was waiting for him where it was warm. Sure enough, Dahlia was sitting at the bar at the side of the restaurant, nibbling at the mixed nuts in the container next to her. She wore a slinky red dress and black heels. Her legs were crossed, and one of her shoes was scuffed. Ben took a deep breath and rolled his shoulders back. Sure, he was a few minutes late, but he'd made it. He stepped into the lobby and grinned.

That was when he saw Mike prop his guitar on its stand on the band stage next to the bar and walk over to Dahlia. *Great,* Ben was thinking. He'd been meaning to introduce them so that Dahlia could audition for the band. Mike sat on the stool next to Dahlia, and she twisted in her seat to face him. She leaned forward with a flirty smile. Mike grinned, turning on the charm, and held up two fingers for the bartender. Was Mike ordering Dahlia a drink? Ben charged forward but was stopped by the hostess, a tall woman with pink hair and several nose rings.

"Excuse me, sir, do you have a reservation? There's a cover charge if you want to go to the bar."

Ben pulled his attention away from Mike and Dahlia, who were now laughing together conspiratorially. "Yes, I do have a reservation. Ben Wexler-Lowrey, party of two," he said, peering over the podium at the reservation list. He pointed to his name.

"We called your name ten minutes ago, and you weren't here."

"I'm five minutes late," Ben protested. "Five minutes."

The hostess held up her wrist. "My watch says ten. You'll have to wait until the next table becomes available."

"Fabulous," Ben mumbled. "Can I wait at the bar?"

"Sure," said the hostess. "But there's a ten-dollar cover charge."

Ben winced at the notion of paying good money just to sit down. He pulled the cash out of his wallet and slapped it on the podium. From the corner of his eye, he saw Simon and the band's drummer setting up equipment on the stage. But Mike didn't budge from his seat beside Dahlia, even when Simon began doing a sound check. Ben regulated his breathing and told himself to calm down. Mike was his best friend. They'd never fought over women before. He had no reason to be jealous or assume that Mike would try to steal Dahlia away from him. Mike wasn't like that.

"I see you two have finally met," Ben said once he approached them. "Sorry I was late. My parents needed help at the bakery."

"You're not late; I was early," said Dahlia. "Besides," she said, her gaze becoming soft under fluttering lashes, "this gave me the chance to meet Mike."

"I hope you like jazz," Mike replied, staring back at her with equal fervor.

"I listen to blues all the time," she said.

"How fortuitous," said Ben, feeling like a third wheel. "When are the Monte Cristos due onstage?"

"Right now," Simon barked, sneaking up behind them. "Come on, Mike. You need to do the sound check."

"Oh, right." He didn't take his eyes off Dahlia for one second. "Nurse my drink for me?"

"I'll take care of it as soon as it arrives," she said in a breathy voice.

"Ben Wexlery?" the pink-haired hostess called from the podium. "Is there a Ben Wexlery here?"

"I assume she means me," Ben said. "I think our table is ready."

"Let's just eat here," Dahlia suggested. "They serve food at the bar, right? We'll get a better view of the band."

"Okay." Ben wanted to be agreeable—plus the food served at the bar was cheaper. "I'll go tell the hostess we'll sit here." He left for one minute to cancel their table, and when he came back, Mike was at the bar again, engaged in conversation with Dahlia.

"Of course I've heard about the Essentially Ellington High School Jazz Competition," Dahlia was saying. "I went to Roosevelt High School in Seattle, and they win all the time."

"Not my junior year, they didn't." Mike grinned. "Harper Landing High went all the way to Lincoln Center in New York City and took home first place."

"I was in choir." Dahlia crossed and uncrossed her long legs. She leaned toward Mike, seemingly unaware that Ben had returned.

Ben cleared his throat. "You both like music. That's been established." He stuffed his hands in his pocket.

"Jonas, party of three," called the hostess.

Ben whipped around and saw Marlo walk through the lobby with her parents. She wore a royal-blue sweater dress, black boots, and a wool coat. Her hair was wound into a coil at the nape of her neck, and a jaunty hat rested on her head, pulled all the way down over her ears. Marlo followed Chuck and Laura through the maze of tables until they reached a booth at the opposite side of the restaurant.

"Oh look," said Dahlia. "Marlo's here."

"Ben and Marlo have been sworn enemies since first grade," Mike said as he rested his elbow on the bar.

"Kindergarten," Ben muttered, not that either of them was listening to him.

"When they were on a soccer team," Mike continued, his eyes glued on Dahlia, "Marlo made fun of Ben for putting his shin guards on upside down."

"Chuck made fun of me for doing that," Ben corrected. "Not Marlo."

"That sounds like Mr. Jonas." Dahlia took a sip of her long island iced tea, which had just arrived. "But his bark is worse than his bite."

The cliché made Ben cringe, but he didn't say anything. Plus, he didn't agree with her. Belittling six-year-olds was no way to coach. He flagged down the bartender so he could order himself a drink.

"Uh-oh. It looks like I need to go," said Mike at the sight of Simon frantically waving from the stage. "I'll be back after our first set."

That did it, as far as Ben was concerned. "This is a date," he declared, waving his finger between Dahlia and himself.

"It is?" Mike's eyes widened in shock and fell as a look of disappointment overtook him. "I'm sorry. I didn't realize."

"Didn't you hear me tell Dahlia that I was sorry I was late?"

"I thought you were talking to me." Mike rubbed the back of his neck. "You said you were going to come to watch the Monte Cristos tonight."

"Oh." Ben could see how Mike had been confused. "It's a misunderstanding, that's all."

"Yeah," said Dahlia, not bothering to hide the disappointment on her face. "But if I was here by myself, I would have totally let you pick me up from this bar."

A half smile flitted across Mike's face before he looked somberly at Ben. "Sorry, man."

"Mike Lu!" Simon hollered from across the bar. "Get your butt over here."

"No problem," said Ben.

Mike sighed and walked away.

Just then the bartender arrived, which provided a welcome relief from the awkwardness. Ben ordered an IPA and sliders, and Dahlia asked for a chef's salad. Once the waiter left, they sat in silence for a moment until a commotion on the other side of the room captured their attention.

"Seitan is disgusting. You know I hate it," Chuck bellowed. "Why would you suggest I order that?"

"Because you need to work on your cholesterol," Laura said in such a shrill voice that it carried across the room. Marlo sat beside her, covering her face with her hands.

"There they go again," Dahlia said, shaking her head. "Oh boy."

"Yeah." Ben stared at the way Marlo seemed to shrink inside her coat, which she hadn't taken off. "I wouldn't want to be at that table." As soon as he said it, he realized that he didn't want to be at the bar either—not when the chemistry between Mike and Dahlia had been so palpable that he'd almost seen sparks shoot between them. The Monte Cristos were onstage now, performing a jazz number that would make bluebirds cry. "You and Mike seem to have a lot in common," he said.

"We really do." Dahlia smiled at the mention of Mike. Then she frowned and looked back at her drink. "Sorry," she said.

"Don't be sorry." Ben sighed. "You like him. I can tell. And he likes you."

"Really?" Dahlia's face lit up. "I mean, I'm on a date with you, and you're great and . . ." Her mouth hung open, as if she was unable to finish her sentence.

"But this is weird because Mike is my best friend." Ben opened up his wallet and pulled out the gift card Simon had given him for the Western Cedar. He slid it onto the bar and held out his hand to shake. "I'm going to leave, but feel free to stay. Okay?"

"Can we be friends?" Dahlia asked. For the first time that evening, she looked at him with enthusiasm.

"Sure." Ben nodded.

"Thanks, Ben," said Dahlia as she threw her arms around him in a hug. "You're the best."

"Great," Ben said with a smile that did *not* show his dimples. He could feel Mike's eyes on them from across the room and heard Mike's guitar miss a beat when Dahlia hugged him. But as Ben stood up to go, he bobbed his head toward his friend, and Mike's expression softened. When he realized Ben was leaving, Mike grinned.

Ben walked through the bar and into the lobby. "*Now* do you want a table?" the hostess asked him.

"No thanks," Ben said as he charged through the front door and stepped into the cold. Head turned, looking back at the hostess, he smacked directly into Marlo, who was pacing up and down the sidewalk.

CHAPTER NINE

Marlo bumped her forehead against Ben's pectorals so hard that her hat was knocked off. "Whoa!" she said. "Sorry." She raised her hands to steady herself and ended up placing them on Ben's chest. Marlo felt a buzz of energy pulse underneath her palms. It was like Ben had sent out sparks that tickled her nervous system.

"No, *I'm* sorry." Ben held on to her arms, bracing her as she wobbled. "I should have looked where I was going. Are you okay?" His brown eyes stared at her so intently she felt compelled to look away.

"I'm fine." Marlo squeezed her eyes shut and held her breath. Could this evening get any worse? First, her parents got into a shouting match in the middle of the restaurant, and now Ben was witnessing her humiliation as she slinked outside to escape the embarrassment. "I should watch where I'm going." She fluttered her eyes open and bent over to pick up her hat.

"This evening sucks, and I should be more careful."

Marlo jammed her hat on her head and stood up. "What's wrong with your evening?" she asked.

Ben tilted his head to the side and kneaded the back of his neck. "I think my date just fell in love with Mike Lu."

"Dahlia?" Marlo chuckled. "She's had a crush on him for ages. Oops." Marlo covered her mouth with her hand. "I shouldn't have said that."

Ben sighed. "Don't worry about it. All you did was confirm my suspicions, and I think Mike has a thing for her too."

"Dahlia said nice things about you as well," Marlo added, feeling like she owed him a consolation prize.

"Wow, thanks. I feel so special now." Ben grinned, and Marlo tried not to notice how adorable his dimples were. "What are you doing out in the cold?"

"Avoiding my parents' argument." Marlo fanned her shoes into a V and then pulled them back again. She often fidgeted into ballet positions when nervous. "Are they still going at it?"

"I didn't notice, but I'll check." Ben walked up to the window and stared into the restaurant. "They're going at it, all right," he said. "But at least they're not fighting anymore. I bet the temperature in there went up ten degrees."

"Oh jeez." Marlo stomped to the glass and looked inside. Her parents were now sharing one side of the booth—plus a considerable amount of saliva by the look of it. "I should never have agreed to come with them tonight. Hopefully, someone will enjoy the Copper River salmon I ordered, because it won't be me." She held on to her purse strap and turned away.

"I haven't had dinner yet either," said Ben. "But I know a good place to eat if you like salmon—smoked-salmon chowder, that is."

"Is the bakery open?" Marlo asked. "I thought the Nuthatch closed an hour ago."

"They did." Ben reached into his pocket and pulled out his keys. "But I know the owners."

Marlo's stomach rumbled at the mention of food. "I would love some chowder," she said. "Are you sure your parents won't mind?"

"Not in the slightest." He waved his hand, motioning her forward. "Come on. I think we have some sourdough bread bowls left too."

"Yum. Just let me text my parents first." As soon as Marlo hit send, she felt freer.

A hot meal was too good an opportunity to pass up—at least, that was what Marlo told herself. Following Ben toward Main Street had nothing to do with how good he looked in slim-fitting pants and a polo shirt, his jacket unzipped like he was impervious to the cold. In the brief moment she'd been pressed against him, Marlo had smelled the clean scent of soap mixed with something exotic, like a jungle. Which was strange, because Ben was the least exotic person she knew. He was as familiar as turkey and gravy. Ben was someone she'd overlooked or, worse, looked down upon. But now she found her gloved hand twitching, eager to slip into the crook of his arm. Marlo kept her hand safely stowed in her pocket where it belonged and looked down at her boots as they marched in step with his leather shoes.

"I read your article about the senior center," she said. "Do you think they'll come up with the funds for a solar-paneled roof?"

"They already have a grant from the rotary club for half of it." Ben turned when they reached Main Street. The Nuthatch Bakery lay ahead of them, but the lights were off, and there was a CLOSED sign on the front door. "Then, for the second half of the roof, they're selling dedications for five hundred dollars each."

"Like sponsoring a park bench, only for electricity," Marlo said, remembering the way Ben had worded it in his article. "I think that's brilliant. It's environmentally friendly, but it'll also make the senior center cheaper to operate in the future. I wish we could do that at the Cascade Athletic Club, but the up-front cost would be too steep."

"You never know," said Ben as he led Marlo away from Main Street and down the alley behind the bakery. "You guys probably use a ton of electricity for the cardio equipment and the air-conditioning. You might recoup your money quickly and start saving sooner than you realized. It might be worth having the solar company come out and take a look." They were at the rear entrance now, and motion-sensor lights flicked on as Ben unlocked the door. "After you," he said, waving her inside.

Walking into the Nuthatch Bakery's kitchen was like wrapping herself up in a blanket of cinnamon rolls. "What's that delicious smell?" Marlo asked as her eyes adjusted to the dim light coming from the glowing exit signs.

"Lots of things." Ben flicked on the lights, revealing a gleaming industrial kitchen with stainless steel counters, two sinks, and a commercial dishwasher. "There are the preassembled scone and muffin doughs ready to finish off in the morning, the sourdough starter, the rising baguettes, and . . . oh yeah—the cinnamon rolls are proofing. My dad will get here at three a.m. to finish everything off."

"I knew I smelled cinnamon." Marlo's mouth watered.

"Do you want one? There might still be one or two out front. We move them to the day-old rack once the fresh ones are ready."

Marlo removed her hat and unbuttoned her coat. The kitchen was warm and cozy. "I'd never say no to a cinnamon roll."

"Carbs don't scare you?"

"Nope." Marlo shrugged out of her coat.

"Here, I'll hang that up for you." Ben took her hat and coat and hung them on a hook by the desk. He stashed his jacket next to it. "Let me warm up that chowder, and then I'll hunt for the pastries. Here," he said, pulling out a desk chair. "Take a seat."

"Thank you." Marlo sat down and watched Ben work. First, he washed his hands and dried them on a paper towel. Then he opened the enormous refrigerator and took out a large glass pitcher filled with a blush-colored liquid. "Do you need any help?" Marlo asked.

Ben shook his head. "No thanks. It'll warm up on the stove in no time." He poured the chowder into a small saucepan and lit the gas range. "I'll be right back with the bread," he said, pushing through a swinging door into the retail space.

Marlo swiveled in the desk chair and admired the pictures hanging on the bulletin board behind it. She studied several portraits of all four Wexler-Lowreys taken at a professional studio as well as on a beach. The most recent family picture was from Ben's sister's graduation. Marlo couldn't recall her name. Since the sister was older, she'd only been at elementary school with them for a couple of years before she'd headed off to middle school. The best part of the bulletin board, besides the pictures, was Ben's articles. There were several clippings from the *Seattle Times*, including stories he'd written about Harper Landing, plus there were a few from the *Western Front*, which Marlo was unfamiliar with. That seemed to be his college paper. But it was a yellowed copy of the *Harper Landing Beacon* that caught Marlo's eye. There was the headline that was seared into her memory bank: **PE Waiver Program Elitist and Unnecessary.** Marlo felt irritation bubble inside, almost as grumbly as her empty stomach, until she started reading.

"Should families who can afford to pay $625 a month be allowed to pull their students out of school early?" the article began. "That is what happened to an elite group of students enrolled in Harper Landing Middle School. These wealthy families acquire their seventh and eighth graders' waivers so that they don't have to suit up in PE uniforms like everybody else."

Even now, after all these years, the thesis annoyed her. Yes, ballet and things like traveling soccer teams, competitive gymnastics, and ice hockey were expensive, but that wasn't the students' faults.

"Excuse me," said a snotty voice behind her. "Who would you be?"

Marlo spun around in her chair and saw a woman wearing sweatpants, a University of Washington hoodie with a huge red-wine stain across the front of it, and thick glasses. At first, Marlo didn't recognize the woman, but then she realized she was seeing a disheveled version of the person from the graduation picture on the wall. "Are you Ben's sister?" Marlo asked.

"I asked you first." The woman put her hands on her hips.

Marlo straightened her posture and raised her chin. She was willing to answer the question, but she refused to be bullied. "I'm Marlo," she said as she crossed her legs.

"We're in luck on both counts." Ben backed through the swinging door holding two bread bowls and a plastic-wrapped cinnamon roll the size of Marlo's head. "There were only two bread bowls left, and—" Ben paused midsentence when he saw his sister. "Grace," Ben sputtered. "What are you doing here?"

"What do you mean, what am I doing here? I live here," Grace snapped.

"In the Nuthatch Bakery?" Marlo asked.

"No, not *in* the bakery." Grace looked at Marlo like she was an idiot. "In the apartment upstairs."

"We're having soup." Ben set the cinnamon roll on the counter and used his free hand to grab two plates for the bread bowls. "Would you like some?"

"You know I hate fish." Grace pointed at the cinnamon roll. "I came here for that."

"Sorry," Ben said with a shrug. "The bun's already spoken for." He turned the flame underneath the chowder down to a simmer. "Marlo, this is my sister, Grace. Grace, this is Marlo Jonas."

"Pleased to meet you," Marlo said automatically, even though she sensed nothing pleasant about Grace at all.

Grace closed her eyes and massaged her forehead. "I just wanted a cinnamon roll," she muttered. "I *really* wanted a cinnamon roll. Or cheesecake. Do we have cheesecake?"

"Mom and Dad don't serve cheesecake." Ben stirred the chowder. "You know that. But I saw some chocolate chip cookies out there."

"Chocolate gives me a migraine." Grace rubbed her temples. "And I already have a migraine. It's my fault for drinking a glass of wine." She pointed to her stained hoodie. "Or half a glass, before I spilled it." She turned to go.

"Wait!" Marlo stood up and retrieved the cinnamon roll from the counter. "You can have it. I don't know what it's like to have a migraine, but I've heard they're awful." She handed the pastry to Grace.

"Thank you." Grace brought the roll up to her nose and sniffed it through the plastic. "I'm a little bit queasy, but I think I can hold this down." Her expression softened. "Sorry to interrupt your date."

"Oh, this isn't a date," Ben said, so quickly that Marlo's cheeks turned pink.

"But I thought . . ." Grace looked from Ben to Marlo and then back to Ben again. "Never mind. I can't think straight right now." She stumbled out of the kitchen and let the door slam behind her.

"So you've met my sister." Ben scooped chowder into a torn-out divot in each bread bowl. "Would you believe she's single?"

"I don't think I saw her at her best," Marlo said. She stood next to Ben, her stomach rumbling so loudly now she was sure he would hear it, and watched him prepare dinner.

"Grace is pretty much like that all the time." Ben selected two spoons and a few napkins from a shelf. "Only slightly less grumpy."

"At least you have a sister," said Marlo. "I wish I had a sibling as a buffer against my parents. Being an only child has its drawbacks."

"I want to hear all about it," said Ben. "Stay here while I get the barstools."

Ben wanted to listen to her troubles? Between that and his offering her dinner, Marlo's opinion of him softened.

He went through the swinging door and came back a moment later carrying two high-backed chairs. Ben set them right in front of the stainless steel counter and sat down next to the stove.

Marlo had never eaten in the back room of a restaurant before. She felt like she was getting a behind-the-scenes tour. She slid onto the barstool and picked up her spoon. Her mouth watered as the fragrant aroma of salmon, onions, potatoes, and cream wafted up from the bread bowl. She took a bite, and the flavors made her salivate even more. Marlo dipped her spoon into the bowl and ate hungrily, letting the calorie-dense meal soothe her stress. "This tastes delicious," she murmured as she ripped off a piece of the bread bowl and dipped it into the chowder. "Thank you."

Ben poured two glasses of water and sat down next to her. "No problem," he said as he tore off a bite from his bowl. "You were talking about being an only child a minute ago. You didn't like it?"

Marlo shrugged. "Not really. It had its perks, I'm sure, like how we always had the money for my ballet lessons, even when I was little and my parents were building a brand-new business. But I had no one to play with until they opened the day care at the gym."

"I didn't know there was day care at Cascade Athletic Club."

"It's not really day care." Marlo blotted her mouth with a napkin. "It's drop-off childcare for when parents exercise. We have a two-hour maximum. But since my parents worked there, I stayed there all day from when I was three years old up to about fifth or sixth grade. By then I was old enough to walk up to the Red Slipper by myself for dance class. My mom signed me up for every class Madame Burke offered because she knew I loved it so much, but also as a way to keep me busy while she and my dad worked."

Marlo looked over at the bulletin board and the clippings of Ben's articles and pointed to the one about PE waivers. "So yeah, my parents might have spent six hundred and twenty-five dollars a month on my ballet lessons, but that's comparable to day care."

"I never thought about it like that." Ben stirred his soup in slow circles. "But your situation was different in that you could walk to the dance studio. Most kids who do elite sports have stay-at-home parents or nannies who drive them all over the place. Like the hockey players who travel to Canada for games or the gymnasts who fly to Arizona for meets. I knew plenty of guys who did that in school."

"That's true," Marlo admitted. "And I guess the class fees weren't the only costs involved with dance. When I moved to pointe shoes, I wore out a new pair every six weeks."

"How much were those to replace?"

"Over a hundred dollars." Marlo curled and uncurled her toes inside her boots. She hadn't worn pointe shoes in over two years, and while her bones and ligaments thanked her, her heart ached at everything she'd lost. "My favorite expense was the costumes we bought each year for the winter and spring recitals. Madame Burke always had a flair for drama, and she selected the most beautiful things for us to wear. Sometimes we borrowed them from her warehouse, but usually we had to buy them brand new so they would fit properly."

"I remember you coming to school with your hair in those curlers."

Marlo's nostrils flared. Her improving opinion of Ben reversed course. "And I remember your Cheetos explosion. That little stunt cost me opening night."

Ben's eyes opened wide. "Shit," he mumbled, covering his mouth with his hand. "I'm so sorry. I swear it was an accident."

Marlo sighed. It was a long time ago, but the disappointment still stung. She folded her arms across her chest. "An accident?"

"Yeah." Ben nodded vigorously. "Mike dared me to pop the Cheetos right when the basketball team came out. He was angry that the basketball team got a pep rally but the jazz and marching band got squat."

"The arts are never appreciated." Marlo unfolded her arms. "You swear it was an accident? On a stack of newspapers swear?"

Ben crossed his heart. "Reporter's honor."

"Okay," Marlo relented. "I believe you."

"Why'd you have to wear curlers for dance?"

"They were for *The Nutcracker*. I had to wear spiral curls, and those are hard to create with hair as straight as mine."

Ben ripped the side off his empty bread bowl. "Grace hates her curly hair. She always tried to straighten it when she was in high school, but then it would puff up again in the rain."

"What was it like growing up with an older sister?" Marlo was tempted to eat the rest of her sourdough bowl, too, because it was so good, but she was full.

"I could never do anything right as far as Grace was concerned." Ben frowned. "She has exceedingly high standards."

"That's hard." Marlo watched Ben's face as he spoke about his sister. Creases deepened in his forehead, and a pained look took over his expression, as if even now, as a grown adult, the wounds of childhood still stung. "How do you get along now?"

"Pretty good, I guess." Ben shrugged. "I do my life; she does hers. We'll always have our parents in common."

"And neither one of you are interested in taking over all this?" Marlo waved her hands.

"Nope. Grace is a scientist, and I'm a journalist. I don't know what my folks will do with their business someday. Sell it, I guess. Julia Harper owns the property, so they won't have to deal with the building."

"I had no interest in running the gym." Marlo crooked the heel of her boots into the barstool's bottom rail. "But now that I stumbled into it, it's hard to say what the future holds."

"On-site day care is a huge benefit." Ben leaned back in his chair. "Think what the world would be like if everyone had that option."

"I never thought about it like that." Marlo sipped from her water glass and considered her circumstances in a new way. At least her family's business was something that meshed with her skill set. No, it wasn't ballet, but it was fitness related. If she'd had to walk into the Nuthatch Bakery and start rolling out piecrust, she would have failed. As much as she appreciated what the Wexler-Lowreys had accomplished, she knew that it took people who were passionate about baking and the restaurant industry to make this business work. "I just wish there was a way that I could fix the Cascade Athletic Club's finances."

"Did you try the survey yet?" Ben asked.

Marlo nodded. "I did. Or I'm going to." She pulled out her phone and tapped the screen. "I have a draft ready, but I don't know if it's any good." Seconds away from showing Ben the survey, she turned her phone over, feeling uncertain. "I don't want to bother you, though. I'm sorry."

"Don't be sorry." Ben stacked the plates and pushed them away. "I'm happy to help—unless you're concerned about proprietary knowledge or something."

Marlo shook her head. "No, I'm not." She took a deep breath and turned her phone over, feeling nervous. Marlo was used to being judged onstage, where every inch of her body and every angle of her long limbs was available for scrutiny, but someone evaluating her business acumen—or lack thereof—was different. "Okay, then." She showed the draft to Ben.

Ben read slowly, his eyes moving from side to side as he took in every word. His mouth opened slightly and then closed again. Ben touched the screen and drew his finger upward, scrolling to the next page. His face bore a neutral expression that was difficult for Marlo to read. She was eager to know what he was thinking. Were her survey questions good or bad? But the only thing she could infer from Ben's demeanor was that he was concentrating and reading with care every word she wrote.

"So?" Marlo asked when Ben set the phone down. "What do you think? How badly did I screw up?"

"I don't think you screwed up at all." Ben flexed his hand, like he had a cramp in it. "There's some wordsmithing I would do to make things clearer, but that's me being a writer."

"That's true." Surprisingly, she wasn't miffed by Ben's comment about improved wordsmithing. In fact, she wished she could print the survey out and give him a red pen.

"The main question I think you're missing is about intention," said Ben. "*Why* do people come to Cascade Athletic Club in the first place?"

"I have something about goals," said Marlo. "I asked if they wanted to increase muscle, lose weight, or focus on flexibility."

"And that was a great question. I think you also mentioned losing inches." Ben scrolled back to find it. "Yeah, you did. But those are outcomes people could get anywhere. What you want to do is remind your audience what makes the Cascade Athletic Club special. Use this survey not only as an opportunity to find out more information about your members but also to reaffirm your relationship with them."

"How do I do that?" Marlo reached into her purse and pulled out the pen and paper she used for her grocery list. "Tell me what to say, and I'll include it."

Ben rested both elbows on the counter, pressed his palms together, and tapped his fingertips. "Okay," he finally said. "I've only been inside your gym one time, so I don't know, but you and Dahlia both mentioned what an important place it was for seniors, right?"

Marlo nodded. "Some of them come every day and stay for a couple of hours, hanging out with their friends. They never actually become more fit, but they don't decline either. It helps them maintain what they've got."

"Mentally, too, right?" Ben asked. "Since there's a social element?"

Marlo nodded. "It's like when some of the moms come too. They drop their kids off at the day care and come to my barre class fifteen minutes early so they can chat. It's a different vibe than spin class, where people are on their bikes pedaling like maniacs, unable to talk to the person next to them."

"But that's important too." Ben rested his chin on his hand and looked at her. "People who are short on time want to go someplace where they'll efficiently burn a ton of calories."

"Yes," Marlo agreed. "And we let members reserve bikes the night before so they won't show up at five thirty a.m. only to find that there's no room for them in the spin studio."

"May I?" Ben reached for Marlo's pen and paper. He looked down at what she'd written and laughed. "Is this your grocery list?"

Marlo blushed, desperately hoping she didn't have something embarrassing on it. She couldn't remember for sure.

"You eat sardines?" Ben raised his eyebrows.

"I put them in pasta dishes," Marlo explained. "They have omega-3s."

"Hardly anyone likes sardines."

"I love them."

Ben looked up from the paper and stared straight into Marlo's eyes with such intensity that her knees felt fluttery. "Me too," he said. Their eyes locked together for a moment until Ben focused back on the paper. "Okay, let's do this," he said as he began writing in tidy letters. "What do you value most about Cascade Athletic Club? Check all that apply." Ben paused, clicking and unclicking the ballpoint pen for a few seconds. "Number one—working out with friends is important to me. Number two—time spent at the CAC helps keep me mentally fit as well as physically fit. Number three—the CAC values my time and helps me work out efficiently. Number four . . ." Ben paused and looked at Marlo. "Your turn. Final statement."

"I don't know." Marlo shook her head. "You're doing so well, and . . ."

"You've got this," said Ben. "You know your business better than anyone."

"Except for my parents."

"Maybe more than your parents." Ben tilted his head to the side. "Your ideas about competing with CrossFit are good. You've identified a changing market and that different age demographics want different things."

"But all ages can work out at Cascade Athletic Club," said Marlo. "We have something for everyone." She smiled brightly. "That's it! That's what number four could be—the CAC is an inclusive community that welcomes people of all ages and fitness levels."

Ben jotted that down. "Technically, the YMCA does that as well," he said. "But probably the Cascade Athletic Club has fewer children running around."

Marlo laughed. "We never let kids run around unsupervised."

Ben grinned, and his dimples peeked out. "Once you're in fifth grade, the YMCA lets you run wild. Of course, by that point, my parents pulled me out of day care to save money and made Grace watch me." He wrinkled his nose. "Which was about as much fun as you would expect."

"Thanks for your help." Marlo leaned forward, holding her shoulders back and maintaining good posture. "And for dinner. I really appreciate it." She couldn't believe that Ben Wexler-Lowrey had saved her evening or that sitting this close to him was giving her butterflies. But as she stared into his dark-brown eyes, she saw kindness that drew her in further. He was so easy to talk to, and he not only listened to her attentively but offered suggestions that made her smarter. "If you ever want to come to the gym and have a smoothie on me, please let me know." As soon as she'd said it, Marlo remembered that Dahlia worked behind the smoothie bar. "Maybe on Dahlia's day off," Marlo corrected herself.

Ben shrugged. "That wouldn't be a problem. We ended things on good terms. Besides, if she starts dating Mike, I'm sure I'll see a lot of her since Mike's my roommate." Ben's eyes opened wide, and his mouth dropped open. "Oh shoot." He spun around on the barstool and stared at the clock above the oven. "My roommate." Ben stood up and gathered up the dishes, then rushed them over to the rack in front of the commercial dishwasher. "I've got to go. Katelyn broke her wrist last week, and she can't open her pain-medication bottle without help." He looked back at the clock. "She's due for her meds in twenty minutes. I need to go."

"I'll put the barstools away." Marlo rushed to help. Five minutes later they left through the back door and headed into the alley. "Thanks again," Marlo said, staring into Ben's eyes. She wasn't hoping he would kiss her. Absolutely not. That thought never occurred to her. But when Ben's lips parted, the flutters in her stomach emerged into full-grown butterflies. She felt hope rise from the soles of her feet and practically lift her off the ground in a cloud of anticipation. She was thrilled at the feel of Ben's hand pressed to her back. Her spine arched, eager to deepen the connection.

"Main Street is this way," said Ben as he led her out of the alley. "Watch your step. The paving's a bit rough."

Marlo was glad that darkness shielded her from view. The heat that flushed her cheeks burned red from embarrassment. How stupid was she, thinking that Ben would kiss her? "Thanks," she mumbled as they exited the alleyway. "Tell Katelyn I hope she feels better." She rushed away down the sidewalk without waiting to hear him respond.

CHAPTER TEN

Ben kicked himself for not having the guts to kiss Marlo last night. When she'd stood there at the back door of the bakery, her hat pulled jauntily over her head and her blue eyes gazing up at him, Ben had stared back with equal wonder, like he was seeing her for the first time. Instead of the privileged, bossy princess he'd known, he saw a woman who kept a grocery list in her purse, who helped him clean up from dinner, who offered her food to Grace when his sister was in pain, and who had soft, kissable lips the color of cherries. But kissing her would have been a mistake. Their history proved that. Marlo was a Leaping Lemur, and he was a Sleepy Sloth. She was poised to take over her parents' multimillion-dollar business—even if it was in financial turmoil—and he was contemplating biking sixteen miles in the rain to work this morning to save a few bucks on gas.

"How many pieces of bacon do you want?" Ben called to Katelyn from the kitchen. It was Saturday morning, and he was using all four burners on the stove. The kettle boiled, the nonstick skillet held pancakes, spinach was being sautéed in the stainless steel skillet, and bacon sizzled in the cast-iron pan.

"Two, thanks," Katelyn answered from the living room. She slurred slightly since she was hopped up on pain medicine. Her wrist fracture had been severe enough that she was having surgery Tuesday morning.

Until then it was in a temporary brace and had to be elevated on a pillow.

"Coming right up." Ben used tongs to lift the bacon slices from the pan and drained the fat on a plate lined with paper towels. He loaded two pancakes onto a plate and sliced them into bite-size pieces before drowning them in homemade big-leaf maple syrup that Simon had tapped and processed from a tree in the backyard last year. Ben brewed a pot of MarketSpice tea while he transferred two strips of bacon to the pancake plate, and then he poured the tea into a commuter cup with a tight-fitting lid so that Katelyn wouldn't spill it. He brought the plate, silverware, and mug into the living room and set it on the end table next to the ratty brown recliner where Katelyn sat.

"That smells good." Katelyn spoke in a weak voice. "Thanks." Her hair hung loose in greasy waves, and she wore a pullover sweatshirt and sweatpants that were easy for her to put on one-handed.

"Okay, here's the backup remote." Ben set the controller next to the plate. "And you've already got a box of tissues and a bottle of water."

"Can you open it for me? I can't untwist the cap."

"Right." Ben unscrewed the top of the insulated bottle.

Thunder clapped outside, and the lights flickered. Water pelted against the front windows. The thought of biking to work in that mess made Ben shiver, but he had no other options since his gas budget was empty. "Let me grab you the afghan." He walked over to the couch and pulled off the knitted blanket that Savannah had made. He spread it over Katelyn's feet, stretched out on the recliner. "Anything else you need?"

Katelyn shook her head. "Simon and Mike will be up soon."

"I'm up now." Simon walked into the room wearing cargo shorts, Birkenstocks, and a flannel shirt. "How are you feeling?"

"Not so great." Katelyn nibbled on a piece of bacon. "The pain meds make me queasy."

"That's why you need food in your stomach," said Ben. "Eat up."

"How about I get a fire going?" Simon sat down in front of the hearth and pulled back the rusty screen in front of the old brick fireplace. He stuck his head inside and looked up.

"What are you doing?" Katelyn asked.

"Opening the flue." Simon pulled his head back out. "We haven't used it since spring." His arm was coated in black dust. "I'll go out to the shed and get some wood."

As soon as Simon left, Katelyn motioned with her good arm for Ben to come closer, and she whispered something.

"What was that?" Ben asked, crouching down next to her. "I couldn't hear you."

"I said, What am I going to do about Simon?"

"What do you mean?" Ben looked confused.

"I've got a ten-thousand-dollar out-of-pocket maximum before my insurance kicks in, and Simon's offered to pay for it so that my surgery can happen on Tuesday. But I don't want to be in debt to him like that." Katelyn sighed and looked down at her injured arm. The fingers were swollen and a slightly different color than her good hand.

"Can't you ask your parents?" Ben scratched the back of his head. He knew that Katelyn and her folks didn't get along, but they owned a successful dental practice and had plenty of money to help.

"I *did* ask them." Katelyn sighed. "I called them when I found out about the surgery. They said they'd pay for everything if I go back to school and finish my degree."

"Boom. Problem solved."

"But then I'd have to take their money," Katelyn whined. "And listen to their advice."

"Here we go." Simon walked in from the kitchen carrying a huge pile of wood. "By the way, Ben, there's a squirrel's nest out there for you to take care of."

"Why me?" Ben asked.

"Because I can't do it." Simon shuddered. "You know squirrels scare the snot out of me."

"Sure." Ben's stomach twisted. "I'll deal with it after work." He turned his attention back to Katelyn. "You're only eighteen credits away from your degree, Kate. That's nothing. If you go back full time and quit the espresso stand so you can concentrate, you could graduate in one quarter."

"Quit my job?" Katelyn's lower lip quivered. "But then I wouldn't see Hunter anymore."

"I've got a hot date tonight." Simon snapped a twig in two. "Did I tell you?"

"Hunter doesn't appreciate you," Ben continued, ignoring Simon, who always had a hot date since he was constantly trolling Good Catch for fresh women. "Working at his espresso stand will take you nowhere."

"But you know how much I love him." Katelyn reached for a tissue and wiped her nose. "And I just know that one of these days, he's going to notice me and realize that the perfect woman has been there all along, right under his nose."

"It's with a barre instructor," said Simon in a loud voice, refusing to be left out of the conversation. "You should see her picture; she's hotter than the fire I'm about to build." He tossed a log into the fireplace and knocked over the pyramid he'd assembled.

"That's interesting," said Ben as he frowned at Katelyn. "I wish there was something I could say that would make you listen to reason."

"Reason doesn't matter when you look like Marlo Jonas." Simon whistled. "She's got legs for days."

"Wait. What?" Ben spun around and looked at Simon. "Your date is with Marlo Jonas?"

"Marlo Jonas," Katelyn said with a sneer. "My nemesis."

"I didn't realize you two knew her." Simon stuffed newspaper between the logs in his reassembled pyramid.

"Sure," Ben said in what he'd intended to be a disinterested tone of voice but that sounded more like a falsetto. "We go way back." He felt his insides rage. Ben took a deep breath to steady himself. Marlo going out with Simon meant nothing to him.

"Simon, how could you?" Katelyn asked. "Out of all the people in Harper Landing, you pick Marlo?"

"What?" Simon shrugged. "The ladies love me—what can I say?"

"That's my cue to leave." Ben grabbed his raincoat and safety vest from the coat closet and put on his bike shoes. He stomped on his Delta cleats over to the charging station in the kitchen and collected his cell phone and found his helmet where he'd left it on a chair.

"You're not going out in that storm, are you?" Katelyn asked as Ben opened the front door. "You'll be drenched."

"Don't worry about it," Ben said, just as thunder crashed in the distance. "It's another gorgeous day in the Pacific Northwest."

Despite his bravado, the sixteen-mile ride to Seattle was miserable. Rain meant the temperature was in the low forties, so at least it wasn't freezing, but the windchill factor was icy as a cold front blew down from Alaska. The Interurban Trail linking Harper Landing to Seattle was slippery. As soon as Ben entered King County, homeless encampments began popping up to the left and right of him. Seeing unhoused people struggling against the cruel weather put things in perspective for Ben. He was grateful to have a home, a decent job, and good health.

The thunderclouds parted by the time he reached Denny Way, and when he locked his bike, the rain stopped. The break in the weather was too late for Ben's wardrobe, however. He was sopping wet. When Ben reached his work area, he didn't bother turning on his computer yet. Instead, he searched for the emergency clothes he kept underneath his desk and headed for the men's restroom to change.

Ten minutes later, in dry clothes and sitting at his desk, Ben's thoughts drifted over to Simon's date with Marlo. Why hadn't she mentioned it to him last night at dinner? As soon as he asked himself that question, he knew it was unfair. It wasn't any of his business who Marlo went out with. Still, she might have mentioned it considering that the Monte Cristos had been performing at the Western Cedar. Or had Marlo not made the connection? Perhaps she hadn't realized that it was Simon up there onstage. Or maybe she'd been too preoccupied with her parents' argument to notice.

Ben logged into his work email and scrolled through his messages, but Marlo kept popping up in his head. Her wager with Chuck was to date someone who was outside what the Jonas family considered to be traditionally attractive. Did that mean Marlo thought Simon was ugly? No, not ugly. Marlo wouldn't be that judgmental. But she might consider him to be outside the parameters of what she usually found to be attractive. Ben grinned when he realized that, even though he knew he was being a jerk to Simon. Besides, it didn't matter what Simon looked like or if Marlo found him attractive. Knowing Simon, their date would be a disaster. Marlo was serious about finding someone worthwhile to build a relationship with, but Simon's goal was to date as many women as possible.

Ben knew he should explore his dating options too. So a few hours later when he was in the lunchroom eating a turkey-and-cheese sandwich he'd bought at the shop down the block, he opened up the Good Catch app on his phone and checked his notifications. Today was Saturday, November 15, and Ben hadn't opened up the app since Friday the seventh when he'd gone out with Brittany. It hadn't occurred to him that she hadn't texted him on his phone after their date, but then again, he couldn't remember giving her his number. All their communication had been through Good Catch, which explained why there were a dozen notifications from her.

Hey Mr. Muscle, she wrote. I had a great time last night. Wanna do it again?

Uh-oh. Ben realized he'd better figure out what to say. He clicked on her next message.

It's Saturday night and I'm lonely for you, Brittany wrote, adding a kissy face emoji at the end.

Shoot. Now Ben felt like a real turd. Why hadn't he checked his Good Catch notifications before now? It wasn't fair to Brittany to leave her hanging like this.

The next message was from one o'clock in the morning last Sunday. Instead of text, there was only an image. Ben's mouth dropped open when he clicked on the picture and saw what she'd sent.

"Who's sending you boob shots?" a voice asked from behind him.

Ben swiped away from the picture and turned toward Savannah, who had sneaked up unnoticed. She wore a floor-length skirt and a knitted cape. Each item on its own was eccentric in a cool bohemian way. Yet worn together, the combination made her resemble Laura Ingalls. The way she'd braided her frizzy blonde hair in a plait around her crown didn't help. If anything, it added to the pioneer vibe.

"Hi, Savannah." Ben tried not to wrinkle his nose at the scent of her body odor. She reeked of apple cider vinegar, which Savannah swore helped her survive cold-and-flu season.

"So? Who sent you that racy pic?"

"It's from a woman I went on one date with a couple of Fridays ago. One date was enough."

"One date, and she's sending you cleavage shots?" Savannah grabbed a bite of turkey from Ben's sandwich and popped it in her mouth. "That must have been a hell of a date." She pulled out a chair and sat next to him.

"It was awful. And now I need to figure out how to deal with her."

"Good." Savannah nodded. "Make it a clean break so she doesn't hang on and pester you like that balloon woman."

"Goldie doesn't pester me."

Savannah raised her eyebrows. "Did she or did she not try to bribe the security team down at the front desk with a bundle of balloon flowers so she could come surprise you on your last birthday?"

"Yeah, but I mean . . ." Ben shrugged. "Some people would say that was sweet."

Savannah slapped her palm on the table and looked straight into Ben's eyes. "She was only wearing a trench coat and body glitter."

"It was summer."

Savannah narrowed her eyes at him. "She could have gotten you fired."

"Okay, okay. Point taken." Ben tapped on the next message from Brittany. Before he could read it, Savannah snatched the phone out of his hands.

"Babe, I need you. Eggplant emoji. Wineglass emoji," Savannah read in a high-pitched breathy voice. She glared over the screen at him. "What exactly did you do on that first date?"

"Nothing!" Ben held out both hands for emphasis. "She slobbered all over me, and that was it."

Savannah shook her head. "Don't talk about women like they're puppies." She scrolled to the next message. "Brittany says, 'Is this because I didn't tell you I have a daughter?'" Savannah made a face. "She didn't tell you she had a kid?"

"Nope. Not that it would have mattered to me, but still . . ."

"It shows a lack of integrity that she'd hide something like that." Savannah wrinkled her nose and tapped the screen. "Uh-oh," she said. "I'm not sure I should read this message aloud in a workplace setting. Too many expletives."

"Great." Ben banged his head on the table. "Just great. How should I respond?"

Savannah clicked on another message. "Fancy that. More expletives."

Ben moaned. "What am I going to do?"

Savannah chewed on her thumbnail. "I'm thinking."

"This is why I hate dating."

Savannah examined her thumb, apparently satisfied with her gnawed nail. "Don't overthink it." She handed the phone back to Ben. "Just say, 'It was nice meeting you, but I'm not what you need. Best wishes, Ben.'"

"Can you repeat that?" Ben struggled to text fast enough to keep up with her.

"Sure." Savannah slipped her arms under her cape. "'It was nice meeting you, but I'm not what you need. Best wishes, Ben.'"

Ben typed the last letter and hit send. "Thanks." He exhaled loudly. "You made that seem so easy."

"It *was* easy. Like when you and I broke up. I'm not what you need, and you're not what I need, and that's okay." The corners of her mouth lifted into a huge smile. "If we were still together, I wouldn't have met Xander. And guess what?" Savannah pulled her arms out from underneath her cape and threw them around Ben in a huge hug. "He asked me to move in with him."

"That's great." Ben squeezed her back. "I'm so happy for you."

Savannah let go of Ben and sat straight in her chair. "We're having a housewarming party next Friday night. Do you want to come?"

"Are you cooking?"

Savannah nodded.

"Hell yeah, I'll be there. Snohomish, right?"

"Right. Xander works at Microsoft in Bellevue but commutes from Snohomish each day." She sighed heavily. "It's going to be a long commute for me, too, but hopefully I can take the bus. That way I can at least be knitting when I'm stuck in traffic."

"You mean *legally* knitting."

"What else am I supposed to do in bumper-to-bumper traffic?" Savannah pulled a strand of frizzy hair that had escaped her french braid out of her face. "Anyhow, yes, it's a long way to commute, but Xander's property is worth it. He has forty acres in the Snohomish River Valley and a barn with six sheep."

"Ah, yes." Ben nodded. "I've heard about the sheep before."

"But did I tell you about the goats? The cashmere goats?"

"He has goats too? You must be kidding."

Savannah pointed her finger and jabbed Ben in the chest. "No puns, Mister, unless you want me to break into clichés."

"I'm happy for you, Savannah—I am." Ben smiled. "You deserve as much joy as this world can hold."

Savannah tucked her head to her chest and grinned with uncharacteristic shyness. "Thanks, Ben. I'm still so thrilled I can hardly believe it. It's nice to have something positive in my life considering everything that's happening with my grandpa."

"How's he doing with his cancer treatment?"

"They've brought in hospice now."

"Home care or at the hospital?" Ben asked.

"He's at home. But I don't want to talk about it."

"Okay." Ben patted her hand. "I'm here for you if you need anything. You know that, right?"

Savannah nodded just as his phone buzzed. A notification from Good Catch popped up on the screen again.

"Uh-oh." Ben glanced at the message. "It looks like Brittany texted me back."

"Let me handle it." Savannah picked up the phone and clicked on the link. She cringed while reading. "Is this woman for real?"

"What did she say?"

Savannah handed his phone back to him. "She says she's going to destroy your parents' business."

"The Nuthatch Bakery?" Ben felt icicles colder than any raindrops from his morning ride creep down his spine as he read Brittany's note.

Nobody says no to Brittany Barrow, she texted. You made a fool out of me, and I'm going to make you and your parents' shabby little bakery pay.

"I don't understand." Ben kneaded the back of his neck. "I never told her who my parents were or that they owned the Nuthatch."

"Well, she probably googled you, don't you think? I bet you googled her, too, although you did a crappy job of it since you didn't find out about her kid."

"It was more of a light googling as opposed to a deep dive."

"Ben, Ben, Ben." Savannah shook her head. "What kind of a journalist are you? You're so smart and yet so clueless."

"I'm clueless?" Ben couldn't believe what he was hearing. "It's your message to Brittany that set her off."

"No, it's not." Savannah crossed her arms. "She would have been set off no matter what you wrote. It's the fact that you waited so long to respond to her that bruised her ego."

"And now she's going after my folks."

"Unless she works for the health department, I doubt there's much she can do."

"She runs two advertising circulars in Harper Landing," said Ben. "One's a pretend magazine; the other's a coupon pack."

"Well, she's not going to be able to hurt the Nuthatch with that type of arsenal. The worst she can do is badmouth your parents to other local business owners she knows."

"But that would be horrible!" Ben raked his fingers through his hair. "Word of mouth is everything in Harper Landing."

"It's nothing a good restaurant review won't fix." Savannah patted him on the back. "And lucky for the Nuthatch, you know the restaurant reviewer at the *Seattle Times*."

"Really?" Ben brought his hands down. "You'd do that for me?"

"Not for you, silly. I'd do it for the Nuthatch. I love that place."

"I've always hoped you'd write a review, but I didn't want to ask," said Ben. "It would have seemed unprofessional for me to bring up a favor like that."

"Well, you're not asking; I'm offering." Savannah nodded and stood up. "I'll add it to my schedule. In the meantime, don't forget about my housewarming party this Friday night. I'll send you the Evite."

"I wouldn't miss it." Ben waved as Savannah walked away, and then he collected his lunch trash. He still had four more hours on the clock before he could go home.

When Ben got back to his desk, he devoted himself to finishing off a story he was writing about a dog-rescue organization in Lynnwood and then clicked over to the paper's Facebook page so he could monitor what people were saying about his most recent articles. The comments were mild that day, and except for the usual trolls, nothing was getting out of hand. That was both good and bad. When comments heated up, Facebook posts got more engagement, and more engagement meant higher traffic for the paper. But since online views weren't nearly as fiscally important as actual subscribers, Ben was happy with the calm because it made it easier for him to write.

Unfortunately, the rain wasn't letting up, and Ben didn't relish the idea of biking home in a dark storm. Uber was out of the question; it would cost too much money. He plugged his bike lights into the outlet by his desk to make sure the batteries were fully charged for his commute.

Once that was taken care of, Ben read his article about the dog rescue three more times. Dyslexia meant that he was horrible at catching typos. He frequently misspelled simple words that he knew how to spell because his brain couldn't see the mistakes. Ben knew that his editor would help catch errors, but he didn't want to make a fool of himself or make him think that he wasn't up to the job. That was the horrible thing about poor spelling. It made smart people look stupid, even if they weren't. In Ben's experience, great spellers—like his sister, Grace—loved to lord it over him, as if they had earned their abilities instead of being naturally gifted with them.

Nobody had worked harder to learn how to spell than Ben, absolutely nobody. He'd gone to elementary school for seven and a half hours a day like every other kid he'd known, but then Ben had clocked an additional five hours a week working with his dyslexia tutor after school. She'd taught Ben how to break words into phonemes he'd memorized one by one. He'd studied pictures of how mouths moved when they made each sound. He'd built words with letter tiles on a magnetic board while he'd sounded them out loud. Homophones had been the hardest things to master. *Heir* versus *air*, *stationary* and *stationery*, *faze* or *phase*? To this day those words tripped him up, and the worst were *there*, *their*, and *they're*. He knew what the differences were—he really did. But when he typed fast, they slipped out of his brain and through his fingers in the wrong form.

Ben took a deep breath and was about to email the article to his editor when he decided to proofread one more time, using a trick his tutor had taught him fifteen years ago. He began at the end of his article and worked back through the words, checking for errors. As far as he could tell, he'd caught them all, but he could never be too sure. If he'd been writing from home, Mike would have checked for him. Mike had read all of his articles up at Western Washington University when Ben had written for the *Western Front*. He was dependable like that. If Ben called Mike now, he knew he'd help him out, but one glance at the clock told him there wasn't any time. Ben hit send and hoped for the best. He was collecting his bike gear when his phone rang.

"Hello?" Ben answered without looking at the number. He thought it might be Katelyn, who was having a hard time texting at present.

"Ben," said a cheery voice. "I'm down in the lobby."

"Uh . . . who is this?"

"It's me, silly," said the woman. "Goldie."

Ben pulled the phone away from his ear and looked at the screen. Sure enough, there was the contact picture of Goldie wearing a balloon crown and holding three cats. Shoot. He really should screen his calls. "Um . . . hi, Goldie. Why are you in the lobby?"

"I just got off work at Archie McPhee's, and when I swung by the building, I saw your bike parked here and thought you might want a ride home since it's raining so hard."

Ben tugged his collar away from his neck. Archie McPhee, the famous Seattle joke-and-novelty shop where Goldie worked when she wasn't doing her balloon gig, was near the Woodland Park Zoo and at least twenty minutes north of the *Seattle Times* offices on Denny Way. "I don't understand," said Ben. "Why'd you drive south?"

"What do you mean, why'd I drive south?"

"You live in Lynnwood. That's north of Archie McPhee's."

"I had to fuel up, and that fried-chicken place on Denny Way and I have a deal," said Goldie, breathing heavily into the phone.

That didn't make any sense at all, but Ben didn't want to argue. "Um . . . okay," he mumbled. Where was Savannah when he needed her? Ben had no idea what to say to get himself out of this situation. "I'll be downstairs in five minutes." He put on his jacket and vest and grabbed his bike lights and shoes just in case. On the elevator ride down to the lobby, he devised a plan to tell Goldie that he needed to bike home to hit his mileage goals for the year. But when Ben stepped out of the elevator, the electricity flickered.

Lightning flashed outside, illuminating the windows with super-natural light, and thunder crashed a few seconds later. Goldie stood in the center of the room, in front of the security desk, wearing a shiny purple raincoat made out of vinyl. Her platinum-blonde curls were closely cropped around her head, and she had enormous eyelashes that Ben thought might have been fake but was unsure of the specifics. The bright-red lipstick she wore clashed with her purple coat and gave her a clownish aesthetic that Ben knew she worked hard to achieve. "Benny!" Goldie shrieked when she saw him and frantically waved her hand.

The curmudgeonly security guard with the thick gray mustache raised his eyebrows at Ben but didn't say anything until Ben had crossed through the turnstile. "Have a great night, *Benny*," he said with a chuckle.

"Hi, Goldie." Ben kept a firm hold on his helmet and shoes so that both arms were occupied.

She hugged him anyway and planted a kiss on his cheek. "Isn't it lucky I was in the neighborhood?"

"Yeah." Ben nodded. "So lucky."

"I'm parked right in front of your bike."

"But that's a red curb." Ben followed her out to the sidewalk. Rain pelted him in the face, along with what might have been hail or graupel, a type of snow pellet that happened when water froze on snowflakes. The temperature was dropping fast.

"It's red? Oops." Goldie latched her arm through Ben's and pulled him toward her bright-yellow Volkswagen Westfalia. She didn't let go until they reached the van and she needed to slide the door open.

Ben unlocked his bike and rolled it across the sidewalk. "Are you sure about this?" He pointed at his muddy tires. "I don't want to get your interior dirty."

"No problem." Goldie opened the passenger door for him.

Ben lifted his bike up and stuffed it into the van. The smell of cats was so strong that even the rainstorm couldn't wash it away. Once he was sure his bike was safe, Ben closed the side door and climbed into the velour-covered passenger seat. He buckled the lap belt and braced his feet on the floor.

Goldie wasn't a crazy driver like Savannah was, but the Westfalia was an unreliable vehicle, especially since it ran on waste cooking oil. When Goldie pulled out into traffic, Ben smelled french fries.

"So what's the deal you have with the fried-chicken restaurant?" he asked.

"I provide balloon entertainment for them once a month, and in exchange they let me pick up their used oil whenever I want." Goldie beamed a smile. "No money changes hands at all, except when I collect tips from the restaurant patrons." She patted one of the many pockets on her raincoat where Ben knew she kept balloons. "Let me tell you, the rooster I blow up is especially popular at that place."

"Eat chickens. Play with chickens . . ."

"Exactly." Goldie nodded. "So hey, I've been meaning to talk to you about your new girlfriend."

"I don't have a new girlfriend." Ben sneezed. The cat hair was getting to him.

"You don't?" Goldie's clownish smile became even wider. "That's great news."

Shoot, Ben thought to himself. He hadn't meant to get her hopes up, but halting Goldie's enthusiasm was like stopping the weather. "I'm taking a break from dating," he said, which wasn't exactly true but was true at that very second.

"That's probably a wise idea until you learn to make better choices." Goldie nodded her approval. "That woman, Brittany Barrow—she's a piece of work."

"You know her name?" Ben wiped his nose on his sleeve since he didn't have a tissue. "First and last?"

"Yup." Goldie lifted her chin. "It took me a while to figure out where I knew her from, but then I remembered Zach Barrow's birthday party last June. Brittany hired me and a hypnotist to come and perform for a bunch of unruly twelve-year-olds in her backyard."

"Brittany doesn't have a son, but she does have a little girl named Porsche."

Goldie snorted derisively. "What a horrible name to give a human being. But no, Porsche isn't a little girl; she's in high school. A freshman, I think."

"What? How's that possible? Brittany told me she was twenty-six." Ben quickly did the math. "That means she was twelve when she gave birth to her daughter?"

"Ah, Benny." Goldie chuckled and shook her head. "Never trust someone who names their daughter after an automobile. Brittany might as well worship the American dollar. Her backyard was a shrine to the capitalistic norms oppressing society. You should have seen the size of their trampoline."

"Trampolines are fun," Ben protested. "Mike had one growing up."

"Hoarding that type of recreational equipment for private use is materialistic and wrong." Goldie grimaced. "And combine that with a basketball hoop, an outdoor pizza oven, and a hot tub, and you've got a family obsessed with privilege and comfort."

"Wow." Ben had no interest in ever seeing Brittany again, but now he wanted to hang out in her backyard. "So how was work today?" he asked, changing the subject. He kept Goldie talking about Archie McPhee for the rest of the ride home and was grateful when they reached Harper Landing, because there were only so many stories about selling fake dog poo that a person could listen to. Ben knew he needed to do something to end things with Goldie for good and stop getting her hopes up. The problem was, he didn't know how to accomplish that without being the bad guy. Then he remembered the language Savannah had given him to deal with Brittany.

"Goldie," Ben said as he unclicked his seat belt. "Thanks for the ride, and, um . . . it was nice of you, and it was also nice knowing you, but—"

"Nice knowing me?" Goldie asked. "What the hell is that supposed to mean?"

Ben gripped his bike helmet in sweaty hands, losing confidence. He never should have gone off script. But then Savannah's words came back to him right when he needed them most. "I'm not what you need," he said sincerely. "But I wish you all the best."

"What?" Goldie's lips curled. "You don't mean that. We're friends. You said we could be friends."

"Not anymore," Ben blurted. "I'm too allergic to cats." He jumped out of the passenger seat and slid open the side door to grab his bike.

"You can get allergy shots," Goldie cried. "Or take Zyrtec."

Ben sneezed. "Sorry, Goldie." He lugged his bike to the ground. "I'm afraid of needles, and Zyrtec makes me sleepy. It's best for my health if we never see each other again."

"What about Allegra?"

Ben shook his head. "It's over, Goldie."

Goldie opened up her door. "It doesn't have to be over," she said as she put one foot outside. "I'll—"

"No," Ben said in a firm voice. "We're too different. I have a credit card I never told you about."

"What?" Goldie yanked her foot back into the vehicle.

"And I *like* it," Ben said, twisting the knife. "I use it to pay bills so it earns me points."

Goldie's eyes narrowed into two slits. "You know credit card points are a capitalistic plot designed to enslave people to credit. I've told you about that before."

"It's too late for me, Goldie." Ben reaffirmed his grip on his handle-bars. "I'm already a goner. My biggest dream now is to open a platinum card."

"You wouldn't," Goldie sneered.

"Oh, I would." Ben hopped on his bike. "Drive safe." He pedaled up the driveway and into the side yard, securing the gate behind him.

One thing was certain as he listened to Goldie drive away—Ben had reached his tipping point when it came to crazy ex-girlfriends. Maybe he didn't deserve someone as stunningly gorgeous and easy to talk to as Marlo. But if he could date someone who smelled clean and didn't talk nonstop about herself, that would be great. When it came to kissing, it was unlikely that Ben would ever find a woman whose lips made him mourn missed opportunity like Marlo's did, but at least he could find someone who didn't literally style themselves to look like a clown. Was that too much to ask?

CHAPTER ELEVEN

"I hope you like avant-garde theater." Simon took off his sport coat and draped it on his seat. "I know the director, and if this production of *Waiting for Godot* is half as good as *Our Town* was last year, then we're in for a treat." His green feather earring fluttered as he spoke.

Marlo couldn't remember what she'd heard about that performance of *Our Town*, but she knew it hadn't been good. She was also unsure of what Simon meant by *avant-garde* when it came to the theater but didn't want to admit it for fear of sounding stupid. She knew that modern dance had been considered avant-garde when it had been new. It had been a rejection of the constraints of classical ballet. But how did that apply to community theater? "*Our Town* is a classic," she said.

"And James—that's my friend who's a director—James completely reimagined it by putting the whole cast on pogo sticks."

"Pogo sticks?" Marlo raised her eyebrows. It was all coming back to her now. The women in her barre class had laughed about it for weeks. Melanie Knowles, who helped run the Harper Landing Moms Facebook group, had said that so many people had made fun of it that the volunteer admin team had had to add a keyword alert for *pogo sticks* because the group feed had been one satirical meme after another and feelings were being hurt.

Simon closed his eyes and lifted his chin like he was reliving the play in his memory. "Picture it," he said, holding out his hands. "A dark stage and one tiny light bulb swinging in the center. Then you hear the bounce, bounce, bounce of a pogo stick, and you know that magic is about to happen."

"It sounds unique."

"Yeah, babe, it was." Simon nodded.

Marlo thought it was way too soon for Simon to be calling her *babe*, especially since they'd only officially met in person thirty minutes ago, but she didn't correct him. "I remember you saying that arts were your passion," she said instead. "You're a potter and a musician, right?"

"That's right." Simon flung his arm around the back of Marlo's seat, and she leaned forward slightly to maintain her personal space. "I also brew beer, raise bees, and create mosaic patio furniture in my spare time."

"Wow. You're a regular Renaissance man. Do you cook too?"

Simon's proud smile faded in an instant. "No, but I'm hardly ever home. Most nights I'm out with the ladies. Unless, of course, my band has a gig."

"Fascinating," said Marlo with the straightest face she could manage. So far this date was going better than the one with Hunter last week, but only because they were in a public place and she had no reason to suspect that Simon might kill her.

"I hear you know Katelyn Grouse," said Simon.

"Yeah, I do. How do you know her?"

"She's my roommate." Simon almost stumbled over the word *roommate*.

"Wait . . ." Marlo wrinkled her forehead. "I thought Katelyn was Ben Wexler-Lowrey's roommate."

"She is." Simon nodded. "But I own the house."

"So you know Ben too?" Marlo felt a rush when she said Ben's name, which was ridiculous of her, and she knew it.

"Sure, I know Ben." Simon folded his arms across his chest. "He made Katelyn's breakfast this morning." Simon scowled. "But when I built her a fire, brought her favorite slippers, *and* french braided her hair, she barely noticed."

"Oh." Marlo wasn't sure what to say. "How's Katelyn feeling? I heard she broke her arm."

"Wrist," Simon corrected. "It was her wrist. She fell off her bike coming up from the ferry."

Marlo shuddered, imagining the pain. "That's awful. Poor Katelyn."

"I'm surprised to hear you say that." Simon tilted his head to the side.

"Why? It sounds like a horrible accident."

"Katelyn said you were sworn enemies."

"What?" Marlo shook her head. "No way. We always got along great in high school. I mean, we weren't exactly best friends, but I didn't dislike her."

"She said something about a mean comment in her yearbook . . ." Simon raised his eyebrows but didn't say anything further.

Marlo scoured her memory bank, trying to think what Katelyn might be referring to, but finally shrugged, giving up. "I don't know what she's talking about." Marlo opened up her program and searched for some way to change the subject. "Oh, hey," she said. "George Fiege is in this. His wife was my fifth-grade teacher." Marlo looked for a wheelchair to see if she could spot her teacher. Sure enough, Mrs. Fiege was sitting over to the right in the front row. "That's her," Marlo said excitedly. "Do you mind if I go say hi?"

"Of course not." Simon looked down at his phone. "Go ahead."

"Thanks." Marlo stood up and squeezed her way down the row of seats until she reached the aisle. Mrs. Fiege had been one of her favorite teachers because she had come to both of Marlo's recitals when she'd been in fifth grade as well as her first performance for the Pacific Northwest Ballet. Instead of making a scene and embarrassing her like her parents had done, Mrs. Fiege had brought her bouquets of pink roses. Marlo had one bud from each pressed into her scrapbook of memories.

"Mrs. Fiege," Marlo said, crouching down beside her so they could be at eye level. "It's so good to see you. I saw you at Julia's wedding, but we didn't get a chance to talk."

"I told you to call me Shelly." Mrs. Fiege reached her arms out for a hug. "It's good to see you too."

Marlo hugged her back gently. Mrs. Fiege smelled like Estée Lauder perfume mixed with hemp cream. "I saw in the program that your husband is performing."

"That's right." Mrs. Fiege smiled, but it was the same smile she used during standardized testing week.

Marlo recognized that fake smile immediately. "Are you excited?" she asked.

"Thrilled," Mrs. Fiege said with a sigh. "George is *so* happy, and he's worked *so* hard on learning his lines that I hate to burst his bubble. But I don't know if Harper Landing is ready to accept something so avant-garde."

"More avant-garde than last year's production of *Our Town*?"

"Wait until you see what the director has planned now. I'm worried he's sending my dear husband out to make a fool of himself."

"Oh, Shelly, it's going to be fine," said a bright voice from behind them. Julia Harper stood in the aisle. Her blonde hair was swept back into a ponytail, and she carried an enormous purse over her shoulder. "Hi, Marlo," she said. "'I haven't made it back to barre class yet, but I'll be there soon because I hit the buffet pretty hard on my honeymoon cruise."

"And I'm sure every bite was worth it." Marlo stood up and hugged her friend. "Fitness is about taking care of yourself, not beating yourself up for being human."

"I'm choosing to believe that's true." Julia nodded. "Are you joining us? We have an extra seat because Aaron's not coming. We were going to leave Jack with Paige Lu tonight, but she has a head cold."

"I wish I could sit with you, but I'm on a date." Marlo looked up into the audience and saw Simon staring at his phone. "I'd better be going."

"Enjoy your date," said Mrs. Fiege.

Now it was Marlo's turn to fake smile. "I'll try." She walked up the aisle and shimmied across the seats until she reached her spot next to Simon. "Sorry about that," she said once she'd sat down. "Mrs. Fiege is special to me."

"No worries." Simon put away his phone. "Say, can I ask you a question?"

"Sure." Marlo shrugged, curious about what Simon wanted to know.

"Were Katelyn and Ben serious when they were in high school?"

"Serious how?"

"As a couple, I mean." Simon fingered the edges of his feather earring.

"I don't think so." Marlo settled back in her seat. "They went to prom together—I remember that. Sometimes they'd hold hands in the hall. But they weren't the type of couple whose PDA made other people nauseous." *Not like my parents,* Marlo thought privately.

"Huh." Simon shrugged. "So *that's* not it."

Marlo was about to ask him what he meant when the lights dimmed. "I'm excited to see this," she whispered. "I read *Waiting for Godot* in college. Thanks for taking me."

He held a finger over his lips to shush her. "It's starting."

Marlo sank back into her seat, annoyed with Simon for shushing her. The play *wasn't* starting—not yet, at least. The curtains hadn't parted, and the older couple next to them was still complaining about the price of Dungeness crab at the Western Cedar. Marlo pointed and flexed her toes, trying to steady herself. The truth was, she was curious to see *Waiting for Godot* because she'd read it in a course she'd taken at the University of Washington on twentieth-century French literature.

Samuel Beckett was from Ireland, but he'd originally written the play in French. It was about two characters, Vladimir and Estragon, who wait for a man named Godot who never comes.

"Ladies, gentleman, and patrons of the arts," said a voice from off-stage. "Thank you for joining us at the Harper Landing Players' production of *Waiting for Godot*, by Samuel Beckett. Please take this moment to silence your cell phones."

Marlo pulled her phone out of her purse and turned it off. She'd danced in too many performances where someone's phone had rung and disrupted the ambiance. The couple next to her tried to turn off their phones, too, but couldn't figure it out.

"Would you mind helping me, dear?" asked the white-haired lady.

"Of course." Marlo pressed the button on the side, and the phone powered off.

"Thanks, sweets." The woman smiled and passed the phone to her husband. "Didn't I see you at the senior center the other day?"

Marlo nodded. "That's right. I ate lunch there on Tuesday."

"Shh!" Once again Simon hushed her. "No talking in the theater."

"The play hasn't started," the woman scolded. "I'll talk if I want to."

Marlo shrank back in her seat. She didn't approve of the way Simon had spoken to her, but she understood his desire for good manners at the theater. "Sorry," she mouthed.

The houselights went down, and a spotlight lit up the red velvet curtain. The mumbles across the audience died out completely, and when there was perfect silence, the curtains parted. George Fiege sat on a pile of burlap, struggling to put on his shoes. He wore a baggy brown suit and a fedora, but that wasn't the most noticeable thing about his wardrobe. Long straps wrapped around dumbbells hung from his arms and shoulders. Three Velcro leg weights were attached to each leg. Mr. Fiege, portraying the character of Estragon, wasn't just waiting for Godot; he was *weighting* for Godot. When Vladimir arrived onstage a few moments later, he dragged kettlebells behind him.

Marlo pressed her lips together and raised her eyebrows so high that she felt her hairline tighten. She covered her mouth with her hand to hide her laugh. She wondered what her French lit professor would make of this. The director was certainly exploiting the *comedy* in tragicomedy. Or was he? Marlo glanced across the audience the best she could, considering her eyes were still adjusting to the dim light, and noticed that nobody else was laughing. She looked back onstage, where the cast was continuing to perform the lines with straight faces. They couldn't be serious, could they? She glanced at Simon and witnessed him clenching both fists like he was trying to help Mr. Fiege carry all that weight on his shoulders.

Okay, then. Marlo tried to open her mind a little wider, but all she saw were two middle-aged men struggling to move. Halfway through the first act they seemed to give up altogether and remained rooted in one spot, sweat pouring down their faces. Mr. Fiege's hat fell to the ground accidentally, and his balding head glistened in the harsh light. Marlo looked over at Mrs. Fiege and saw her wearing her standardized-testing smile again. Next to her, Julia was cringing. That made Marlo feel better. At least she wasn't the only person who recognized that this performance was horrible. She wasn't sure what the white-haired lady to her right thought, because the woman was snoring.

Suddenly, in the middle of a dramatic pause onstage, the opening bars to "Hooked on a Feeling" by Blue Swede rang out across the still auditorium.

"Shoot!" Simon scrambled to pull his phone out of his pocket, but since he was wearing cargo shorts, he had to unzip multiple pockets sewn right next to each other before he could find his phone. "My apologies," Simon called.

"What happened?" The old woman next to Marlo jerked awake, but her husband kept sleeping.

Marlo scooted down in her seat as the whole room glared at them. For once she let her posture deteriorate into something that would have made Madame Burke cry.

"All better now," said Simon, finally turning off his phone.

Up on stage Mr. Fiege and his castmate kept going like nothing had happened. Marlo appreciated their commitment, and it was what she would have done, too, as a dancer. But this wasn't ballet; it was theater. Now the audience had missed a whole page of lines, and the already confusing performance was even more indecipherable than before. Still, after a couple of minutes, Marlo got back in the groove again and was able to follow the dialogue. That was, until Simon's phone rang again, clearly still hooked on a feeling.

The phone didn't sing the words, but Marlo imagined them when she heard the music.

This time, Simon stood and bulldozed his way across the row of seats, stepping on people's feet and squishing past them until he reached the aisle. The door at the back of the auditorium opened and closed a second later with a thud.

Marlo tried to soothe her embarrassment by reminding herself that at least Simon wasn't a psycho killer, but at the same time, she regretted that she wasn't on a lonely beach in Port Inez where nobody could witness her humiliation.

The play limped along until intermission, and Simon still hadn't returned. Marlo waited while the patrons next to her slowly crept out of the row and up the aisle. She saw Julia and Mrs. Fiege stuck at the bottom, unable to move through the traffic. Marlo knew that she should probably knee and elbow her way to the lobby and find Simon, but she wished she could hang out with her friend and favorite teacher instead. She waved to them from afar, and they waved back. Then, Marlo left her seat and went to seek Simon.

The theater lobby was packed with patrons holding compostable paper cups filled with wine or coffee. Two lines snaked through the crowd—one for the drink station, and one for the women's restroom. Marlo searched for Simon's red hair and fanciful earring but didn't see him. She made three slow laps around the room and also poked her head outside, where it was raining hard enough to drown rats, and decided he must be in the men's restroom, where she couldn't see him. Desperate for relief herself, Marlo joined the line for the women's restroom and pulled out her phone. Maybe Simon had texted her via the Good Catch app, she figured.

It took a full sixty seconds for her phone to boot back to life, but when it did, she saw that yes, notifications were waiting for her from Good Catch. Marlo tapped on the link as the line inched forward and saw a note from Simon in her dashboard.

> Sorry to leave you hanging, Babe. Katelyn needed me and I had to go.

Marlow stared at the text in disbelief. What a jerk! Simon had been her ride home. I hope she heals fast, Marlo texted back. Sorry, it didn't work out between us. She hit send and then blocked Simon's profile, which made her feel better.

"Ladies, gentleman, and critics," said a voice over the loudspeaker. "Please return to your seats. The show will begin in five minutes."

Marlo let out an exasperated sigh. She was still in line for the women's restroom and had just now reached the door. Peering inside, she saw two stalls and three ladies in front of her, including the woman with white hair.

"You young people and your phones." The old woman made a clucking noise with her tongue. "What's so interesting that you can't put them down?"

"I was checking my messages," said Marlo. But then she felt mad at herself for defending her actions. She could be on her phone if she wanted to be.

"Where's your boyfriend?" The woman stepped into the restroom as the line moved forward.

"He's not my boyfriend. But the man I was with had an emergency and had to leave early." Marlo was ready to bail on the whole evening herself. She wished she had her coat with her, but it was back in the theater. Otherwise, she'd Uber home as soon as she could.

"Oh gosh, is there still a line?" Mrs. Fiege rolled up in her mechanized wheelchair. "It was too crowded to get out of the theater until now."

Julia was right next to her. "We just barely missed all the people returning to their seats."

"I was hoping to get a glass of wine." Mrs. Fiege looked over longingly at the beverage station, which now had a CLOSED sign hanging off the espresso machine.

"Don't worry, Shelly." Julia patted her enormous purse. "I left the house in such a rush that I grabbed the diaper bag by mistake."

"I'm not that desperate for the restroom," said Mrs. Fiege.

Julia blushed. "No, of course not." She looked down at her friend. "Unless you are? In which case I'll go clear a path for you."

"You can have my spot," Marlo volunteered. "I'm sorry I didn't offer it sooner."

Mrs. Fiege shook her head. "I can hold it a while longer. But mainly I'm thirsty. Do you have a bottle of chardonnay in there, Julia?"

Julia unzipped the diaper bag. "How about apple juice? It's organic." She reached into the generous tote and pulled out a juice box. "Oh look! White grape juice. That's almost as good as wine."

"If you're two years old," Mrs. Fiege laughed. "But I'll take one. Thanks."

"Want one, Marlo?" Julia held out another box.

"I'd love one, thanks." Marlo took the drink and set it on the sink next to the faucet. It was finally her turn in line. When she was finished using the toilet, she gave up the stall to Julia and washed her hands. She took her time, waiting for Mrs. Fiege to emerge. She didn't want to leave without saying goodbye. Plus, she didn't look forward to returning to the theater late by herself.

"Well, what do you think of the play so far?" Mrs. Fiege asked as she rolled to the sink. She stretched her arms out as far as they could go to reach the faucet.

Although technically the restroom had an ADA-compliant stall, the sink hadn't been designed for wheelchairs. Now that Marlo noticed it, she realized that the paper towel holder was way too high for Mrs. Fiege to access. "The play's been interesting," said Marlo as she pulled out a strip of paper towels for her teacher. "Did your husband have to lift weights to train for it?"

Mrs. Fiege nodded. "He sure did, and you should have heard George go on and on about how much his muscles hurt after each practice."

"That's why I keep telling him to join the gym," said Julia as she stepped up to the sink. George Fiege was her accountant. "Cascade Athletic Club offers the SilverSneakers program, right?" She looked at Marlo for confirmation.

"That's right." Marlo nodded.

"So see?" Julia asked. "It wouldn't cost any money, so George has no good reason not to."

"I'm the reason." Shelly shrugged. "He won't go without me, and I do so much physical therapy as it is that going to the gym sounds like torture."

"What about swimming?" Marlo tugged down the edge of her sweater that had crept up. "We have a saltwater pool."

"I love swimming," said Mrs. Fiege. "But I haven't swum in ages. Is it a zero-entry pool where I could switch chairs and roll right in?"

"No." Marlo shook her head. "Unfortunately not. But we do have a pool lift. Mr. Fiege and one of the lifeguards could help you into that chair, and then we'd gently lower you into the water."

"It's a beautiful pool," said Julia. "The temperature is perfect."

"And our women's restroom is spotless and completely ADA compliant," said Marlo. "Even the steam room and sauna."

"Heat's not good for my MS," said Mrs. Fiege. "But my doctor did suggest swimming." She leaned back in her seat. "I just don't relish the idea of shopping for a bathing suit. There's no way that the one I bought ten years ago will fit. I've lost so much weight since then."

"You could order one online." Julia slung her bag over her shoulder.

Mrs. Fiege tapped her chin. "I'll think about it. I would like to see George get more exercise besides walking Midas to the dog park on Saturdays. Plus, swimming is fun."

The three of them left the small restroom together and entered the empty lobby. Marlo wished more than ever that she had her coat with her so that she could leave, but she didn't want to hurt Mrs. Fiege's feelings since her husband was the star.

"Your date probably thinks you fell in," said Julia.

"He already left." Marlo slurped apple juice. "There was some sort of emergency."

"And he bailed on you?" Julia scrunched up her face. "What a jerk."

"*Jerk*'s not the word I was going to use—but that too." Mrs. Fiege sighed and stared at the closed doors to the auditorium. "Well, I guess we'd better go back in there. The big barbell scene is coming up next."

Barbells? That wasn't something Marlo remembered from her French lit class, but she kept quiet. "No offense to your husband, Mrs. Fiege, but drinking juice boxes with you two in the restroom has been the best part of this whole evening."

"Oh, honey," said Mrs. Fiege as she rolled to the doors. "You need to get out more."

"I'm trying," said Marlo.

"Take a firm hold of life, and enjoy every minute," said Mrs. Fiege. "The best moments of youth are the ones you don't expect, and the worst are the opportunities you bail on."

"Okay," Marlo said noncommittally. But she knew that her teacher was right. She thought back to her dinner at the Nuthatch Bakery with Ben last night and how tingly she'd felt when she'd thought he was going to kiss her. That had been the happiest she'd felt in a long time—until Ben had turned away. Why hadn't she grabbed him by the arms, pulled him close, and shown him what she wanted? Maybe because the first step was admitting that truth to herself. Marlo wanted Ben Wexler-Lowrey. She didn't want Ryan, or Hunter, or Simon, or some other weirdo she met on Good Catch—she wanted Ben. And the next time she saw him, she was going to tell him that.

CHAPTER TWELVE

It was Monday morning, and Ben was in downtown Harper Landing doing a story on the Forgotten Hug, the up-and-coming antique store on Third Avenue. He sat on a midcentury modern dining chair, polished to a shine with orange oil, and turned off the recording app on his phone. "I've got what I need for the article," Ben said as he put down his pencil and closed his spiral notebook. He'd enjoyed interviewing Dawn Maddox and finding out how this thirty-five-year-old single mom had turned her Etsy shop into a business with a physical storefront. "That part about you being a former dancer at Lottie Burke's studio is a great detail."

"As soon as I saw that the original site of the Red Slipper was available to rent, I knew it was a sign from the universe telling me to be bold." Dawn held up a china teapot. "More tea?"

Ben, who preferred coffee but who had already had a cup because he didn't want to appear rude, declined. "No thanks." He stood up. "I'm ready for the tour now."

"Great." Dawn rose from her chair. The aquamarine tunic she wore was the same color as her eyes. "I'll show you around."

Ben followed her out of her office into the main room. Neatly arranged aisles snaked through vintage furniture, cut-crystal glass displays, and racks of embroidered linens. Mirrors on one side of the room made the space feel bigger, and quilts hung from the former ballet barre.

"It looks like you're giving the antique stores in Snohomish some serious competition," Ben commented as he admired a first-edition copy of *Charlotte's Web*. Ben loved how Charlotte used spiderweb journalism to save lives.

"That's right." Dawn nodded and led Ben to a rack. "But what sets my shop apart is my collection of vintage Nordic sweaters. I search estate sales all across Washington to find them and then sell them here in the store as well as online."

Ben picked a hanger off a rack and was surprised at how much it weighed. The intricate pattern caught his attention, but what struck him the most was the ornate pewter clasps buttoning the cardigan in place. To him, it looked like something a fisherman would have worn in the 1900s. When he saw that the price tag said $200, it sent a shock through him. "How many of these do you sell each week?"

"I sell five or six a day online." Dawn picked up another one, which was a crew neck instead of a cardigan. "They last for decades because of the quality of the wool. There's a strong Scandinavian community in Seattle, and I usually find stock in people's attics and then sell it all over the world." She put the sweater back on the rack. "But if you think these are cool, wait until you see what I found in the storage room."

Cool wasn't the word Ben would have used to describe the sweaters, but he knew that Savannah, his mom, and maybe even Katelyn would love them. Goldie would have said that Dawn was exploiting a culturally rich community for her personal economic gain, but Ben didn't see it that way. He thought Dawn was clever for figuring out a way to match supply with demand. "Where's the storage room?" he asked.

"It's upstairs." Dawn led Ben up a narrow flight of stairs. "I found all of Madame Burke's leftover costumes from the Red Slipper." They were at the top of the stairs now, in a lofted space that held artwork. Paintings, gilded mirrors, and statues were artfully arranged in a path that zigzagged through the loft. Ben didn't feel claustrophobic, but there were enough items for sale that he didn't notice the tiny door in the corner until Dawn reached out and opened it. She raised her hand and pulled a chain, and a weak light bulb flashed on.

"Sorry it's dark in here, but I think that was to protect the fabric." Dawn held the door open for Ben and let him enter first.

Unlike the orange-oil scent of the rest of the shop, the storage room smelled dusty, like someone had shaken out all the pillows on a couch. It took a moment for Ben's eyes to adjust to the dim light, but once they did, he saw five racks of costumes, organized in groups according to color. Sequins sparkled like disco balls, and netting puffed out from beneath gigantic skirts. One wall was covered in tutus of every color. But a framed poster caught Ben's eye. There, immortalized in the beauty of her teenage youth, was Marlo, elevated on pointe shoes wearing a smile of pure delight. "Wow," he said, staring at the fading colors. Ben looked at teenage Marlo with new eyes. Instead of judging her for preconceived notions that had turned out to be false, he saw her for what she was—a high schooler dancing dozens of hours a week who went home to deal with a difficult home life. She wasn't a prima donna; she was a hardworking person, just like him.

"Aren't these costumes fun?" Dawn asked. "They're a piece of Harper Landing history right here in the attic."

"I know someone who would love to see them." Ben looked down at Dawn and grinned, flashing his dimples in what he hoped was a winning manner.

"Who?" Dawn asked.

Ben pointed at Marlo's poster. "The woman right there—Marlo Jonas. She was just telling me that Madame Burke's costumes were one of her favorite memories from childhood."

"I know Marlo." Dawn squinted at the portrait. "She's my barre instructor. I don't know why I never recognized that was her." She shrugged. "I need to get my vision checked. And sure, you can show her, but it'll have to be fast. This inventory is selling out in my Etsy shop as fast as I can box it up to mail."

"Could I call her right now?" Ben took his phone out of his pocket.

"Absolutely." Dawn turned around to go. "I'd better get back to the showroom. I have some Etsy orders to pack up."

"I'll go with you." Ben followed her out of the storage room but held back when he reached the loft. He wanted to be able to speak to Marlo in private since it was the first time he was calling her. But as soon as he looked at his phone, he realized that he didn't have her number. He tried googling her name, but she was unlisted. He ended up calling the Cascade Athletic Club directly. Then, as he listened to the phone ringing, Ben panicked. What if she was teaching a class? What if she wasn't interested in the costumes? Or, worse, what if her parents answered the phone?

Feeling like he was thirteen years old, Ben looked down at the carpet and caught a glimpse of himself in a mirror resting on the floor. Man, his shoes were dirty. He should have—

"Hello? Cascade Athletic Club," said a chipper voice, interrupting Ben's thoughts.

"Hi. Is Marlo Jonas there?" Ben asked.

"She's at the smoothie bar. May I ask who's calling?"

"Ben Wexler-Lowrey." Ben paced through the narrow walkway, clenching and unclenching the hand that gave him writer's cramp. "If she doesn't want to—"

"One minute," said the person at the front desk. Ben couldn't tell if the voice was male or female.

After what seemed like an eternity later, Marlo picked up the phone. "Marlo Jonas speaking."

"Marlo? Hi. This is Ben. But I guess they told you that already. Anyway—"

"Ben?" Marlo asked. "Ben Wexler-Lowrey?"

Jealously, he wondered how many Bens there were in her life and why she felt the need to be specific. "Yes, it's me. I'm calling from that new antique shop on Third. The one where your old dance studio used to be."

"The Forgotten Hug," said Marlo. "I've been meaning to go in there. Is it nice?"

"Yeah, if you like stuff like this." Ben looked over the loft's railing to the scene below. "I'm calling you because there's a room here that's full of Madame Burke costumes, and I thought you'd like to see them before the owner sells them."

"I'd love to see them," Marlo said, excitement filling her tone. "I've got a break in my schedule. Can I come over right now?"

Ben looked at his watch. He didn't need to turn in his assignment until three thirty that afternoon, and he was working from home that day. "Sure. I'll be here. There's even a framed poster of you."

"Well, *that's* embarrassing."

"Why are you embarrassed?" he asked.

"I just am. I'll see you in ten minutes, and thanks." Marlo hung up the phone before Ben had a chance to say goodbye.

While he was waiting, Ben figured he might as well do some Christmas shopping. He wandered downstairs and looked at the kitchen gadgets. There was an old-fashioned eggbeater that he thought his dad might have fun with, plus a hand-embroidered apron with the Harper Landing ferry on it and the expression **I BELIEVE IN FERRIES** underneath. That was a classic town joke that his mom loved. Both were reasonably priced and within Ben's budget. The store was closed on Mondays, but he asked Dawn, and she said she didn't mind ringing a few things up. They were just finishing the transaction when Marlo arrived.

"Hi, Marlo." Dawn gave the bag to Ben and smiled at Marlo. "Fancy meeting you out of the barre studio."

"I do emerge from the cave on rare occasions." Marlo removed her hat and gloves and stuffed them in her purse. She wore floral leggings and a thick pink sweatshirt underneath her raincoat. "Hi, Ben." Marlo's cheeks were almost as pink as her hoodie.

"Hi." He gazed at her without moving.

"You were going to show her the costumes?" Dawn prodded. "Upstairs?" The corners of her mouth wiggled as she watched Ben and Marlo stare at each other.

"Oh, that's right." Ben spun around and headed to the stairs. "Wait until you see."

Ben felt as much as heard Marlo follow him. She smelled like baby powder and hand soap. He couldn't hear her footsteps because of the Ugg boots she wore, which landed soundlessly on the old wood floor.

"Being here brings back a lot of memories for me," Marlo said in a wistful voice. "I know Madame Burke would be sad that it's no longer a dance studio, but she would have loved the quilts hanging off of the ballet barre."

"Where do kids go to take dance lessons now?" Ben reached the top of the steps and waited for Marlo to catch up.

"There's a new studio in Lynnwood, and the YMCA offers classes as well." Marlo climbed the last step. "If I had more business sense, I'd open up a studio of my own, but I still have so much to learn."

"Someday soon, maybe," said Ben. "You could have classes at the gym for kids."

"Maybe." Marlo bit her bottom lip and looked off into the distance. "That could be a unique way to bring in revenue. Parents could work out Saturday morning while their kids were at dance class."

"If only you had a former professional ballerina to teach them."

Marlo grinned. "I'll think about it." She took a step closer to him. "You're always giving me good ideas about the club. Thanks."

"Pretty ironic considering I've only been to the Cascade Athletic Club one time."

"My offer still stands. You can come to spend the day at the club with me whenever you want." She put her hands in her pockets. "I mean, *if* you want."

Ben wished her hands were still free, because he was tempted to hold one. Her standing that close to him made his pulse beat fast. He wanted to slip his arm around her slim waist right then and there and pull her close for a kiss that would make it difficult for them to breathe. "The club would be fun," he finally managed to mumble out. "Come on." He waved his hand. "Let me show you the costumes."

Ben opened up the narrow door and flipped the light switch on. He took a deep breath as Marlo passed him. There was that sweet scent of baby powder again, mixed with a faint whiff of sweat, like Marlo might have already taught a class that morning. Hell, knowing Marlo's schedule, she might have taught two classes, or even three. Ben wondered if all that spinning meant she might like cycling the Interurban Trail with him one day. Not in November when the weather was wretched but next summer when the sun came up. Then he kicked himself for planning that far ahead. As if Marlo would want to spend a long-future month with him when they'd barely talked to each other their entire lives until now.

"Oh my goodness, this takes me back." Marlo leaned into the clothing racks, stretched out her arms, and hugged them. "It's like I can feel Madame Burke's love for me, right here in this room." When she stood up, tears were rolling down her face, and Ben didn't think they were because of the dust. "She always wanted the best for me—for all of us." Marlo wiped her eyes with the back of her sleeve and lifted her chin. "'Stand up straight,' she'd tell us. 'Put on a smile, and remember to breathe, because the show must go on.'"

"Did you see the poster?" Ben pointed at the wall. "How old were you there?"

Marlo laughed when she saw herself. "I was eighteen and a senior in high school. I'd just auditioned for the Pacific Northwest Ballet Company and was waiting to hear back. It was the same day Madame Burke took promotional pictures for *The Nutcracker*, and I had to rush back from the city to make it on time."

"That sounds like preparation for what you do now," said Ben. "Rushing from one class to the next."

"Kind of, yeah. When you're passionate about an extracurricular like I was, the skills you learn stick with you for the rest of your life." She took a deep breath and looked at him. "Like you and the school newspaper. You spent so much time on that as a teenager, and look how much you've accomplished now. I read all of your articles."

"You do?" Ben was stunned—and flummoxed. It made him anxious thinking that she read things he wrote. He would have to bug Mike for extra help proofreading now. But if he was honest with himself, it also made him feel happy. A warm glow pooled over him that started in his chest and filtered out to his fingertips. Marlo Jonas thought he was a good writer. The toughest critic of all thought he had worthy things to say.

"I do." Marlo cleared her throat. "Do you remember the bet I made with my dad at Julia's wedding?"

Ben nodded. "Yeah, I remember. I'm still dealing with the aftermath of the similar wager I made with my mom."

"Well, I hope you're luckier than me, because I've failed." Marlo inched her Ugg boots closer to where Ben stood. "The thing is, I was supposed to fall for someone who didn't make my knees turn to mush every time I looked at him. I was supposed to be better than that, and I wasn't."

"You weren't?" Ben clenched his jaw. Simon hadn't mentioned details about his date with Marlo the other night. He'd been too busy helping Katelyn decipher her course catalog and register for classes. But Ben knew that Marlo and Simon had gone out. This must be about that.

Marlo lunged forward and put her hands on the side of his chest, surprising him. She tilted up her face and pressed her lips against his before he even realized what she was doing. Marlo was kissing him! Right there in front of the tutus. Ben was too stunned to think, but he didn't have to. He dropped the package of Christmas presents he was holding, wrapped his arms around her, and pulled her in as tight as he could. His mouth hungrily explored hers as he held her firmly against him. Ben tilted his head, deepening the kiss, and closed his eyes as he felt his body respond to senses that overwhelmed him. She tasted like peppermint, she felt like heaven, and the touch of her lips against his own ignited his heart.

But as quickly as it had begun, the kiss ended. Marlo darted back and bumped into the costumes, knocking hangers off the rack. She put her hand over her mouth and looked at him with shock.

His chest heaved up and down as he fought to catch his breath, and Ben struggled to make sense of any of it. "I'm sorry," he said, trying to make things right. "I didn't mean to—" But before he could finish his sentence, Marlo closed the distance between them again. Her hands entwined around his neck, and her fingers raked through his hair.

Ben's eyelids shut, and he held her tight, his hands roaming her back and stroking the soft fabric of her sweatshirt. Her hip bone jutted into his thigh, and he marveled at how close they were. But it still wasn't near enough. He wanted to consume her, to turn the both of them inside out until they were one being so they wouldn't explode. Ben had never felt that way kissing another woman, not with Katelyn, nor Savannah, and especially not Goldie. This was something different. Something unreal. Ben felt like they were two magnets drawn together.

Time stopped. Earth may have ceased turning so far as Ben knew. Every part of Ben was entranced by Marlo. He couldn't believe that the most beautiful woman he'd ever met was kissing him with desire. No, not just desire, but tenderness too. She trembled, and this time, when she pulled back for air, she braced her arms against him to hold herself steady.

"I'm a little bit dizzy," she admitted before resting her cheek against his shoulder.

Ben used the opportunity to tickle her neck with kisses, which made her giggle. "It's hot in here," he whispered. "No wonder you're dizzy. I'm about to keel over myself from shock."

She sighed and hugged him tighter. "I don't know what I'm doing, but please don't let go."

"I wouldn't dream of it." Ben closed his eyes and let his inhalations match the pace of her breathing. No sooner had he caught his breath than his lips found her forehead and her cheekbone and then made their way to her lips, which were parted and ready for his tongue. Ben felt like a teenager making out in high school, only he'd never done this in high school, not with the intensity of a neutron star ready to collide and explode.

"Knock, knock," said a voice behind them. The light bulb went out, plunging them into darkness, then flicked back on again.

Ben and Marlo jumped apart. Ben turned away from the doorway and tried to calm himself down. When the light returned, he saw Marlo, cheeks aflame, tugging down her sweatshirt where moments ago his hands had been exploring the smoothness of her bare skin.

Dawn stood in the doorway, an amused smile on her face. "I thought you guys might have gotten lost in here," she said. "I came to see if there was anything you wanted before I sell off the lot of it?"

"The picture," Ben said, pointing to the framed poster on the wall. "I'll take that."

"And I'll, um . . ." Marlo bent down to pick up the costumes she'd knocked off the rack. "I'll take one of these," she said, holding up a red velvet leotard.

Ben's pulse raced as he imagined what she'd look like wearing that. He bent down to pick up the Christmas presents he'd purchased and patted his hair as casually as possible, because he knew that it must be rumpled. "How much for the poster and costume?" he asked Dawn.

"They're on the house," she said with a smirk. "But come on, you two, it's cold in here. The heater doesn't reach the attic." She stepped back and held open the door.

The room didn't feel cold to Ben. It might as well have been one hundred degrees. He let Marlo go ahead of him and then lifted the poster off the wall and followed her out. Ben admired Marlo's backside as she walked down the stairs. The poster and package were awkward to carry, and he was mindful where he stepped so that he didn't accidentally knock over an antique.

"I'll look forward to that article," said Dawn, right before they left. "Thanks for writing about the Forgotten Hug."

"No problem." Ben smiled guiltily. "Thanks for the poster." He opened the door for Marlo.

"Well," said Marlo as they stood on the sidewalk. The cold made her pink cheeks appear even rosier.

The icy air blowing off Puget Sound was a shock to Ben's system. He wanted to gather Marlo up into a hug and protect her from the elements, but he couldn't because he was holding the poster and package.

"Did we do that?" Ben asked. Outside in the light of day, it seemed even more shocking than it had been in the storeroom.

"We did." Marlo put on her hat. "I mean, *I* did." She looked down at her feet.

"I'm pretty sure I did too," said Ben, "and that I'd like to do it again." He grinned and thought fast. He'd be in the newsroom Saturday and Sunday, but Friday was free. "Would you like to go out Friday night?"

"I'd love to." Marlo smiled, and Ben had never seen her look that happy.

But too late, Ben remembered that he already had plans for Friday. "Oh, wait," he said. "I promised my friend that I'd go to her house-warming party. It's okay, though," he said quickly. "I can bail on that."

"Can you bring a date?" Marlo stepped closer toward him and away from the wind.

"Sure, but it's in Snohomish. I think there are sheep involved. You probably wouldn't—"

"Sounds like fun." Marlo pecked him on the cheek. "But Friday's a long way off. I have to work tomorrow night, but I'm free Wednesday. Would you like to come over to my apartment for dinner?"

"Absolutely." Ben readjusted his grip on the frame because it was slipping. "Text me your address and the time."

"I don't think I have your phone number, but I can find it on Good Catch."

"I didn't see you on Good Catch."

Marlo curled up her shoulders. "That's because I blocked you."

Ben laughed. "You blocked me, huh? It didn't look like you were blocking me up there in that storage room."

Marlo blushed. "Nope." She kissed him softly on the lips. "I'll see you on Wednesday," she said before she walked away at a fast pace toward the marina district.

Ben stood rooted to the spot, watching her go. He didn't move a muscle until she'd rounded the corner and was out of sight. That was when, as Ben turned to walk toward his car, he remembered that he'd biked. How was he supposed to ride home holding this picture frame and his parents' presents? He couldn't, because it was impossible. So he took his next-best option. He walked over to Main Street, where the Nuthatch Bakery sat between two stores, Paige's Pages and the Wanderer's Home. Mike was most likely working at one of them, and he'd let Ben stash the poster in his car for sure.

CHAPTER THIRTEEN

The last person Marlo had cooked for was Ryan, who'd hated everything she'd made. If she served brown rice, he wouldn't eat it because he was doing Whole30. If she made lettuce-wrapped grass-fed bison burgers, he'd say he was vegan. Whatever fad was popular at his CrossFit gym was the diet Ryan was currently on, and he never had the courtesy to communicate that to Marlo ahead of time. He'd just show up for dinner and make her feel like a jerk for not accommodating his food restrictions. That was why Marlo made extra sure she knew what Ben could eat when she'd texted him her address.

I'm an omnivore, he'd written back. Anything you make will be great, even roadkill.

I haven't run over any raccoons lately, she'd responded.

That's good, Ben had answered, because the @HarpLanPDScan Twitter feed would have gone nuts.

That text exchange had happened Tuesday morning, and Marlo hadn't heard from Ben since. It made her nervous. Was he second-guessing what they'd started? But then she realized he'd messaged her last, so perhaps he was waiting for *her* to respond. Marlo was too stressed to overanalyze it any further. She focused on peeling ginger for the stir-fry she was making.

Marlo wore a black apron with a faux pink tutu sewn onto the front. She felt ridiculous in it, but it was the only apron she owned, and she didn't want to get her outfit dirty. Under the apron, she had on an ivory sweater, her favorite skinny jeans, and shearling-lined Birkenstocks. Marlo intended to slip into heels at the last minute, but no way did she want to cook in three inches of pain. She finished peeling the ginger and diced it into small bits on the cutting board. Bowls lined up on the counter held snap peas, bite-size pieces of broccoli, leafy green bok choy, and a drained can of mandarin oranges. The oven timer rang, and Marlo removed a sheet pan of toasted almonds just in time. The parchment paper liner was singed from the heat.

Ben would be here any minute, and Marlo was annoyed that the rice cooker hadn't come to temperature yet. If it didn't heat up fast, the rice and stir-fry would be done at two different times. Marlo drank a swig of water and used a fork to flip the salmon in the marinade she'd made of coconut aminos, soy sauce, rice vinegar, and brown sugar. Almost too late, she remembered to take out the marionberries so they could defrost and be ready to serve with ice cream. Marlo dug into the back of her freezer for the container of berries she'd picked in Snohomish last August. She had a bag of blueberries, too, but marionberries were fancier.

The doorbell rang right as she was dumping the berries into a colander to drain. Marlo untied her apron and looked for a place to put it. She was on her way to the closet where her washer and dryer were stacked when the doorbell rang again. "Coming!" she called. With no time to make it to the closet, Marlo bunched up the apron, the silly pink tulle sticking out like cotton candy, and stuffed it into the first place she saw, which was a basket next to the couch that held afghans. At the last moment she remembered to light her spring-meadow candle on the mantle. Then she raced to the front door and flung it open.

Ben stood at the threshold holding two dozen red roses. His raincoat was drenched. "Hi," he said, with a huge smile on his face. "I hope I'm not late." He handed her the roses, spotted with raindrops on the covering cellophane. "These are for you."

"They're gorgeous." Marlo accepted the flowers and marveled at how beautiful they were. She hadn't been given flowers in over two years, not since she'd quit dancing. "This was thoughtful," Marlo started to say, but she was interrupted by Ben sweeping her into his arms and kissing her. She lifted onto her toes so she could reach and slid her free arm around his neck. Ben smelled like soap and rain. His wet raincoat steamed between them as they took their time with the lingering kiss.

"Sorry," Ben said when they finally parted. "I got you all wet from my jacket." He unzipped his raincoat.

"I don't mind. Wool dries quickly." Marlo brushed droplets off her sweater, and as she did so, she glanced at her feet, which were still shod in her shearling-lined Birkenstocks. She'd forgotten to slip into her heels! Not only that, but her feet were hideous. She was so long overdue for a pedicure that she'd been wearing grip socks to teach barre class for the past three weeks so nobody would see her toes. "Um . . . ," Marlo muttered, suddenly flustered.

"Where should I hang this?" Ben held up his jacket.

"I'll put it on a kitchen chair so it can dry." Holding the roses with one hand, Marlo took his coat in the other. She hurried to the kitchen and draped his jacket over the chair where she'd sat earlier that day to put on her sandals. Her heels should have been nearby. But when Marlo scanned the wood floor, she didn't see them.

"Ooh," Ben said, "are those blackberries?"

"Close." Marlo was still frantically searching for her heels. Sadly, it was no use. She couldn't find them anywhere. "They're marionberries," Marlo said as she gave up on finding her pretty footwear. She opened up a cabinet and took out the Waterford Crystal vase Madame Burke had given her when she'd signed her contract at the Pacific Northwest Ballet.

"Duh. I see the color now. They're too red to be blackberries." Ben looked at the multiple dishes of vegetables on the counter. "You've been busy. Do you need any help?"

Marlo filled the vase with water while she cut elastic off the rose stems. "Could you open a bottle of wine? There's a rack on the counter." She plunged the roses into the water and arranged them into a nice display. The roses were too tall to put at the center of the kitchen table, so she put them on the coffee table in front of the couch instead.

When she returned to the kitchen, Ben was holding the bottle of Chateau Ste. Michelle chardonnay she'd purchased at their tasting room in Woodinville with Ryan a couple of months ago. It had been a double date with Ryan and his coworker from T-Mobile. He and his friend had gotten wasted while Marlo had been stuck making small talk with the coworker's girlfriend, who worked at Pottery Barn. The only good thing that had come from the afternoon was the bottle of chardonnay and the discount Marlo had gotten buying the faux-angora blanket that was in the basket next to her couch.

"Is this okay?" Ben asked.

"Sounds great." Marlo opened the knife drawer and pulled out the corkscrew. "Here you go." She selected two wineglasses from the cabinet above and gave them to him as well. The rice cooker was bubbling now, spewing steam through the vents. "Dinner will be ready in twenty minutes." Marlo lit the burner under her wok. She added a tablespoon of sesame oil and threw in the garlic and ginger first, then the salmon.

"Mmm. That smells good. What type of salmon is it?"

"Sockeye. My dad caught it this summer on his boat." Marlo broke up the fish into bite-size pieces with a wooden spoon and then threw in the broccoli and snap peas.

"Do you ever go out on the water with him?"

"No, not really." Marlo shrugged. "My mom's vegetarian, so she hates to fish, and my dad prefers boating with his buddies."

"Mike's dad has a boat. He takes us crabbing in the summer."

"That sounds like fun." Marlo opened the refrigerator and took out a mason jar of homemade chicken broth. She used a spoon to scrape off the fat and then poured a cupful of broth into the wok.

"There," said Ben as he pulled the cork out of the chardonnay. "That one was tricky." He poured two generous glasses of wine.

Marlo's first sip was more like a gulp, but it helped settle her nerves. She dumped in the bok choy and covered the wok with the lid. "Alexa," she called out. "Set the timer for seven minutes."

"You have an Alexa?" Ben looked around the room, trying to find it.

"An Echo." Marlo pointed at the small device next to the toaster. "I use it to listen to music, mostly."

"I've always thought about getting one of those." Ben stared at it. "What else can it do?"

"It reads the news or audiobooks. It's an alarm clock and stop-watch. Oh yeah, and it can also help with spelling." She put her hand on her hip and raised her voice. "Alexa, how do you spell supercalifragilisticexpialidocious?"

Alexa spelled out the letters in a clear voice, and Ben looked impressed. "Wow, I need one of those. I'm a horrible speller."

"Spelling is easy. Writing is hard," said Marlo. When she saw Ben flinch, she immediately recognized she had said something wrong, but she didn't know what it was. She'd just complimented his talent as a writer, after all. "Google Home and Siri can do that stuff too," she said.

Ben pulled out his cracked cell phone. "My phone's a dinosaur and doesn't have any of those features, but it has a recording function for when I do interviews, so that works for me."

"Whatever works, right?"

"Yeah." Ben's eyes drifted over to the Echo, but then he put his phone away and reached for her hands. "I can't believe you're cooking me dinner. Thank you for this."

"It's not a big deal." Marlo shrugged as she blushed.

Ben tugged her toward him, and they kissed, the taste of wine still on their lips. Marlo thought fleetingly of the juice boxes she had shared the Saturday before with Mrs. Fiege and Julia. Chardonnay was so much better, she confirmed, and she wondered what her former teacher would think about her kissing Ben.

"Can I ask you a question?" Marlo asked when their lips parted. She was still in his arms, leaning into him as he rested against the counter.

"Sure. You can ask me anything."

"Why'd you say that you couldn't cook in your Good Catch profile?"

"Because I can't."

"That's not true. I've seen you in the kitchen at the bakery."

"Heating up soup. No biggie."

Marlo narrowed her eyes at him. "Stop selling yourself short."

Ben winced. "There's something you should know about me," he said. "I hate clichés."

"Duly noted, but that doesn't change the meaning of what I said. Why not be proud of your accomplishments instead of downplaying them?"

"But baking is different than cooking," said Ben. "I mean, sure, I can follow recipes, but it's not like I have a Michelin star."

"It's not just cooking." Marlo gazed up into his brown eyes. "You said in your profile that you weren't athletic, and I know that's not true either."

"I'm horrible at sports." Ben shuddered. "Remember the Angry Hornets?"

"That was years ago. And my dad is an awful coach."

"True." Ben frowned.

"Now you're a guy who bikes to Seattle and back. That's hard core. I don't understand why you'd think that you weren't athletic."

Ben shrugged. "I guess because in my mind, I still associate organized sports with athleticism."

"Well, you need to broaden your definition, Mister." Marlo jabbed her finger into his chest. "Dancers are athletes, too, but ballet's not an organized sport."

"Good point." Ben grinned.

The timer sounded, and Marlo turned away to deal with the stir-fry. She clicked off the stove and unplugged the rice cooker. Then she took out serving utensils and two plates. Usually when she and her folks ate dinner, they ate buffet style and served themselves food directly from the stove and kitchen counter, but now she panicked, realizing how gauche that appeared. It would be better to put the rice and stir-fry into fancy bowls that she set on the table. But Marlo didn't have serving dishes like that. She owned her parents' castoffs.

"Shall I grab my plate from the table?" Ben asked as Marlo stared at the food.

"Yeah, that would be great." Marlo lifted the lid of the wok and wedged a spoon inside. She waited while Ben went first, scooping out rice and the entrée onto his plate.

"This looks and smells delicious," he said as he mounded the stir-fry over the rice. "I can't wait to taste it."

"It's something simple," said Marlo, brushing off the compliment. She served herself and followed Ben to the table. It was dark out, but she'd left the window shades open so they could see the twinkling lights from the ferry shuttling people back and forth to Port Inez. Marlo took a bite and was relieved to find that the food was as good as it smelled. The vegetables were crisp and tender, and the salmon had absorbed the perfect amount of marinade. But she couldn't shake the feeling that something was missing.

"Oh, I left my wineglass on the counter," said Ben. "I'll grab yours too."

"Thanks." Marlo unfolded a napkin and put it on her lap. Maybe the wine was what had been nagging her. She smiled when Ben put the glass in her hand.

"Cheers," he said.

"You can do better than that," she said. "You're the writer who hates clichés, after all."

Ben sat down next to her. "You know how to pressure a guy, don't you?" He grinned, and his dimples flashed. Ben lifted his wineglass in another toast. "Here's to my enormous good fortune that you've lost your bet with your dad."

"I'll drink to that." Marlo clinked glasses with him and sipped her wine. "Shoot!" She set down her wineglass so hard that some of the chardonnay sloshed out. "The toasted almonds!" Marlo hopped up from the table and raced to the kitchen counter, where the slivered nuts still lay on the parchment paper. "I meant to mix these into the stir-fry at the last minute so they wouldn't be soggy," she said as she carefully carried the paper to the table without spilling them.

"Sprinkling them on top works too." Ben leaned back so she could scatter some on his plate.

"Spoken like a true chef." Marlo garnished both of their plates and tossed the parchment paper into the recycling. "I'm sorry I messed up," she said as she sat back down. "I wanted tonight to be perfect."

"It *is* perfect." Ben reached over and rubbed her back in slow circles. "Or shall I say exceptional? Shooting for perfection can drive a person nuts."

"True." Marlo nodded. She loaded broccoli onto her fork and deliberated if she should tell Ben the realization she'd come to after a great deal of thought. If it had been Ryan or any of the other self-absorbed guys she'd dated over the years, she would have passed, but Ben was different. He was easy to talk to and always made her feel understood. "I was looking back at our past," she said slowly, "and I think my perfectionism is why we spent all of those years not being friends."

"Because of Ms. Hanline?"

"Ms. Hanline?" Marlo wrinkled her forehead. "No. Because of the fourth-grade recorder concert. I made myself crazy mastering that dance routine, and then . . ." Marlo crumpled her napkin without meaning to. "You know . . ."

"I burped into the microphone?" Ben asked with a straight face.

Hearing him say it aloud made Marlo feel silly for holding a grudge all those years. It was funny, now that she thought about it. But at the time it had felt like he'd sunk her battleship. "Yeah," she giggled. "You torpedoed me."

"Oh boy." Ben hung his head. "Marlo, I'm so sorry," he said when he looked up again. "I know you must have worked hard on that dance. But me ruining your performance had nothing to do with you. It was all about me. I couldn't read the notes to 'Ode to Joy,' and so I improvised."

"By burping?"

Ben shrugged. "It seemed like a good idea at the time. I *was* nine, after all."

"I understand blanking because of stage fright." Marlo reached out and squeezed his hand. "But why couldn't you read the notes? Our music teacher drilled that song into the whole class for months."

"I—" Ben's face froze, and for a moment he said nothing. His mouth hung open like the universe had hit the pause button on a supernatural remote control and glued him in place. Then he shuddered and unstuck himself. "I have dyslexia," he said calmly. "But it wasn't diagnosed until fifth grade when Mrs. Fiege noticed something was wrong and insisted that the school district evaluate me."

"Dyslexia?" Marlo didn't know what to say. The only familiarity she had with dyslexia was Bella Thorne from the Disney show *Shake It Up* and the true-to-life story line that dealt with the actress's dyslexia. Since it was about dance, all Madame Burke's students had been obsessed with that show.

"Yeah," Ben said quickly. "And our problems didn't start at that fourth-grade recorder concert; they began in Ms. Hanline's class when you'd lean over my desk, correct my work for me, and make me feel like an idiot."

"I don't remember that, Ben." A huge lump formed in Marlo's throat as she realized how much she had hurt him. "I'm so sorry."

"Yeah, well, we were both five, so I'll forgive you," Ben said with a soft smile. "Now I should get one of those Echos, because I could really use the help with spelling. Assistive technology is critical for me. I wouldn't have my job without spell-check."

"Wait," said Marlo. "Is that why you misspelled my name on my latte cup in high school?"

"Huh?"

"You wrote Jon*ass*, and I thought you did it on purpose."

"Crap." Ben squeezed his eyes shut. "No, I most definitely did *not* do it on purpose. I have trouble with double consonants."

"I thought you were being a jerk. But it turns out I was the jerk, back in kindergarten." Marlo frowned. "I don't remember anything from that year except for how mean Ms. Hanline was."

"She wouldn't let us go out to recess unless everyone at our table group had their work done. Remember Antarctica?"

"Was that the name of our table group or something?"

Ben nodded. "Yup."

Now that Ben was talking about this, a key turned in her memory bank, and images slowly filtered out. "I think I was trying to help," said Marlo. "But in a bossy five-year-old-girl kind of way. I don't think I meant to hurt your feelings."

"I'm sure you didn't. We were in a bad situation. If anyone's to blame, it's Ms. Hanline for not recognizing the early signs of my dyslexia."

"It sounds like your first-, second-, third-, and fourth-grade teachers screwed up too," said Marlo. "I can only imagine all of the hurt you went through during those years."

Ben nodded. "Yes."

It was no wonder Ben didn't click the boxes for *can cook* or *athletic*, Marlo realized. His childhood had trained him to feel inferior about himself.

"But look at all you've accomplished since Ms. Hanline's class," said Marlo, feeling angry at the way Ben had been mistreated. "You're a brilliant writer, and you do an important service to your community.

Thank goodness it's you covering the news in Harper Landing and not some person from Seattle or Tacoma who has no idea what matters to us."

"I appreciate you saying that, but there are drawbacks to being a journalist too."

"Like what?"

"Low wages. People hating on you online. A struggling industry. Long hours. These days you practically have to wait for someone to die to get a job at a newspaper. I'm not joking. I have two friends from college who didn't get jobs until reporters died and the positions became open."

"I had no idea," said Marlo. There was so much about Ben and his life that she needed to learn, but she wanted to discover every bit of it. "Do you love it? Being a journalist, I mean."

Ben nodded. "I wouldn't want any other job. Which sucks, because it means I'll probably always be poor."

"Not unless you marry a sugar mama." Marlo laughed. "Your mom had it all wrong. She shouldn't have dared you to date beautiful women; she should have challenged you to find rich ones."

Ben folded his arms across his chest. "Says the gorgeous woman with a view of Puget Sound."

Marlo twirled her fork in the air. "This condo belongs to my parents." But she felt like she owed Ben the rest of the truth, especially after he'd revealed his secrets to her. "They don't charge me rent, though. When I was a ballerina and made pennies, they helped support me financially then too. I never would have been able to eat otherwise."

"Is there a chance you could go back to ballet?" Ben asked, right before eating the last bite of his dinner.

Marlo shook her head sadly and told him about her injury. Once she started talking about it, she couldn't stop. She described the surgeries and the failed graft, the year of agonizing physical therapy, and the horror she'd felt when her doctors had told her she'd never be able to dance on pointe again. "That's how I ended up working at my parents' club," she said. Her cheeks felt wet, and she wiped tears away with her napkin. "It's not something I wanted at the time, but I'm growing to accept it."

As soon as she said it, she realized she meant it too. The Cascade Athletic Club was special, and it was important not only to her family but to the people of Harper Landing. Plus, it had afforded her a comfortable life all these years. Ben had chosen a profession that gave him purpose but that also brought hardship. If Marlo stuck with her job and took over for her parents one day, she'd be rich. She could be a wife and mother who paid for all of the fancy things she'd had growing up: dance lessons, birthday parties, new school clothes, and more. She could donate money too. It would be her writing the checks to sponsor first-grade soccer teams and buying school auction baskets. She'd take her father's place at the rotary club and underwrite scholarships to the University of Washington.

The problem was, to make any of those dreams happen, she had to help the Cascade Athletic Club navigate away from the rocky financial situation it was in now. She'd already begun that process by investigating the kitchen permit. Yes, their current permit did allow for small kitchen appliances. They could even have a bread machine if they wanted, and Marlo thought that the aroma of fresh bread might be its own advertisement. She had put her mom in charge of researching tapas recipes. She'd also located a signage company. The new menu for behind the smoothie bar would have bigger, easier-to-read letters. There would also be a printed menu in braille and a kids' version with pictures. That way it would be accessible to everyone.

Her next step was to analyze the survey results, which were trickling in after she had sent the email Monday morning. She still wasn't entirely sure what she was looking for in that analysis, but she knew who could help. She gazed at Ben with even more appreciation than she'd had before. He was honest, trustworthy, loyal, and smart. He'd already given her tips to help the club, and she knew that if she asked him to study it, he'd probably see solutions that her family had never considered.

"You're wrong, Ben," she said as she slid her hand up to his arm. "I mean about the toast."

"Huh?" He raised his eyebrows.

"You said I'd lost my bet with my dad, and sure, I thought that, too, considering how I can't seem to keep my hands off of you."

"I don't understand—not that I don't appreciate you manhandling me," he said with a grin.

"The bet wasn't just about looks; it was about me seeking out a man with a good heart despite what he looked like, and you have the best heart of anyone I know."

"I don't know about that."

"It's true. Dahlia told me about how you helped Katelyn in the middle of your date. You've helped me every time I talk to you. I read your articles, and I see how much you care for our community. You were even nice to your sister when she was being crabby."

"Grace is always crabby. That's just her."

"And being kind is who you are." Marlo squeezed his biceps, at least the part that her fingers could reach. She stood up to gather the plates.

"Let me help with that." Ben collected the dishes before she could stop him. He followed her into the kitchen and put them in the dishwasher.

"Are you ready for something sweet?" Marlo opened up the freezer to take out the ice cream.

"Always." Ben sneaked up behind her, nibbled her neck, and made her giggle and forget all about the ice cream thawing on the counter.

CHAPTER FOURTEEN

Ben did not, under any circumstances, want to admit that he was lost, but the back roads of Snohomish were hellishly confusing. A combination farm town and bedroom community forty minutes north of Seattle, Snohomish was known for three things: antique shops, pumpkin farms, and paragliding. Like many parts of Western Washington, Snohomish had been logged in the late 1800s. Now the valley was ripe with produce instead of timber. Ben and Marlo drove down narrow country roads for twenty minutes, and it felt like they'd twisted through every corn maze in the valley, but Google Maps said they were still on track to make it to Savannah's housewarming party on time.

"Thanks for coming with me tonight." Ben glanced at Marlo sitting in the passenger seat next to him and felt like he'd won the lottery. Her long brown hair was curled into fluffy waves, and she had on a slim-fitting black coat that matched her jeans. "Especially since this event we're going to is so weird."

"Why is it weird? I thought you said it was a housewarming party." She held up the gift-wrapped houseplant in her lap. "That's why I swung by the Gnome's Backyard and picked up this succulent."

"It *is* a housewarming party, and that was thoughtful of you to bring a gift, because that didn't occur to me."

"It did now." Marlo grinned. "I wrote both of our names on the card."

"Wow. You're good."

"I'm just happy to be meeting your friends. How do you know them, again?"

"Well . . ." Ben scratched the back of his head. "That's what I meant about it being weird. Savannah is my coworker at the paper, but we also dated for a few months last year."

"You're taking me to your ex-girlfriend's housewarming party?" Marlo looked down at the houseplant. "I bought a gift for your *ex-girlfriend*?"

"She's more of a friend-friend now," Ben said hastily, "and she's moving in with her new boyfriend, Xander, who works at Microsoft."

"Oh." Marlo fiddled with the edge of the tissue paper that was bunched up around the present. "That kind of makes it better." She looked at him closely. "This isn't the woman your mom said made balloon animals, is it?"

"Goldie? No." Ben shook his head. "I'd never make you spend an evening with *her*."

They turned onto a road that brought them closer to the river. It was so dark that it was hard to read the signs, and without his phone guiding him, Ben would have been totally lost. The road stopped at a dead end. Hundreds of twinkling lights lit up a house with a wraparound porch. To the left of the house was a barn with a small animal pen in front of it. Parked cars lined up in a ditch next to the pavement. Savannah hadn't been kidding when she'd said Xander owned a hobby farm. This place must be a paradise for her.

"Do they have horses?" Marlo asked as she stared at the barn.

"Sheep, I think." Ben parked in the ditch and prayed he'd be able to unpark later that evening. His Kia didn't have all-wheel drive, and yesterday's rain had turned the ground into gumbo mud. "We don't have to stay long, I promise." He opened his door first and then rushed to help Marlo. The passenger side was the muddiest, and he helped her around the hood so she wouldn't slip. "Thanks for coming with me," he said once they were on firm ground. He wrapped his arms around her as best he could, considering she was holding a houseplant, and kissed her softly on the lips. It was too cold for anything else. The temperature had dropped to the high thirties. Ben took Marlo's hand in his own and was glad she was wearing gloves, because his fingers were freezing. He wore his winter coat but had left his gloves in his raincoat pockets.

As they walked up the gravel driveway to Savannah's new home, he mentally calculated how quickly they could get in and out of the party. Five minutes of greetings. Ten minutes of eating food—Savannah was an amazing cook, and appetizers were her specialty. Then, maybe another ten minutes of mingling. This was Ben's chance to introduce Marlo to coworkers from the *Seattle Times* that Savannah might have invited. With any luck, they could leave the housewarming party in thirty minutes. But then what? Where would they go? Payday wasn't until next Friday, and Ben had used up all of his extra cash on a haircut, a half tank of gas, and the Kia's first carwash of the year. Now he was broke again, which meant he couldn't afford to take Marlo to a bar in downtown Snohomish, a trendy restaurant in Bothell, or even for a drive to Seattle for a walk underneath the Space Needle at night.

Ben squeezed Marlo's hand as they approached the porch steps. "We won't stay here long," he repeated. "Maybe afterward, we could drive to Mukilteo and park in front of the lighthouse. It's supposed to be beautiful at night."

Marlo smiled, a giggle escaping before she could contain it. "Are you asking me to go parking with you?"

Ben grinned back at her. "Why yes, I believe I am."

Marlo lifted onto her toes and kissed him on the lips. "I'd love to go parking with you." She slipped her free hand around his neck.

The temperature rose twenty degrees for Ben, no matter what the thermometer outside said. He pulled her closer, hungry for the taste of her lips and longing to hear the sound of her heartbeat against his. Kissing her underneath the stars, on a cold November night, made him feel like they were at the center of a giant snow globe that the universe had shaken up with glitter. The world was a magical place, full of endless possibilities, and he'd never noticed it before. Holding Marlo in his arms and feeling her soft lips press against his made him feel like the luckiest guy on earth. Anything was possible—anything at all.

"Are you going to stand there making out like teenagers, or are you coming inside to say hello?" called out a voice from behind them.

Ben felt Marlo jump a step back, ripping out of his arms. He looked up at the front porch, where Savannah stood, hands on her hips, tapping her foot and wearing an amused expression.

"Sorry," he said sheepishly. "We were just about to come in." Ben put his arm around Marlo's shoulders and gave her a small squeeze. "This is Marlo," he said, uncertain of whether to introduce her as his girlfriend yet or not. "Marlo, this is Savannah."

"Marlo from the Leaping Lemurs?" Savannah raised her eyebrows.

"What?" Marlo asked. She looked at Ben.

"Um, yeah," said Ben as he tugged at his collar. "I told Savannah how we've known each other since kindergarten. You were a Leaping Lemur. I was a Sleepy Sloth. You don't remember that?"

Marlo shook her head sadly. "Sorry."

"I don't know how he remembers this stuff either," said Savannah as she waited for them to come up to the porch. "The only thing I remember about kindergarten was my teacher's perm." She opened up the front door and stepped aside so they could pass.

Entering Savannah and Xander's home was like walking into a log cabin. There were wood-paneled walls, a wide-planked wood floor covered with braided rugs, and an enormous stone fireplace with a built-in wood stove at the back of the room. The glass door of the stove glowed with a merry blaze. Ben recognized pieces of furniture that belonged to Savannah, like her antique rocking chair and her bookshelves, plus her knitting basket, and they were blended in with soft leather couches that must have belonged to Xander. But the most distinctive feature of the room—not in terms of size, but in wow factor—was the spinning wheel. Ben had never seen one in person before and was curious to inspect it.

"What a beautiful room," said Marlo. "Congratulations on your new home." She offered Savannah the houseplant. "This is for you."

"Thank you." Savannah took the succulent and admired the leaves. "It's the same color as my sweater." Indeed it was. Savannah wore a tunic-length sweater over corduroy pants and high-heeled granny boots. Ben had never seen Savannah wear heels before, which explained why Savannah wobbled unsteadily with each step she took. Her hair was braided around the crown of her head like normal, and her cheeks were flushed, either from the warmth of the fire or the excitement of the gathering.

The house was packed with people, some of whom Ben recognized from work. "Where's Xander?" Ben searched the room. "I can't wait to meet him."

"He's in the kitchen." Savannah waved her hand, beckoning them inside. "Come, follow me, and I'll introduce you. I'll also show you where you can put your coats and purse."

They walked with Savannah through the living room, and Ben nodded to people he knew as they passed.

"This fireplace is stunning," said Marlo when they reached the hearth.

"Isn't it?" Savannah caressed the stonework. "The river rock was collected on site, and the wood-burning-stove insert fits perfectly. Do you like my dragon?"

"Huh?" Ben scratched his head.

"I love it." Marlo pointed to the cast-iron dragon resting on the stove and blowing out steam through its nostrils.

"Here, hold this." Savannah thrust the houseplant into Ben's hands. "I'll add another cinnamon stick." Using a hot pad, she lifted the dragon's head off its kettle. Savannah pulled a cinnamon stick out of her pocket, dropped it into the water, and assembled the dragon again.

"So that's where that delicious smell is coming from," said Marlo. "As soon as we walked in here, I smelled apple pie."

"I have some of those too." Savannah smiled. "Mine aren't as good as Ben's. His crusts are Instagram worthy."

"And yet he thinks he can't cook," said Marlo.

"I know, right?" Savannah took back her plant and hooked her arm around Marlo's, pulling her into the kitchen. "Sometimes Ben's too humble for his own good."

"I can hear you guys talking about me," Ben grumbled, walking behind them.

Half a dozen platters covered the kitchen island, each with a different hors d'oeuvre. There were hand-rolled sushi rolls, dolmas made from fresh grape leaves, crispy fried wontons, and a gorgonzola cheese torte that made Ben's mouth water as soon as he saw it. Savannah had brought many of these recipes in to work for various functions, and Ben knew that she'd chosen her favorites, even if they didn't necessarily follow a theme. Two apple pies plus a grasshopper pie rested on the stovetop, and the kitchen sink was full of ice and booze. Savannah must have been cooking for two days straight, and her grocery bill was probably astronomical. She'd only worked at the paper a couple of years longer than Ben, and he knew her salary wasn't much higher than his. This house, and this party, must have cost a fortune. Ben hoped that Xander was a keeper, because his Microsoft money was making all of Savannah's dreams come true.

"Honey, look who's here," said Savannah as she set down the succulent next to the toaster. "This is my friend, Ben, and his girlfriend, Marlo."

Ben's stomach clenched when he heard the word *girlfriend*. Hopefully, Savannah and her big mouth wouldn't scare Marlo off. He checked out Marlo's reaction from the corner of his eye, and thankfully, she seemed unscathed. Marlo smiled and shook hands with the petite man in front of her.

"Any friend of Savannah's is a friend of mine," said Xander, pumping Marlo's hand up and down with vigor. He was just over five feet two, and Savannah towered over him in her heels. "Savannah's told me all about you," said Xander, offering his hand to Ben.

"You as well," said Ben as they shook.

"I knew as soon as I met Savannah at the Evergreen State Fair that she was the one." Xander let go of Ben's hand and threw both arms around Savannah, giving her a squeeze that knocked her off balance for a moment and made her laugh.

"You met at the fair?" Marlo asked.

"That's right." Xander grinned. His short blonde hair was graying at the temples, and he wore a blue-and-gray Nordic sweater that made him look like an elf. Ben wondered idly if he might have bought it from Dawn at her shop. It even had pewter buttons. "I entered my wool in the fiber-arts category," said Xander. "Savannah was one of the judges."

"That was August." Savannah beamed. "We've been together ever since."

Xander kissed Savannah on her cheek. "As soon as I saw her wearing a crocheted halter top, I said to myself, 'Holy smokes, this woman is mine.'"

"And he can knit too!" Savannah exclaimed. She was smiling so hard that she squinted. "Wait until you see his sheep."

"Your sheep, too, now, baby." Xander squeezed her tighter.

"I want to see sheep," said Marlo. "Are they still awake?"

Ben, who'd heard all about Xander's sheep, was curious, too, but not enough to go back outside into the cold.

"They're sleeping now, but that shouldn't matter," said Xander. "Sheep will sleep anywhere they feel safe, even outside on a cold night like this. We bring them into the barn at night, though, because of coyotes. We'll take everyone out to the barn for a tour later."

"Can you believe it?" Savannah asked, still grinning from ear to ear. "Letting the sheep out to pasture is my new morning routine. I'm in seventh heaven."

"Drop another cliché and I'm bringing out the puns," said Ben.

"We have two cashmere goats as well," said Xander with a twinkle in his eyes. "And I'm not kidding."

Savannah elbowed him in the ribs. "Stop," she said with a laugh. "But look at me, keeping you guys here in your coats. You must be sweltering. Here, I'll show you where you can put them." Savannah kissed Xander one more time and then led Ben and Marlo down a hallway, past a bathroom, and into the master bedroom in the back, where a queen-size bed was covered with coats. "Here you go." She pointed at the pile.

"Thanks." Marlo set down her purse.

"I'm really happy for you, Savannah," said Ben as he unzipped his coat.

"I know you are," she answered. "Listen, I hate to ask you, especially since you brought your new girlfriend with you tonight, but I need a favor."

"What?" Ben asked.

"My grandma's coming." Savannah clasped her hands together like she was praying. "She'll be here in a few minutes, and I need someone to watch her."

"You want me to babysit Liz?"

"Not babysit." Savannah shook her head. "Keep her company. Make her feel welcome. I have guests coming and going, and I can't be there to hold her hand the entire time."

Ben didn't want to say yes, but he was equally unwilling to say no, especially since he'd met Liz before. "How's your grandpa doing?"

"Not well." Savannah looked at the pointy toes of her high-heeled granny boots. "He has hospice nurses watching him tonight. They told Grandma Liz that it would be good for her to get out of the house for the evening, for her mental health. My mom was supposed to bring her, but you know how flaky my mom is. She picked up an extra shift at the Tulalip Casino instead."

"I'd love to meet your grandmother," said Marlo. "What's her name?"

"Liz Anker." Savannah looked at Marlo with relief. "Are you sure you don't mind?"

Marlo shook her head. "Not in the slightest. I love grandmothers. My mom's mom lives in Minnesota, and my dad's mom died before I was born."

"And you know me," said Ben, flashing his dimples. "Old ladies love me."

"It's true," said Marlo. "He had to turn off his old-lady magnet at the senior center last week so he wouldn't be swarmed."

"Which is why I keep telling him to lean into his yarn followers on Twitter," said Savannah as she led them out of the room. "Embrace your fan base. Write more articles about what they want to hear."

"Like yarn bombing?" Marlo asked.

Savannah froze in her tracks. "Ben, how could you?" She gently punched him in the arm. "That was a secret."

"He didn't say a word," said Marlo, pointing to yarn faces pinned to the wall. "But I recognize that artwork from the yarn-bombing article he wrote about Mill Creek."

"I wouldn't know anything about that," said Savannah with a sly grin. "Come on into the kitchen and get some food before my grandma gets here."

Ben and Marlo barely had time to load up their plates and grab a drink before Liz arrived. Ben had met Liz before, last year at Savannah's birthday dinner, but he was shocked at how much she'd aged over the past twelve months. Liz was sixty-five years old and quite fit for her age. Her blonde hair showed thick roots of gray, and her face was lined with worry. She had on jeans and a turtleneck sweater that was as grim as her expression. Savannah glanced over to where Ben and Marlo stood by the spinning wheel and nodded. Then she escorted her grandmother into the kitchen for some food.

"Are you sure you don't mind grandma-sitting?" Ben whispered to Marlo. "Sorry I dragged you into this."

"It's fine. I'm happy to help." She squeezed his arm. "One of the most important values my father has taught me is to be kind to senior citizens."

"It's still weird for me to think of your dad as a good person instead of the coach who yelled at me for doing cartwheels."

Marlo frowned. "You were six, and he shouldn't have yelled at you. My dad loves to win, and sometimes that makes him a jerk." She patted Ben's chest. "But if you had been sixty-six, he would have invited you for pizza and a pool party after."

"To be fair to Chuck, he did invite us for a pool party. That was the only time I've been to the club."

"Which is why you should come to visit me on your day off next week," said Marlo. "Either Monday or Tuesday, right?"

"Monday would work." Ben picked a wonton off his plate. "I promised my parents I'd help with the pre-Thanksgiving rush on Tuesday. They've got three hundred pies to bake." He popped the hors d'oeuvre in his mouth and enjoyed the savory crab filling.

"Monday would be great. I want to show you around but was also kind of hoping . . ." Marlo lifted her shoulders and smiled guiltily.

"Hoping what?"

"Hoping that you could look at our books and the survey results and anything else you think is important. I'm working on a plan to help the club, but I could use some guidance. Right now the Cascade Athletic Club is dangerously close to running in the red."

"Sure." Ben nodded. "I'll take a look. But I doubt I'll be able to help."

"Your business management minor has already proven to be a lot more useful than my dance degree," said Marlo. "At least in terms of the advice you've given me so far."

"And here's Ben," said Savannah in a loud voice as she and Liz walked up to them. "You remember Ben, right?"

"Your old boyfriend Ben?" Liz raised her eyebrows in shock. "Of course I remember Ben. Not many people's cars break down in my driveway and need to be towed away the next day. My neighbors still talk about it."

"Sorry about that." Ben felt his ears turn red with embarrassment.

"I'm just messing with you." Liz laughed and set down her plate of food on the spinning wheel's seat. She opened her arms up wide. "Come give me a hug, you rascal." She enveloped Ben in a warm embrace. "I still remember that potpie you made me with leftover chicken while we waited for the tow truck to arrive."

"It's good to see you, too, Liz." Ben hugged her back. He was about to introduce Marlo when she beat him to it.

"I'm Marlo," she said, holding out her hand. She looked at him and winked. "Ben's new girlfriend."

He felt a zing of energy when Marlo said that.

"You sure can pick 'em." Liz shook Marlo's hand. "Aren't you a pretty one!"

"Thanks," said Marlo.

"Where'd the two of you meet?" Liz asked.

"Kindergarten," Ben explained.

"Oh?" Liz sat down on a folding chair nearby. "Are you from Harper Landing too?"

"I am." Marlo sat down next to her. "Where do you live?"

"Everett." Liz scraped gorgonzola cheese onto a cracker. "My husband was a machinist for Boeing. But I've always loved Harper Landing. Before he got sick—" Liz paused, and a haunted look took hold in her eyes. "Before Jim got sick with colon cancer, we dreamed of opening up a yarn shop in Harper Landing. I even had the site picked out. It was where a dance studio used to be."

"The Red Slipper?" Marlo asked.

"Yup." Liz nodded. "That's the one. An antique shop beat us to it. Anyhow, that's where I was going to open my yarn shop. I had the name all picked out and everything."

"What were you going to call it?" Ben asked.

"Hip to Knit." Liz shrugged. "It was probably a stupid idea. Everyone buys yarn online or from Jo-Ann's these days."

"I think it's a great idea," said Marlo.

"There's a property that's newly available," said Ben. "It's where the Sugar Factory candy store used to be."

Liz shook her head sadly. "Not that it matters now." She looked at Marlo. "What do you do for a living? Are you a reporter too?"

"No. I teach fitness classes at the Cascade Athletic Club."

"Oh?" Liz smiled. "I recognize that name from the SilverSneakers list. Right now I go to the YMCA because it's closer. At least, I used to go when I had more time."

"Who wants to see the sheep?" Xander called out to the room. He and Savannah already had their coats on.

"Me!" Liz jumped to her feet. She and Marlo had raised their hands at the same time. A few minutes later they were all bundled up in their coats and heading out to the barn.

"This is so much fun," Marlo whispered as they made their way down the gravel driveway. "I love meeting your friends."

Ben felt warmth in his heart that was strong enough to beat out the cold. Was this what being in love felt like? Watching the way Marlo had interacted with Liz had confirmed all the good things he'd already thought about Marlo. Not only was she gorgeous, but she was just as beautiful on the inside as out.

But when they walked past his aging Kia, parked next to all of the expensive-looking SUVs, Ben remembered the truth of his situation. He didn't have a high-paying tech job like Xander. He couldn't whip out his credit card and make all of Marlo's dreams come true. Even if Ben gave up journalism, he wouldn't be able to take care of Marlo at the standard she was accustomed to. An icy wind blew across his face, and Ben felt like he'd been slapped. Nausea crept up on him, and it wasn't from the greasy appetizers or the smell of sheep dung. It was his brain, whispering to him again and again, *You're not good enough.*

CHAPTER FIFTEEN

Marlo was nervous, and she wasn't normally nervous—not at work, anyway. The Cascade Athletic Club was her second home. She'd practically grown up here next to elliptical trainers and bench-press machines. Yet here she was pacing back and forth in front of the lobby, sweating through her navy-blue fleece jacket with the Cascade Athletic Club emblem embroidered on the chest. Ben was supposed to arrive in five minutes, and Marlo knew that if he didn't arrive soon, she'd spontaneously combust. The pressure building inside her to see him was that intense.

"Stop pacing," said Laura from her seat behind the front desk. "You'll scare away the guests."

Marlo paused in place but couldn't keep her foot from tapping. "Sorry," she said. "Ben should be here any minute."

"Ben who?" Laura wore a navy-blue fleece jacket, too, but Laura had accented her uniform with a chunky necklace that looked like it was made of fishing lures, plus crystal bangles on each wrist. Her long gray hair was pulled into a side braid that hung over her left shoulder. Laura had glasses on and was reading the latest issue of *Yoga Life Today*, which happened to have a goat on the front cover.

"Ben Wexler-Lowrey." Marlo's pulse skipped a beat. "I told you we were dating, right?"

"Ben, like Cheryl and Nick's son, Ben?" Laura closed her magazine.

"That's right."

Laura laughed. "I guess you lost your father's bet, then. Ben's a stud muffin."

"Mom!" Marlo's cheeks turned bright red. "Nobody says *stud muffin* anymore. It's demeaning."

"You're right." Laura shook her head. "I shouldn't say *stud muffin*. That makes him sound like one of those pumped-up maniacs like Ryan who can deadlift a gazillion pounds but couldn't pose in warrior three for thirty seconds without toppling over." She snorted and looked back at the article she'd been reading in her magazine. "Have you told your father yet?"

"No." Marlo chewed on her thumbnail and then pulled her hand away. "And I didn't necessarily lose the bet with Dad either. Ben has an amazing heart. I chose him because of his inner qualities, and that's it."

"Uh-huh." Laura smirked. "Then why are you wearing that low-cut sports bra?"

"What?"

"Don't think I can't see it there, peeking out underneath your tank top."

Marlo looked down at the fleece jacket she was wearing and saw that it was partially unzipped. "I don't know what you're talking about, Mom. You're the one who bought this outfit for me from Lululemon last Christmas." Marlo had always loved it because the sports bra matched the floral leggings, and the navy top was the same color as their Cascade Athletic Club jacket. But she didn't usually wear this ensemble when she had a spin class to teach.

"I bought you that outfit for Pilates and barre class, not spin." Laura wagged her finger, and her bracelets jingled. "With that bra you'll give your students a show when you lean across the saddle. Is Ben coming to spin class with you?"

"Maybe." Marlo patted her head to make sure her hair was smooth. She'd put it up in a ballet bun today so it would be out of her way.

"Well, go ahead and zip your jacket down farther so he gets a good view," said Laura with a wink. "I like that guy. He's got a good sense of humor, and he appreciated all of my stories about the commune." Laura held up the magazine and showed Marlo the cover. "You know," she said, "I'm wondering if the answer to our financial problems might be the skills from my past."

"What?" Marlo asked as she fiddled with her fleece.

Laura pointed at the picture. "Goat yoga. People would pay extra to have a premium experience."

"With goats?" Marlo raised her eyebrows. "Mom, Ben took me to see some goats on Friday, and they were cute but smelly."

"Ben took you on a goat date?" Laura nodded approvingly. "I told you I liked that guy."

"Yeah. Ben's great. But back to the goat idea, I don't see how that concept would work with our club. We don't have livestock facilities for one thing, and you probably need special permits or something." Marlo couldn't believe she was having this discussion but was relieved her father wasn't there. It would probably lead to a huge row between her parents, which would inevitably lead to making out on the front desk of the lobby and freaking out all of the SilverSneakers guests—or inspiring them. Marlo wasn't sure which would be worse.

"I'm sure we could make it work." Laura waved the magazine. "Goats are the future."

"It looks like I got here just in time," said Ben as he walked up to the front desk. "Did Marlo tell you about the cashmere goats we played with Friday night?"

"She did." Laura reached over and squeezed Ben's biceps. "I knew I liked you."

"Mom!" Marlo felt her cheeks turn beet red. "Ben's not here to talk about goats—or to be groped."

"I'm not?" Ben asked with a wink.

"Come on," Marlo said, blushing even harder. "Let me show you around."

"Not so fast." Laura brought out a manila folder. "Ben needs to sign the liability waiver first."

"He's not going to sue us," Marlo protested. "Ben's my guest."

"And like all guests, he needs to fill out the waiver," Laura said in a no-nonsense tone. She uncapped a ballpoint pen and offered it to Ben.

"But—" Marlo started to protest.

"It's fine." Ben picked up the pen and began reading the paperwork. "I'm sure the Cascade Athletic Club paid good money to your lawyer to set these procedures in place, and it's smart to follow their advice."

"Okay." Marlo stared at Ben and felt her nerves jitter. Their Friday-night visit to Savannah's housewarming party had been amazing. Parking at the Mukilteo lighthouse afterward had been incredible. But they hadn't seen each other since. Ben said it was because of his work schedule, but Marlo worried he was avoiding her. She never should have asked him for help looking at the survey results and accounting books. He probably thought she was just using him for advice. And to a degree, she had been, hadn't she? But not now.

Marlo hadn't tackled the survey results yet, but she had brought the financial records home with her every night and had been slowly making sense of them. She'd started with the current year and had been working her way back in time. Analyzing how the club had operated over the past decade was giving her a better sense about changes to make in the future. Childcare was great, but maybe Martha Reynolds's idea of eldercare could work too. Or perhaps they could save on electricity by investing in solar panels. Then there was their advertising budget. Marlo wondered if moving some of that money to social media campaigns might be a good idea but wasn't sure, so she was studying it.

"There," said Ben as he put down the pen. "How's that?" He slid the paperwork over to Laura.

She perused the forms carefully. "Looks great." Laura smiled. "Have fun, you two."

Marlo's palms felt sweaty. She wasn't sure if she should reach for Ben's hand. Everything felt awkward. Marlo was uncomfortable, and not just because her seamless bikinis were sliding into wedgie territory underneath her yoga pants. "Can I show you around?" she blurted out in a squeaky voice.

"Sure." Ben patted his gym bag. "Is there a place I can put this first?"

"Of course." Marlo strode forward. "I'll show you the men's locker room. I mean, I won't *show* you the men's locker room, because obviously I can't go in there, but—"

Ben touched her arm and stopped her babbling. "I've missed you," he said, falling into step beside her.

"I've missed you too." Marlo took a deep breath. "Sorry, I'm so nervous."

"You're nervous?" Ben looked up at the two-story murals of the Cascade Mountains. "This is the first time I've been here since I was six. If anyone has the right to be nervous, it's me. I feel like YMCA riffraff that sneaked in."

"No." Marlo reached for Ben's hand, and his sweaty palm pressed against her own felt natural, unlike her anxiety-ridden doubt. "Don't be ridiculous." She leaned her head against his arm. "Everyone's welcome here." She led him straight upstairs to the entrance of the men's locker room and squeezed his hand before letting go. "We recently installed built-in combination locks, so you don't need a padlock. Just pick one that's set to zero-zero-zero because that means it's available. I'll be right here."

"See you in a jiff." Ben headed through the door and came back five minutes later wearing cotton athletic shorts and a plain white T-shirt. He held a pair of bike shoes. "When's spin class?"

Jennifer Bardsley

"Not for twenty-five minutes." Marlo hooked her elbow around his arm and pulled him toward the Pilates room. "I thought we could—"

"Ben Wexler-Lowrey!" Chuck stood at the doorway to the men's locker room with sharp eyes on both of them. "I thought that was you." He raised his bushy eyebrows when he saw Marlo. "What's going on here?" Chuck asked. "Is this something I should know about?"

Marlo tightened her hold on Ben's biceps. "I'm showing him around the club." She lifted her chin and flashed a "What are you going to do about it?" look.

"Hi, Coach Jonas," said Ben, in a tone that was hard to read. "This is an impressive facility you have here."

Chuck grunted and took two steps closer, his eyes scanning the two of them until his gaze came to rest on Ben's bike shoes. "Are those Delta cleats?"

Ben nodded. "I wasn't sure if I'd be able to clip into the bike here or not, but I brought my shoes just in case."

Chuck's focus shifted to Marlo. "I told your mother investing in the upgraded pedals was a good idea. She thought they were too much money, but ha!" Chuck pounded his chest. "I was right."

Marlo felt relief pour over her body from her head to her toes. She'd been worried there for a second that her father would let loose one of his insensitive comments. But so far, so good.

"What have you been up to recently?" Chuck asked. "Still writing?"

"Yes sir." Ben nodded. "I've also been waking up at three a.m. each morning to help my dad bake pies. The Nuthatch has been over-whelmed with orders for Thanksgiving."

Marlo felt better when she heard that—not that Ben was operating on so little sleep, but that he'd been busy while they'd been apart. Maybe he hadn't been avoiding her. It could be that he was just exhausted.

Chuck slapped Ben on the back so hard that the cleats on Ben's bike shoes rattled. "Don't work too hard, young man. Be sure to hit the sauna later before you leave."

"Thanks," said Ben as Chuck marched away.

"Okay, then." Marlo took a deep breath and tried to recenter. The clock on the wall said she only had twenty minutes until class began, and she was supposed to be there ten minutes early to set up. "I was going to take you to the Pilates room." She led him downstairs.

"Pilates?" Ben asked.

"So we could be alone," Marlo explained.

Ben grinned. "Hello, Pilates."

Marlo laughed. "But now I only have ten minutes before I have to arrive to class."

"I thought you said we had longer than that?"

"You have longer—I need to be there ten minutes early to check the bikes, turn on the fans, hook into the sound system, et cetera." She sighed. "After spin class, I teach barre, but then I don't have any commitments for three hours." She started walking in the opposite direction of the Pilates room so that she could show him the cardio and weight machines. "Let me give you a quick tour so at least you can see everything."

"Oh!" said Ben. "Look who it is!"

Marlo turned her head and saw several familiar faces headed toward them from the lobby. It was Aaron Baxter, Julia Harper, and their baby, Jack, along with Mr. and Mrs. Fiege.

"Mrs. Fiege!" Ben waved and rushed forward, bringing Marlo along with him. "I'm so glad to see you. How've you been?"

"Well, if it isn't my second-favorite reporter." Mrs. Fiege smiled, and she reached for Ben's hand.

"Second favorite?" Ben tilted his head. "Who snagged the top spot?"

"Anderson Cooper." Mrs. Fiege closed her eyes, and she purred. "He's a hard one to beat," she said when she fluttered her eyelids open.

"I'm going to pretend you didn't say that, Shelly," Mr. Fiege grumbled.

"Welcome back from your honeymoon, Aaron," said Marlo. "Are you guys dropping Jack off at the childcare center?"

Aaron's muscled arms hugged the baby tight. "No, we're here to swim."

"I reserved our lanes," said Julia. "And I gave George and Shelly my guest passes."

Ben stood up and smiled at Jack. "What a cutie." He covered his face with his hands and surprised the baby with a game of peekaboo, making Jack laugh.

"I can't believe you talked me into finally buying a bathing suit," said Shelly. "But now that you have, I'm looking forward to getting back into the water."

"And I'm looking forward to seeing you in that one-piece." Mr. Fiege whistled. "You're like a fine wine, my dear."

"Oh stop." Mrs. Fiege blushed. "Not in front of my students."

"Oh. Here, wait." Ben handed his cleats to Marlo and trotted a few steps over to a sanitation station and pumped hand sanitizer on his hands. "It was so busy at the wedding that I didn't want to ask," he said. "But . . ." He held up his clean hands. "Would it be okay if I held Jack for a few minutes?"

"Sure." Aaron passed the baby over. "Would you mind holding him while I change into my swimsuit?"

"I'd be happy to." Ben nestled Jack in his arms. Jack looked at him for a second like he might start crying, but then Ben made a funny face, and the baby laughed.

Motherhood had never been on Marlo's radar until that moment, not in an immediate sense, at least. It had been a far-off notion, like buying life insurance or learning to cook soufflés—not something she'd actively wanted until she saw Ben hold Jack in his arms. He was so naturally good at it—from the way he held Jack face out so that he could look at the world around him and not be bored, to the way Ben bounced Jack up and down and distracted the baby with babble while Julia and Aaron walked away.

Ben's obvious nurturing side made Marlo think about the way she had been parented. Marlo's father loved her; she knew he did. Underneath Chuck's gruff exterior was a big softy with a huge heart for his community. Chuck's bark was always worse than his bite. But Ben had a never-ending well of patience bubbling up inside him. Maybe it was because of how hard he'd worked to overcome his dyslexia that he was so understanding, or perhaps it was written into his DNA. Marlo didn't know. But what she knew for certain as she stood there was that she had the strongest feelings for Ben that she'd ever had for any person in her entire life. Each moment she was with him, they grew more potent.

Marlo looked up at the murals of the Cascade Mountains guarding them and renewed her commitment to the task at hand. Protecting her family's business was more important to her than ever. It was the key to making all of her dreams come true—and that dream included starting a family with Ben someday.

"I need to go now," she told Ben. "But the spin studio's this way when you're ready." She pointed in the right direction. "Take your time. Bike number ten will be waiting for you." She walked over and kissed Ben on the cheek, which caused her to breathe in Jack's sweet baby aroma. "See you in a bit," she said, feeling wistful.

"I'll be there as soon as I can." Ben grinned and wiggled the baby, making Jack giggle. "Won't I, buddy?"

Marlo laughed along with them. But underneath her smile was a want so keen that she'd never felt anything like it before, not even when she'd been training to be a ballerina. *Save the club. Marry Ben. Have a baby.* Her happily ever after was waiting for her so clearly that it felt like she could reach out and brush her fingertips against it.

Marlo made it to the spin studio two minutes later, right on time to prep for her class. She turned on the accent lights, flipped the switches for every fan, and rested Ben's bike shoes on bike number ten. Then she turned on the sound system and slipped the mic over her head, testing it to make sure it worked. She synced her phone so that the playlist was ready and used sanitizing wipes to clean off the instructor bike before adjusting it for proper fit.

"Hi, Marlo," said a woman wearing black leggings and a gray tank top. Her blonde hair was shaped into a short pixie cut, and she had three towels covering the handlebars of her bike.

"Alison, good to see you," said Marlo. "How's Laurie doing?" Alison and her wife, Laurie, had twin boys who were in Orca Street Preschool. Laurie worked for the city of Seattle, and Alison was a firefighter for Harper Landing.

"Great," said Alison. "Laurie's doing the graphic design for Seattle's new PR campaign about carpooling."

"I look forward to seeing it," said Marlo. "Laurie's talented."

"She sure is." Alison nodded.

Marlo straddled her bike and began pedaling to warm up. She nodded at a few more guests as they arrived. At this time in the morning, it was usually self-employed people, work-from-home parents, and retirees. Marlo wasn't surprised to see Brittany come into the studio wearing shiny silver leggings and a sports bra cut even lower than hers. Brittany hopped onto bike number eleven and began pedaling like a fiend.

"Hey, Brittany," Marlo called out in what she hoped was a friendly manner. Normally she got along great with the business entrepreneur. She still did, because Marlo was professional with all of her students. But Marlo had lost respect for Brittany ever since she'd overheard her in barre class bragging about lying to someone on Good Catch about her age and family situation. Marlo had been on some weird Good Catch dates herself, but at least Hunter and Simon had been honest.

"Looking good, Marlo," said Brittany. "Are you teaching barre after this?"

Marlo nodded. "That's right. You must have my schedule memorized."

Brittany grinned proudly and arched her back. "I have an excellent memory. My IQ is in the one hundred fifties—that's the 'very superior' category." She took a sip of water before continuing to boast. "I might do a double and catch your barre class after this. Spin class isn't that hard."

Marlo forced herself to smile and vowed to destroy Brittany with the hardest spin class ever. She'd intended to only do six interval sets and three hills in the forty-five-minute class, but now she decided to double that.

"Pick up your cadence, class," she called into the mic. The studio was packed, and every bike was taken except for Ben's. "This class is starting." Marlo clicked on her playlist, and Macklemore and Ryan Lewis boomed over the speakers singing "Can't Hold Us." She loved Macklemore because he'd grown up in nearby Seattle, and his lyrics always had heart.

Ben entered the class a couple of minutes later and grinned at Marlo. She blew him a kiss and pointed to bike number ten, which had his shoes resting precariously on the saddle.

Ben froze when he saw the bike and then grimaced, causing Marlo to wonder what was wrong. Had she injured his shoes by accident? Or maybe Ben didn't know that the pedals flipped over and one side was for locking in Delta cleats and the other side was a traditional cage for normal gym shoes. Then Marlo saw Brittany look at Ben and sneer. What was *that* all about?

Ben walked up to his bike, picked up his shoes, and balanced on one foot at a time as he snapped them on. Without one more glance at Brittany, he adjusted his bike, clipped into the pedals, and began riding. He didn't have a towel or water bottle with him, which made Marlo nervous. Spin class was challenging enough without proper hydration. But Ben pedaled hard and kept up just fine. She could tell from the instructor dashboard on her display that he jumped into the first interval without any problem. Five minutes later, he still hadn't broken a sweat.

Brittany, on the other hand, was gasping for breath fifteen minutes in. She gripped the handlebars with white knuckles as Marlo led the class through the hardest workout she'd ever taught. Marlo looked around the studio, checking to see how her other students were faring. "Today's a hot one," she announced. "How's everyone doing?"

Alison gave her the thumbs-up, even though her T-shirt was drenched with sweat.

But some of the other students were fading, especially the older ones, and Marlo knew she needed to ease up. As much as she wanted to crush Brittany for that comment about her spin class being too easy, it wasn't fair to make it too hard for the rest of her students.

"Turn your resistance knob to the left, and let's recover on a flat road," said Marlo. "Now's the time to drink some water." Since she was the instructor and could hop off the bike whenever she wanted, she brought her water bottle over to Ben's bike and offered it to him.

"Thanks," said Ben, immediately taking a sip from her bottle. He gave it back a few seconds later.

Meanwhile, on the bike next to Ben's, Brittany spewed out a gulp of water, spraying it so far that it hit Marlo in the face. "Oops," she said in a snide tone. "Sorry."

What a bitch, Marlo thought. She fought to keep her expression neutral. "No problem." Marlo walked over to the clean basket of towels and helped herself to a fresh one to wipe off the spittle. She rotated through the room and checked on her students, offering them encouragement and suggestions, but skipped Brittany before jumping back on her bike. The rest of the class was uneventful, and Marlo was proud when she saw her students' stats. They'd worked hard and burned a ton of calories.

After class, Marlo wiped down her bike and hung around to answer questions. From the corner of her eye, she saw Brittany push past Ben as she bulldozed her way out of the studio, a grim look of determination on her face. "What was that about?" Marlo asked him once she and Ben were alone. "Do you know her?"

Ben wrinkled his nose like he smelled something rank. "We went on one date together a couple of weeks ago, and it was awful. All she did was talk nonstop about herself, and she lied to me about having kids."

"But you're great with kids." Marlo wiped the sweat off her brow. "Why should that matter?"

"It shouldn't," Ben agreed. "But she didn't tell me about them at all, and she said she was twenty-six."

"You're the guy she was bragging about in barre class?" Marlo stopped at the water station and filled up her bottle.

"Oh man." Ben winced. "What did she say?"

"I don't remember, except for her boasting about lying. I guess things didn't end well between you two."

"Nope." Ben shook his head. "They didn't."

Marlo glanced at the clock. She needed to be in the barre studio fast, or she wouldn't have time to set up. "I have one more class to teach before I'm free to hang out. Would you like to come to barre with me, or would you rather do something else?"

"That depends. Are there any men in the class?"

"Sometimes."

Ben raised his eyebrows. "Define *sometimes*."

"Sometimes Matt Guevara, the owner of the Gnome's Backyard, stops by a class to supplement his yoga routine."

"And he's the only guy who ever goes to your barre class?" Ben leaned down to drink from the water fountain.

"At the moment. But you could double that number."

Ben turned off the drinking fountain. "I'm going to be honest," he said as he stepped aside to let someone else access the water station.

"I think I'd rather do the weight machines. I never get a chance to use them, and I was looking forward to that."

"Fine," Marlo said with a teasing pout, which Ben disrupted by kissing her softly and with a tenderness that made her heart melt.

"See you in an hour?" he asked when their lips parted.

Marlo nodded. "I'll be in the barre-and-yoga room."

Not having time to change, Marlo rushed across the gym to the space where her barre class met and was relieved to see that her mom had left the lights set up for her and the sound system on. She loaded her playlist, got out her exercise band and ball, and double-checked her mic.

"Hi, Marlo," said Melanie Knowles as she found a space at the barre.

"Hey, Melanie, how are you doing?" Marlo asked. "Anything dramatic happen on Harper Landing Moms Facebook recently?"

Melanie nodded excitedly. "Oh my goodness, yes. Did you hear that Costco ran out of turkeys this morning?"

"Wow. Really?" Marlo shook her head. "No, I didn't know that."

"Don't worry, though," said Melanie. "Safeway still has them."

"Good to know," said Marlo. "Thanks."

"Are you guys talking about the turkey shortage?" someone asked. It was Dawn Maddox. "A customer at the Forgotten Hug was just mentioning that to me last night."

"I cannot even believe this is happening," said Melanie as she held on to the barre and stretched. "You'd think they'd be better organized for the holiday rush."

As thrilling as the conversation was, Marlo was glad that it was time to start class. She stepped up to the mirror and turned on her playlist. Running through the traditional ballet postures of first and second position was like revisiting old friends. High-rep movements with light weights helped bring her students' heart rates up and toned their limbs. By the end of class, everyone was stretched out and happy.

Maybe that was why when the final track came on—"What a Feeling" by Irene Cara, from the movie *Flashdance*—Marlo was primed to take a trip down memory lane.

"This is the song Madame Burke always ended her recitals with!" Dawn exclaimed. "Come on, Marlo, I know you know it. The finale routine was always the same."

Marlo felt the old choreography ignite her feet, begging to be released. "I can't," she said. "I'm not wearing leg warmers and a ripped T-shirt."

"I will if you will," Dawn dared.

Never one to back down from a challenge, Marlo dropped to the floor, rolled across the ground, and slid out into the splits. She popped up a second later and spun into six perfect pirouettes. "You're on," said Marlo as she kicked up her foot as high as it would go.

"Show off!" Dawn said with a laugh, but she, too, leaped into the center of the studio floor and joined the choreography.

"Bravo!" Melanie shouted, whipping out her phone. The rest of the class cheered and circled around them to watch.

Endorphins washed over her, fueling her brain with glee, as Marlo danced through the familiar routine. Her grand jeté was crappy. Her knees couldn't handle leaping anymore, so it was more of a wide step forward. But that didn't matter. Dancing across the wood floor made her feel happy, especially with a former Red Slipper student like Dawn dancing next to her. By the end of the song, the whole room was clapping.

"Teach us that next time," said Melanie as she pulled down her phone. "Is it okay if I post this on Harper Landing Moms?"

Marlo looked at Dawn, and Dawn looked at Marlo. "Sure," said Marlo, "I guess."

"Be sure to put that I'm the owner of the new antique shop in town. You can tag the store," said Dawn.

"That was amazing!" Ben called from the corner of the studio.

Jennifer Bardsley

Marlo turned around, surprised to see him there. Laughing, she ran across the floor and jumped into his sweaty arms. "It was fun." She kissed him on the cheek. "I'm glad you got to see it. Are you ready for lunch?"

"I wish." Ben's smile faded into a serious expression. "My mom just called me, freaking out."

"Oh no. What's wrong?"

Ben grimaced and lowered his voice. "Someone called the health department and said that the Nuthatch Bakery has a rodent problem," he whispered. "They even showed a supposed picture of our smoked-salmon chowder bowl with a rat in it."

"Yuck!" said Marlo. "And that's ridiculous. I've seen the kitchen, and it's spotless."

"I know." Ben sighed. "And I also know who did this to us."

"Wait." Marlo looked up at him in horror. "You don't mean . . ."

Ben nodded. "Yup. Brittany."

CHAPTER SIXTEEN

Ben stared at the picture again and felt rage boil inside him. It was Tuesday afternoon, and he was in Grace's apartment, sitting at her kitchen table with his family. Cheryl was crying, and Nick kept wiping his eyes with the back of his sleeve when he thought nobody was looking. Downstairs in the bakery, health department inspectors were combing over every inch, looking for infractions. But it was the photograph, printed out and lying on the table in front of them, that really burned. It was a bread bowl of smoked-salmon chowder with a rat tail hanging out of it.

"I don't understand," said Cheryl, her hoarse voice raw with emotion. "You think this woman, Brittany Barrow, kept a dead rat in her car and then drove directly from the gym to our restaurant to stage this picture? Just because you rejected her?"

"You're not that special," said Grace. "I can't imagine anyone going that far because they couldn't date you."

"It might not have happened yesterday," said Ben, ignoring his sister's comment. "Brittany could have staged the picture before then and held it in her arsenal. But she definitely sent it to the health department after she saw me with Marlo in spin class."

"What would you take spin class for?" Grace looked at him like he was an idiot. "Don't you get enough biking during your horrible commute to work?"

"Marlo Jonas?" Nick asked in his quiet voice. "The hot one from the wedding?"

"Not helpful," Cheryl said, raising her voice. "This woman, Brittany Barrow. Her name sounds familiar, but I can't quite place her."

"She owns the *Harper Landing Coupon Pack* and *Harper Landing Delights*." Ben pushed a Christmas cactus out of his way. Grace's table was loaded with plants, just like the rest of her apartment.

"We never advertise with them." Cheryl shook her head. "Do you know how much they charge? It's obscene."

"Maybe that's part of why she hates us," said Ben.

"You." Grace pointed her finger at Ben's chest. "She hates *you*, not us."

"No," said Ben. "I'm pretty sure she had it in for the Nuthatch before she ever met me. You should have heard the awful things she said about it on our date before she knew I was related to the owners. Seeing me with Marlo must have made it worse."

"She probably hated us because we wouldn't advertise with her," said Cheryl. "I told her I thought her magazine was a waste of money."

Grace sighed and looked at her phone. "It's not only the picture and the health department. She's also deployed bots. There are over six hundred fake reviews on Yelp, all slamming us for poor hygiene."

"How do we stop them?" Nick asked.

"We'll have to report them one by one, I guess." Grace adjusted her glasses on the bridge of her nose. "I'll work on that, but, Ben, you should probably make a statement on our Facebook and Instagram page. You're the writer, so come up with something good." It was the closest Grace had ever come to giving a compliment, and for a moment Ben felt proud. "I'll check your spelling before you publish," she added, making him feel horrible again.

"They're not going to find rats," said Ben. "Our cleanliness is impeccable. It's only a matter of time before the inspectors knock on the door and clear us for reopening."

"But the pies," moaned Cheryl. "We won't be able to fulfill our pie orders for Thanksgiving."

"We had over three hundred orders due for tomorrow." Nick shook his head. "We can't disappoint our customers. People are counting on us for the most important meals of the year."

The four of them sat in silence, staring glumly at the picture before Ben turned it over and knocked the table with his fist. "I got it!" he said. "Mom, you still have the cottage bakery license, right?"

Cheryl nodded. "That's right. I keep it current in case your father gets creative in the middle of the night inventing a new cookie recipe that we want to sell the next day."

"There you go." Ben waved his hands excitedly and knocked into the cactus by accident. "Sorry," he said as Grace glared.

"What's the cottage license have to do with any of this?" she asked. "Mom and Dad only have two ovens. They can't bake three hundred pies in twenty-four hours. Without the commercial kitchen, they're screwed."

"No." Ben pointed to the back of Grace's kitchen. "But you've got an oven. Simon has a double oven. And you still have your food handler's license, right?"

Grace nodded. "Only because Mom made me."

"If you're going to be walking into my bakery's kitchen in the middle of the night for a snack, then you'd better have that permit, missy." Cheryl blew her nose. "Keep going, Ben. What are you proposing?"

"Let's split up the work. Dad does pumpkin because those are the hardest to set right. You help Grace make the pecan, here in her apartment. That's probably the smallest order number."

"Correct." Nick nodded.

"I'll do apple at my place because I'm good at crust. Katelyn will help, even though she's down to one hand because of her wrist surgery.

She has her food handler's license from working at the espresso stand, and she'll still be able to operate the mixer."

"Four pies at a time," whispered Nick, mumbling to himself as he worked out the calculations. "If we bake four pies at a time and don't stop baking all night, we could do this."

"Save Thanksgiving," said Ben.

"Save our reputation," Cheryl added.

"But what about the troll reviews?" Grace asked. "Someone needs to report them one by one."

"I bet Simon and Mike will help when they get home from work." Ben pulled out his phone. "I'll text Savannah. She's got restaurant experience."

"Why not call *all* your old girlfriends?" Grace snorted. "Where's balloon girl when you need her?"

"There's no need to mention Goldie at a time like this." Cheryl rose and bumped her head into a hanging philodendron. "These plants!" She rubbed her sore head and moaned. "Honestly."

Two hours later, the plan was fully operational. Ben was at home, preheating the olive-green ovens in Simon's aging kitchen. That meant turning the dial manually since the ovens were so old they didn't have digital displays. Mike and Simon were both at work, but Katelyn was with him, wearing a hairnet and carrying her casted wrist in a sling. She stood at the kitchen counter measuring flour into the KitchenAid mixer Ben's parents had given him as a college-graduation present.

"Kate," Ben said, "I don't know how to thank you."

"Then don't." She looked over her shoulder at him. "Because you don't need to." She passed him the canister of cinnamon. "But you do need to open this for me, because I've only got one hand."

Ben untwisted the cap and handed it back just as Katelyn's phone began to ring on the charging station. "Do you want me to get that for you?" he asked before he looked at the screen. "Um . . . it's Hunter."

Katelyn dug a measuring spoon into the cinnamon. "Ignore it. He already texted me three times today with questions."

"Questions about what?"

"How to replace the register tape. How to unclog the steam nozzle. Would I send him the JPEG file for the custom artwork I did for his logo that he never paid me for in the first place?" Katelyn rolled her eyes. "He said if I come back to work, he'll give me a raise, but if I don't show up today, I'm fired."

"Fired? He can't do that! You're on disability." Ben hated Hunter, but he didn't want Katelyn to lose her job because she was helping bake pies.

Katelyn shrugged. "Yeah, and as soon as my disability runs out, I'm quitting."

"Really?"

Katelyn switched on the mixer. She raised her voice to speak over the whir of the beaters. "It finally occurred to me last night when Simon was putting toothpaste on my toothbrush that you guys do all these nice things for me all the time, especially now that my arm's messed up. But Hunter does nothing." She scraped the bowl with a spatula. "He treats his dog, Buster, better than he treats me."

"That's what I've been telling you for years. What made you finally realize it?"

Katelyn looked at her temporary cast. "Being helpless, I guess. It makes you discover who your true friends are."

"Yeah," Ben agreed wholeheartedly. "It sure does." He wanted to hug her, but that would require washing his hands again. "Okay, back to dough rolling." Ben went to his station at the kitchen table, where a cutting board sprinkled with flour waited for him. The table was covered with four pie tins waiting to be filled. "You're making the crust. I'm rolling out dough." Ben pushed the rolling pin back and forth and tried not to worry. "We need someone on apple duty. I hope Savannah gets here soon."

"Two people on apple duty would be even better," said Katelyn. "Peeling takes forever, even with two hands."

Ben knew that Katelyn was right, but he wasn't sure who else to call. The Nuthatch staff was already at his folks' house helping Nick. The only other person he knew with a food handler's license was Dahlia, and no way was he calling her.

"What did you tell Marlo about this?" Katelyn asked, interrupting his thoughts.

"Nothing," said Ben. "I mean, I talked to her last night when the health department shut us down."

"Temporarily," Katelyn interjected. "Think positive."

"Yeah, temporarily. I spoke with Marlo when that was happening, but I couldn't talk much because my parents were so upset." Ben felt sick inside, not having been able to connect with Marlo since, but he didn't know what to say. First, he'd bailed on her and on helping analyze the Cascade Athletic Club's financial situation, and now he was up to his elbows in flour. He wasn't exactly boyfriend-of-the-year material.

"It's just as well you haven't told her." Katelyn turned on the mixer and raised her voice. "Marlo's such a princess that she wouldn't understand."

"That's not true," said Ben.

Katelyn pointed her rubber scraper at the cell phone–charging station on the counter. "Prove it. Call her right now, and ask her to help. Marlo could peel apples. Any idiot can do that."

"She's not an idiot." Ben clenched his jaw. "And she's probably working right now, and I don't want to interrupt her. Besides, there's the whole food-handler-permit thing and—"

Ben's phone rang, interrupting his ramblings. He wiped his hands on a towel and picked it up, feeling his heart pound when he saw that it was Marlo. "Hello?"

"Ben, it's me," said Marlo. "What's going on? You haven't called me back since last night, and I was worried."

Ben walked into the living room for privacy.

"You don't have much time," Katelyn called after him. "The next batch of dough will be ready in a minute!"

"Was that Katelyn yelling at you?" Marlo asked.

"Yeah, it was, but she's only trying to help." Ben sat down on the couch. "I'm sorry I didn't call, Jonas, but it's a crisis. My family needs to bake over three hundred pies by tomorrow morning, at home, in our houses, or else we'll default on our Thanksgiving orders."

"The Nuthatch is still closed down?"

"That's right. But luckily my mom kept our cottage bakery license current."

"I've got my food handler's permit from when I was trained on the smoothie bar. Can I help?"

"Really?" Ben felt his heart skip a beat. "But don't you have to work?"

"I'll ask my mom to cover my Pilates clients. What's your address? I'll be there in thirty minutes."

Ben rattled off the address and stood up from the couch. "Thank you," he said. "You don't know how much this means to me."

"We can use my kitchen, too, if that helps," Marlo offered.

"I might take you up on that. We'll see how it goes."

"Ben!" Katelyn called. "Dough's ready!"

"Gotta go," said Ben. "I'll see you soon."

He hung up the phone with Marlo just as Savannah arrived. She barged through the front door without knocking and dumped her wool cape onto the couch. "Did someone say *baking emergency*?" Savannah waved a rolling pin in the air. "I've been preparing for this my whole life." She wore a quilted apron with deep pockets over jeans and a flannel shirt. Savannah pushed up her sleeves and charged into the kitchen. "Bakers ready," she announced, like they were in the middle of a baking show on Netflix.

"Hi, Savannah." Katelyn unhooked the stainless steel bowl from the mixer and dumped dough onto a piece of waxed paper on the table.

"Nice to see you, Katelyn." Savannah turned on the faucet and began vigorously washing her hands. "Sorry to hear about your accident."

Ben went back to dough rolling while the two women chatted. By the time he'd laid out the bottom crust on the fourth pie and was pricking the bottoms with a fork so the dough wouldn't bubble, Savannah had peeled through a pile of apples that were ready to be chopped, and Katelyn was dumping more dough on the table to be rolled out. But none of the pies were ready to go into the oven yet, because of the filling backlog. Ben was about to stop what he was doing to begin chopping apples when the front doorbell rang.

"Maybe that's Marlo," Katelyn grumbled.

"Yay," said Savannah. "I like Marlo."

"You do?" Katelyn dumped sugar into the mixing bowl.

"Yeah," said Savannah as she scraped the peeler across apple skin. "My grandma spent a bunch of time with her Friday night and said she was lovely."

Ben rushed into the living room and opened the front door, feeling nervous but excited at the same time. Marlo stood on the doorstep in jeans and a long-sleeve shirt, with her hair pulled back into a ponytail. But it was what she wore over her outfit that made Ben grin. "Nice apron," he said, pulling her toward him for a kiss.

"Mmm," Marlo murmured. "You smell like cinnamon. And sorry about the apron; it's the only one I own."

"The pink fluffy stuff suits you."

"It's called *tulle*, Ben," Savannah said as she poked her head into the living room to wave hello. "Since you're dating a former ballerina, you should learn the correct terminology."

"Hi, Savannah." Marlo waved. Then, she reached into her back pocket and pulled out a piece of paper. "Here's my documentation, sir. A Washington State food handler is at your service."

"Great." Ben grabbed her elbow and pulled her into the kitchen. "We need you to peel apples."

"Yes," said Savannah, dropping the peeler and shaking out her hand. "Please."

Ben felt bad giving Marlo a mundane job, but he didn't know enough about her knife skills to trust her with the chopping. What if she turned out to be one of those people who sliced apples the lazy way, hacking them into square cores instead of cylinders? The Nuthatch had standards, after all, and he knew that Savannah would follow them. But a few minutes later, after watching Marlo peel an apple in one long slice, Ben realized that he needn't have worried. Marlo was fully equipped to be his sous chef—in the kitchen and perhaps in life.

That thought made him jittery with excitement. He looked at the back of her graceful neck bent in concentration and wished he could kiss it. It was kind of her to be here helping him. Katelyn and Savannah showing up was different. He'd done so many things for them over the years that they owed him. But Marlo's generosity came straight from her heart. It was like they were two parts of the same piecrust.

"Okay, Ben, show us how it's done." Savannah slid a filled pie in front of him that was ready to be latticed.

Ben picked up a strip of dough with a zigzag edge and laid it carefully across the sugared apples. He wove strip after strip until the top was Pinterest worthy and then pinched the edges into a tight seal.

"Beautiful work," said Marlo.

"Like always." Savannah handed him another pie to finish.

"I need someone to open the vanilla extract," whined Katelyn.

"I'll help." Marlo walked over to the sink and rinsed her hands. "Let me get the juice off first so I don't make the bottle sticky."

"Thanks." Katelyn handed her the container and waited. "You should probably be wearing a hairnet, you know."

"It's okay," said Ben.

"No, Katelyn's right." Marlo gave the opened vanilla bottle and cap back to her. "Are there extra hairnets I can borrow?"

"Over there in the crate of supplies from the bakery." Katelyn pointed with her elbow. "Unless you think you're too good for hairnets."

"Kate," Ben said in a warning tone.

"It's fine," said Marlo. "I used to wear them all the time when I danced." She fished hairpins out of her pocket and stuck them in her mouth. Ben was impressed to see how fast she could coil her hair into a knot and secure it with the pins. She dug around the box of supplies, pulled out a hairnet, and pinned it into place.

"Nice hair," said Katelyn in a snotty tone.

Ben cringed. Leave it to Katelyn to mention something Marlo had written in her yearbook ages ago.

"Um . . . thanks." Marlo pumped soap into her hands and washed up at the sink.

"I guess I should take one of those too." Savannah set down the knife and walked over to the supplies box next to find a hairnet.

Ben, who hated hairnets, felt put on the spot. He never wore one when he helped at the bakery because he had short hair. But maybe he should now because his parents couldn't afford another health department allegation. "Fine," he said as he set aside the rolling pin. "Peer pressure at its finest." When he put on a net, all three women laughed.

"Well, at least now we all look ridiculous," said Marlo as she peeled another apple.

"Are you saying I look ridiculous?" Katelyn asked, but then she smiled, and Ben could tell she was softening where Marlo was concerned.

The timer buzzed, and Ben took the first four pies out of the oven and set them on trivets to cool. The crusts were golden brown and flaky. He slid four more pies into the oven and kept on working.

"What type of apples are these?" Savannah asked.

"Chehalis." Marlo peeled off a label. "These must have been expensive."

"My dad has a deal with a farmer in Eastern Washington," Ben explained. "Most bakers use Granny Smiths, but heirloom apples are part of what makes our pies special."

"I'll be sure to include that in the restaurant review I'm writing." Savannah slid chopped fruit into a mixing bowl. "Details like that make Seattleites drive to Harper Landing for weekend treats."

"That sounds like a headline right there." Ben lifted a circle of piecrust and carefully laid it out in the dish. "Thanks, Savannah." He looked around the room. "Thank you to all of you."

Outside, a car pulled up and parked in the driveway, and the side door to the kitchen opened a moment later. It was Simon arriving home from work a bit earlier than normal. He had on cargo shorts, sturdy leather shoes, socks, and a green fleece jacket.

"Whoa!" said Simon, wiping his feet on the mat. "Did I interrupt a meeting of the Ben Wexler-Lowrey ex-girlfriend society?"

"Hi, Simon," said Marlo.

Simon nodded politely. "Hi, Marlo."

"It's not an official meeting, because Goldie's not here," said Katelyn. "And Marlo's not part of the club." She turned off the mixer and batted her lashes at Simon. "You're home early. Did you miss me?"

"Babe, I've been thinking about you all day," Simon growled, crossed the linoleum between them in a pounce, and proceeded to seize Katelyn by the waist and nibble her neck.

Katelyn giggled wildly and kissed him on the lips.

"Um . . . ," said Ben. "The rest of us can see you."

"They're dating now?" Savannah asked. "When did *that* happen?"

"I don't know." Ben wove strips of piecrust into another lattice. "I've been working weird hours all week."

"Two days ago." Katelyn slipped her good hand around Simon's neck and sighed. "He took me with him to the Western Cedar to see the

Monte Cristos perform. Dahlia was there too. When Mike and Dahlia left together, it was just Simon and me."

"And that's when I made my move." Simon sucked on Katelyn's ear, and Ben turned away. He'd sensed that Simon had a thing for Katelyn this past year, but he didn't want to watch them make out in the middle of a pie frenzy.

"The best part is that Simon actually cares about my future," said Katelyn. "Unlike Hunter, who treated me like a robot."

"Hunter Darrington only cares about dead bodies," said Marlo as she threw peelings into the compost.

"You're right." Katelyn looked at Marlo and held her eyes for a moment. "He's kind of creepy, now that I think of it. Maybe we should set him up with Goldie."

"Who's this Goldie I keep hearing about?" Marlo asked.

"I don't think we need to mention her." Ben slapped dough on the cutting board and rolled it out harder than he'd intended.

"She's a nutcase, that's who," said Savannah, who then proceeded to tell them about Goldie showing up to the *Seattle Times* dressed like a clown flasher.

Marlo laughed so hard she started crying, and Simon kept shaking his head and muttering, "I told you so."

Ben was relieved when his phone rang and he was able to step away from the circus. "Hi, Mom," he said as he answered it. "How are things going?"

"Not great." Cheryl's voice was full of worry. "The health department is still investigating. First, they had the exterminator out—who found nothing, of course—and now they're following up with the fake Yelp reviews. Grace started to report them, but the pecan chopping has taken more time than I'd anticipated without my food processor. Is Mike home?"

"No," said Ben. "Why?"

"You'd mentioned that maybe he could help report the Yelp stuff."

"Shoot. I forgot to text Mike. Simon's home, though, and I bet he'll help. I'll ask."

"Good," said Cheryl. "I hate to impose, but we're desperate. How are the apple pies coming along?"

"Great. Katelyn, Savannah, and Marlo are here helping."

"Whoa." Cheryl chuckled. "It's like the Ben Wexler-Lowrey cheer squad."

"Don't you start too," Ben grumbled.

"Call me later," said Cheryl, "and give me an update."

"Will do, Mom."

"Love you."

"Love you too." Ben hung up the phone, texted Mike, and went back into the kitchen to wash his hands. Simon was ordering pizza, Katelyn was scooping sugar, and Savannah and Marlo had switched jobs.

"Simon," Ben said as soon as Simon was finished with his phone call. "I need you to hunt trolls."

Simon's face lit up with glee. "Let me get my broadsword."

The crew kept at it for hours. Savannah stayed until eight o'clock. Mike came home an hour later. He couldn't handle food, but he could take out the trash. Simon hunted trolls. Ben, Marlo, and Katelyn kept working until every last pie was assembled. The unbaked pies covered the countertops, the top of the refrigerator, and the kitchen table and even spilled into the living room, resting on the end table and hearth. Katelyn and Simon went to bed at midnight, but Marlo stayed to help with the baking. Every forty minutes they put four more pies in the oven. After the pastries cooled for two hours, they put each in a pink bakery box with the Nuthatch logo stamped on the side.

Ben was exhausted, and he hadn't taught three exercise classes like Marlo had that morning. But he also felt selfish. After half-heartedly urging her to go home, he was happy that she'd refused. Every time they took pies out of the oven, they snuggled on the couch in the living room and dozed off until the buzzer rang.

Ben stretched out on the cushions with Marlo wedged next to him, their bodies fitting together like puzzle pieces. Ben was too exhausted to move, especially as it neared five o'clock in the morning. When the timer beeped for the last four pies, he was so disoriented that he rolled off the couch and banged his head on the coffee table.

"Are you okay?" Marlo mumbled without opening her eyes. She'd taken down her hair, and it fanned out over her shoulders. Marlo reeked of apples and cinnamon. Ben supposed he did, too, but it was a heady scent. Like they'd both been spiced together.

"Shh . . . ," Ben whispered. "Go back to sleep." He double-checked to make sure he hadn't knocked pie boxes off the coffee table when he'd hit his head, and then he tiptoed into the kitchen to turn off the buzzer. The last four pies were glorious, but Ben had no place to put them. By the time he'd cleared space, the pies were a smidge too brown, but there was nothing he could do.

Ben brewed a pot of coffee and felt his senses come back to life as he heard it sputter into the pot. He went back to work, boxing up pies and cleaning up the disaster from the day before. Everything was sticky, especially the floor. Ben brought the mop in from the garage and slid it over the linoleum as he waited for the pies to cool. He drank a cup of coffee and then another. He was due at work in three and a half hours. Marlo was probably scheduled to teach spin. Ben hadn't thought to ask. He felt dumb for not thinking about that before. Just when he was beating himself up for his thoughtlessness, his phone buzzed with a text from Grace. The health department gave the all-clear, she said. They determined it was a hoax.

Awesome news, Ben replied.

Not awesome, texted Grace. We did all that work for nothing.

What are you talking about? Ben typed.

A knock at the front door pulled his attention away from Grace. Who could be there at six fifteen in the morning? The person knocked again, louder this time, and Ben rushed into the living room without reading what Grace had replied.

It was Nick, looking grayer and more wrinkled than Ben had ever seen his father appear before. His shoulders slumped, and he could barely speak because he was so choked up. "Did you hear?" Nick mumbled.

"That the health department cleared us? Yeah." Ben smiled. "That's great news."

"No, not that." Nick shook his head. "All of the orders are canceled." His hand covered his mouth, muffling the words. "Well, not all of them, but they might as well be."

"What?" Ben felt like he'd been punched in the gut. "How could that be?"

Nick stomped into the living room and collapsed into the ratty recliner. Then, when he saw Marlo, who had sprung up to a seated position on the couch, he apologized. "I didn't mean to wake you up," he said. "I didn't mean for any of this to happen." He put his face in his hands.

"What's going on?" Marlo asked.

Ben looked at his phone and read the text from Grace out loud. "The rat photo is everywhere, and nobody wants our pies anymore. All the orders are canceled." Grace had explained it so callously that Ben was annoyed at first, but when he saw Nick's tears, his irritation turned to despair. He'd never seen his father break down like that. Never.

"What?" Marlo leaped to her feet. "That's not right." She paced back and forth in front of the couch. "There must be some way to fix this."

"There isn't." Nick shook his head. "It'll be a huge financial loss, but at least we could donate them to the food bank."

"That would be good publicity," Ben said. "I mean, not that it's about the publicity when you're feeding people with food insecurity."

"That's a great plan B," said Marlo as she pulled her phone out of her purse. "But plan A is to not let Brittany Barrow win, and I think I know how."

A flicker of hope ignited inside him. "How?" Ben asked.

Marlo's fingers typed rapidly into her phone. "I'm messaging Melanie Knowles. Quick, get me the best picture you can of all of the pies, and text it to me fast."

Ben hurried into the kitchen and flipped on all the lights. "On it," he called. "But who's Melanie Knowles?"

"She runs the Harper Landing Moms Facebook group," said Marlo. "It has over five thousand members."

Ben lined up a shot with as many pies in one picture as he could. He took a few more of the lattice top and the wooden crate that said CHEHALIS APPLES, YAKIMA, WA on the side. Then he spliced them all together into one image using a layout app on his phone and texted it to Marlo along with the originals.

"Perfect!" she called back. "Nick, how much do the pies cost?"

"Twenty-five bucks each, but our break-even point is twelve dollars."

"Can I put twenty dollars and say they're on a flash sale?" Marlo asked.

Ben walked back into the living room and plopped onto the couch, his eyes focused on Marlo, admiring how cute and rumpled she looked.

"Sure," said Nick. "That would still be a profit."

"Okay." Marlo tapped her phone. "Done." She sat down next to Ben. "Now we wait to see if Melanie writes back. It's six thirty in the morning, and she has a preschooler, so I doubt that she's awake. Maybe we should—"

Marlo's phone buzzed, and when she read the message, she broke out into a smile. "Melanie's posting it in Harper Landing Moms!"

"I don't know if that will help," said Nick. "Although I appreciate the effort."

"It might." Ben rose to his feet. "The Nuthatch has always relied on word-of-mouth advertising. Let's get these pies to the bakery and hope for the best." He reached out his hand to help his father up and then did the same for Marlo. "Thanks," he whispered into her ear when she nuzzled next to him. "You're amazing."

"I know it," she said with a smirk. "But now's the time to finally fess up."

"What do you mean?"

"Admit it." Marlo tapped him on the chest. "You can cook."

Ben rolled his eyes. "Guilty as charged."

CHAPTER SEVENTEEN

Marlo taught her Wednesday-morning classes, canceled her private afternoon Pilates clients, and came home to her condo to shower. She'd barely toweled off before she crashed onto her bed and slept for five hours. Marlo woke up around five thirty in the evening in a pool of drool, with a horrible crick in her neck that made it hard to move until she stretched. The first thing she did was feed Misty in the bowl next to her alarm clock. The bright-blue fish swam around in circles, swishing in and out of plastic seagrass. Marlo wished she had half of Misty's energy, because at the moment her body felt like lead. But then, as her eyes refocused on the clock and Marlo realized what time it was, she jumped out of bed and raced to the bathroom mirror. Ben was coming for dinner in ten minutes on his way home from work, and Marlo was still wearing the sweatpants she'd changed into after her shower.

Marlo yanked a brush through her hair and styled it as best she could considering it was still damp. She pulled on a pair of skinny jeans and flats and then slipped into a rose-pink sweater with a scoop neckline. There was barely time for makeup, but Marlo managed to swipe on some mascara and brush her eyebrows while she swished minty mouthwash and spat it into the sink. The doorbell rang right as she was rinsing out her mouth. Shoot! Ben was here, and she hadn't started making dinner yet.

"I'll be there in a second!" Marlo hollered as she raced across her condo to the kitchen. She switched on the oven to four hundred degrees and took out a sheet pan so it would look like she'd been busy. Marlo ripped out a piece of foil and lined the pan. Now it appeared like she had a plan, even though she was completely unprepared. "Stand up straight," she could hear Madame Burke say. "Put on a smile, and remember to breathe, because the show must go on." Marlo took a deep breath to settle herself and walked calmly to the front door. When she opened it, she was the picture of composure. "Ben," she gushed, a huge smile on her face. "Hi."

"Hello to you too." Ben grinned and scooped her up in his arms.

Marlo felt safe nestled against Ben's chest, like she had an exoskeleton of strength protecting her from the world. Their lips pressed together, and her heart fluttered. When their tongues touched, her pulse raced faster. Her hands explored his shoulder muscles and slid down his back, feeling the cold from outside that still clung to him. She lifted up onto her toes for a better reach and closed her eyes as everything around her melted away. Then she heard the oven beep, signaling that it was preheated.

"What are you making?" Ben asked. "I'm starving."

Marlo froze. "It's a surprise." She patted her hands on his chest and thought fast. She had no idea what she was preparing for dinner. When she'd texted Ben this morning in between classes about dinner, she had been planning on grocery shopping after work. That was before she'd fallen into a coma in her bedroom. "Why don't you relax on the couch while I cook? You must be exhausted."

Ben yawned. "I *am* a bit sleepy." He rubbed his eyes. "I kept writing the same sentence over and over again at work."

Marlo steered him into the living room and onto her soft velvet couch. She offered him the remote control so he could watch TV.

"No thanks." Ben waved it away. "But if you have the budget and survey results from the Cascade Athletic Club, I'll take a look at them. I promised you I'd help, and then Brittany happened."

"Don't worry about it. I've been figuring it out myself, although I'd still love your help." Marlo walked over to the desk where she'd left her purse and fished out the financial records. "How did the pie selling go today? Did you hear?"

"They sold out." Ben grinned and took the papers from her. "I can't believe I forgot to tell you. That shows how tired I am."

"You've been awake for a billion hours in a row, so I understand." Marlo brushed her knuckles across the stubble of his cheek.

He caught her hand and kissed it. "It was the Harper Landing Moms Facebook group that did it. When they heard that the Nuthatch Bakery was in trouble because of a coordinated attack against us, the orders poured in. The line for pies stretched out the door and all the way past Wanderer's Home."

"That's great. All of that hard work paid off."

"Not just hard work." Ben kissed Marlo's palm. "Your brilliant business idea. Those pies wouldn't have sold without you."

Marlo rumpled the top of Ben's head. "It was nothing. I'll go make dinner. Would you like a glass of wine in the meantime?"

Ben shook his head. "No thanks. It would put me to sleep."

"A nap wouldn't be such a bad idea." Marlo pulled the packet of spreadsheets out of his hands and put them on the coffee table. "Doze off if you want. Dinner won't be ready for at least half an hour."

"Oh no." Ben took back the papers. "I promised you I'd help, and I mean it. Especially after you helped rescue my family's business."

"All I did was peel some apples." Marlo rolled her eyes. "No big deal." She rushed off to the kitchen before he could protest.

Marlo opened the cabinet and took down the cooking spray. She misted the foil-lined pan with olive oil so that whatever she ended up cooking wouldn't stick. Then she hunted through her fridge and freezer for a miracle. There were bits and pieces from previous meals she'd made over the past few days, plus some takeout from Sunday brunch with her parents at the Western Cedar, but nothing that screamed "Serve this to company" or "Make the hot guy on your couch think you're a genius." The pantry was even worse, unless Ben liked olives and Raisin Bran. But then in her freezer she found meatballs and frozen vegetables and knew she was saved.

Marlo cranked the oven up another twenty-five degrees and dumped the meatballs and veggies onto the foil in two strips. She seasoned everything with salt and pepper and sprinkled olive oil over the vegetables. Then she slid the pan into the oven and adjusted the timer for thirty minutes. Marlo set the table, poured tall glasses of ice water, and sliced up two oranges from the fruit bowl on her counter. She popped two pieces of bread into the toaster and put a stick of butter on the table. At the last minute, she grabbed a bottle of ketchup for the meatballs and set that on the table as well. Voilà! Not bad for someone who'd been asleep since noon. The timer rang just as she was finishing up, and she took the sheet pan out of the oven and put it on the stove. "Dinner's ready," Marlo called. "Come and get it." When there wasn't any answer, she went into the living room to investigate.

Ben was sound asleep on the couch, the spreadsheets still in his hands. He looked so peaceful sleeping there that Marlo was unwilling to disturb him. She knew how hard he'd worked and how big his sleep deficit had become. So instead of waking him, she sat on the end of the couch and pulled his feet onto her lap so he could stretch out all the way. Ben moaned and rolled over, causing the papers to flutter to the floor.

Marlo sat there for several minutes, enjoying the sound of Ben's deep breathing and the fact that he was nearby. But after ten minutes, she grew bored. The remote was on the opposite side of the couch, so TV wasn't an option, and Marlo's phone was on its docking station in her bedroom. The only entertainment available, if you could call it that, was the paperwork from the club. Marlo stretched out her foot and grabbed the papers with her toe and then slid them over to where she could reach them without disturbing Ben.

She started with the survey results, which she'd read as they'd come off the printer but hadn't properly perused. Most of the responders seemed to fall into two categories: older people who enjoyed staying at the club for several hours at a time, multiple days a week, and younger people who valued efficient workouts. That younger demographic seemed to want to get in and out of the Cascade Athletic Club fast. They didn't have time to catch up together in the sauna or join a game of doubles at tennis. To them, the club wasn't a place to socialize as much as it was a place to sweat. But one answer that almost everyone selected was this: "The CAC is an inclusive community that welcomes people of all ages and fitness levels."

Marlo read and reread that statement. She thought about Aaron, Julia, and their baby, Jack, swimming next to Mr. and Mrs. Fiege. She pictured the SilverSneakers members gossiping in the lobby wearing tracksuits and drinking coffee. She remembered Martha Reynolds at the senior center expressing her wish that there could be eldercare as well as childcare. Maybe Marlo had been wrong to think that trendy fitness boutiques were their prime competition. What made the Cascade Athletic Club special was also what made it unique: its inclusivity combined with high-end facilities.

Group fitness classes weren't the answer at all, Marlo realized. They needed to lean into their strengths instead of copying what other places were doing. There could be a bridge club for SilverSneakers, for example—bridge and tennis, every Sunday morning, for a nominal fee. Perhaps they could start offering swimming lessons too. Or maybe family yoga parties on Saturday night with pizza. Laura would love to teach classes like that. Marlo's mind whirled as she brainstormed a list of innovations that would bring new life into the business. She found a pen on the end table next to her and jotted down a dozen ideas. Her dad was a horrible coach in general, especially when it came to six-year-olds, but he was great at teaching skills. Maybe Chuck could offer a skills clinic for soccer, tennis, and racquetball. They could charge people extra who wanted one-on-one instruction.

By the time Marlo put down her pen, she felt invigorated by possibility. She took a deep breath before tackling the budget again. This was her fifth time studying it. Math had never been her strong suit, although she had managed to eke out an A minus in calculus her senior year. Marlo scanned the budget and looked carefully at the columns for projected and annual expenses. The line item for advertising irked her. They were spending $20,000 a year on print ads and giving that money to Brittany Barrow for full-page spreads in *Harper Landing Delights*. Marlo grabbed her pen and circled that figure three times. No way was she giving Brittany another dime. Maybe Facebook and Instagram ads could do the same thing.

The other parts of the budget were harder for Marlo to analyze. The line items for utilities couldn't be helped, for example. Not unless they put solar panels on their roof as Ben had suggested. Maybe someday, but they had no funds for that now. Salaries and compensation weren't an area to pick at either. If anything, Marlo wished they could pay employees like Dahlia more money. Then there was that $200,000 they owed the port commission for their share of the new parking structure. That was what was hurting the bottom line, and it was nonnegotiable.

Ben murmured in his sleep and stretched his legs out farther. Marlo reached into the basket next to her and pulled out the faux angora and spread it over them both. She wasn't sure how long she should let Ben sleep, but she didn't want to wake him. Dinner was cold now, and it didn't matter. She was exactly where she wanted to be. Well, almost where she wanted to be. Marlo carefully slid out from underneath Ben's legs and lay down next to him on the couch, tucking the blanket around her shoulders. It was hard being this close to Ben and not waking him up, but Marlo loved listening to the sound of his heartbeat beneath her ear. He moaned, shifted position, and threw his arm around her. For a second Marlo thought he might wake up. But then Ben let out a loud snore, and she had to suppress the urge to giggle.

Marlo closed her eyes and made a wish—lots of wishes, actually. That Ben would want to be with Marlo as much as she wanted to be with him. That her feelings would be met with equal vigor. That Ben sleeping beside her would be a privilege she'd have for the rest of her life. And that maybe, just maybe, she'd be brave enough to speak the words that were on her heart. She was in love.

Marlo woke up the next morning to the smell of coffee and the sound of Ben whistling a happy tune. Her mouth felt like cotton, and she was fairly certain she had raccoon eyes from smudged mascara. She used her fingertip to wipe away black crud underneath her eye creases. Then she raked her fingers through her hair to comb it the best she could. When she felt satisfied that she wasn't a complete troll, she padded into the kitchen to see Ben.

"You're awake," Ben said with a grin. He'd showered, and his hair was still wet, slicked to the side in a swoop. Ben flipped a pancake in the air like a show-off. It landed on the griddle, and butter sizzled. "Just in time for breakfast."

"Mmm . . ." Marlo wrapped her arms around Ben's waist. "The food smells delicious." She nibbled his neck. "You smell delicious too."

"It's the chocolate body scrub I found in your shower." Ben gave her a side hug. "It looked good enough to eat." He set down the pancake flipper and kissed her properly. "You look good enough to eat too," he said in a growly voice that made Marlo laugh. "Sorry for sleeping through dinner."

"Don't worry about it." She nuzzled her nose against his.

"It looked really good. I love meatballs. I didn't know if you wanted to save them or not, so I put the cookie sheet on the counter."

"They're destined for the trash." Marlo took out the wastebasket and disposed of the meal.

"Dinner looked great. I'm sorry I missed it."

"I'm not. I knew you needed your sleep."

"If I'd known who I was sleeping next to, I would have woken up." Ben's hands took a firmer hold of her back, and Marlo felt herself quiver as he pulled her against his chest. She closed her eyes and snaked her hands around his neck, letting every part of herself press into him as they kissed. Her lips parted, and she toyed with his tongue, overwhelmed by the emotions rolling over her. But then her nose tickled with a funny scent.

Ben shoved her gently away from the stove. "The pancakes are burning!" He turned off the burner and grabbed the flipper. "See? I told you I couldn't cook." Ben lifted up the burnt pancake and dumped it into the trash.

"You were doing fine until I distracted you." Marlo laughed and looked in the mixing bowl, which still held plenty of batter. "I'm going to get dressed while you redeem your reputation."

"Aye, aye, Captain." Ben wiped burnt butter out of the pan with a wet paper towel.

Marlo came back five minutes later wearing black leggings and a purple sweater. Ben handed her a mug of coffee and pulled out her chair. "Breakfast is served," he said.

She looked into her mug. "How did you know I take cream?"

"That's the way you drank it at the senior center." Ben sat down next to her and picked up the syrup. He opened the cap and paused before pouring it. "Happy Thanksgiving. I'm incredibly grateful to be sitting here with you."

"That's how I feel too." Marlo smiled and sipped her coffee. "What does your family do for Thanksgiving?"

"Nothing." Ben sliced into his stack of pancakes. "The bakery is so busy during the holidays that we usually order take-out Chinese food."

"Come have dinner with me," Marlo blurted out before she could second-guess herself. "I mean, you can still do Chinese food with your family, but then come to my house for turkey and pies." Marlo made a face. "Well, maybe not pie. The thought of pie makes me feel a bit ill at this point, but the rest of the dinner ought to be good."

"Yes," said Ben.

"Yes, what?"

"Yes, I'd love to spend Thanksgiving with you." He reached for her hand and squeezed it. "Are you sure your parents won't mind?"

"Are you sure you won't mind my parents?" Marlo hunched her shoulders and wrinkled her nose. "They'll spend half of the time arguing and the other half making out. But there will be wine."

"There will be you, and that's all that matters." Ben kissed her hand and let go. "Besides, maybe we could talk about the port commission's parking structure fee. It seems high to me." Ben picked up a stack of papers that was on the other side of the table. "I read through these while you were asleep."

"I did too," Marlo said. "I mean, when you were asleep last night."

"I know." Ben shuffled the papers until he found the page that Marlo had written on. "I saw your list, and I think these are great ideas."

"You do? Really?"

Ben nodded. "Really. You've identified some great opportunities to increase revenue. But the major savings would come from that port commission fee. I don't understand why the port is charging you a fee that's so disproportionally higher than all of the other businesses along the marina."

"I don't know anything about that," Marlo admitted.

Ben chewed a bite of pancake and looked out at the view of Puget Sound. The Olympic Mountains were crisp on the horizon, blanketed with snow, and presented an imposing backdrop behind the water. "I've been to so many city council and port commission meetings over the past couple of years that they all jumble together," he said. "But something about that fee doesn't make sense to me. When I get home, I'll poke around in my notes and see if I can find out more."

Marlo welcomed Ben's help with the port commission fee, but she wasn't ready for him to leave just yet. She loved having him at her kitchen table. He made her condo feel like home, instead of her parents' investment property. She poured him a fresh cup of coffee. "This is the best breakfast I've had in forever." Marlo set the coffeepot on a trivet, leaned over, and hugged him.

"Wait until you taste my waffles."

Marlo giggled. "I like having you here."

"And I like being here." Ben held her tight. "But something tells me I still have a gigantic mess in Simon's kitchen to clean up."

"Too bad," said Marlo. "The last thing I want to do is boss you around, but Simon's messy kitchen will have to wait." She threaded her fingers through his wet hair and pulled him closer, crushing their lips together in a kiss so hot it could have melted butter.

CHAPTER EIGHTEEN

Chuck and Laura Jonas lived in a part of Harper Landing that Ben had never visited before—the rich part called Burke Woods. Mammoth homes in parklike settings with at least three acres on each lot nestled in a forest of century-old trees. Douglas firs, hemlocks, and cedars scraped against the sky, offering privacy and providing a fortress of woods. Ben was relieved that Marlo was driving, because her shiny Acura fit in much better than his dented Kia. He sat in the passenger seat wearing chinos, a polo shirt, and an itchy sweater. Maybe the sweater had been a bad idea, but Katelyn had said it looked awful, and that had convinced Ben that it might be an appropriate choice for dinner with Marlo's parents.

"My folks have been cooking all day," said Marlo as she fiddled with the windshield wipers. Rain pounded against the windshield, but the temperature was so cold outside that it could snow at any minute. "But they've also probably been drinking all day as they cooked, so . . ."

"They'll be more delightful than usual?"

"Yeah." Marlo nodded. "Something like that. Hopefully, they're sober enough to listen to my ideas about the club and to understand the information you've discovered about the port commission." Marlo drove through a roundabout and exited onto a street lined with massive hedges on either side. "I'm kind of nervous," she admitted.

"Because they're going to hate me, right?" Ben stretched out his hand and tried to rid himself of the cramp that was forming. He'd spent two hours at home on a cleaning rampage in the kitchen followed by sleuthing on the computer, digging through port commission records and uncovering information about the new parking structure. Now the tendonitis in his arm raged.

"They're not going to hate you." Marlo looked at Ben like he was nuts. "My mom already loves you—and my dad, well . . ." Marlo clicked on her blinker before turning left. "My dad's impressed that you brought bike shoes to spin class, so at least there's that." She ran her fingers through her chestnut-colored hair. It was down today and fell in soft waves past her shoulders. "No, I'm worried about my parents embarrassing me, because they love to humiliate me."

"I don't think your parents are that self-aware." Ben scratched his chin. "To me, it seems like they get caught up with themselves and don't consider that anyone else is in the room."

"That's true." Marlo nodded. She slowed down her car and turned right into such a narrow opening that Ben didn't see it at first.

"Is this a one-lane road?" he asked, surprised. He'd never seen something like that in Harper Landing before.

"No, this is my driveway. Or my parents' driveway," Marlo added, correcting herself. "I don't live here anymore."

"It's like we're driving through a forest." Ben stared through the window at the deep woods. He saw giant stumps from old-growth trees that loggers in the late 1900s had abandoned intermixed with towering giants that had been planted afterward.

"Yeah. The trees were what made my mom want to move here, but my dad fell in love with the view. I was ten years old when they bought this place." Marlo slowed the car even further as they crept down the driveway that ended in a circle at the bottom of the hill in front of a large two-story house.

"Whoa." Ben's mouth dropped open as he caught a glimpse of Puget Sound peeking from behind the roofline. The forest was gone now, replaced by manicured landscaping. Rhododendrons, Japanese maples, and neatly pruned juniper bushes framed the gray-shingled home and its wraparound porch. "This place is beautiful," he said.

"I've always thought so too." Marlo parked in the driveway and grabbed her purse from the back seat. Before she unlocked the doors, she looked seriously at Ben. "Let's have a code word in case you want to leave in a hurry."

Ben cracked a smile. "A code word?"

Marlo nodded. "I usually escape to my room when my parents are being obnoxious, but—"

"I don't mind escaping to your room with you," Ben interrupted. He brushed her cheek gently with his palm. "Sounds like fun."

"Oh yeah?" Marlo leaned forward and kissed him. Ben felt the temperature in the tiny car heat up as he strained forward in his seat belt to wrap his arms around Marlo. He detached the belt and it zipped back, pinning his shoulder back at an awkward angle.

Marlo laughed and pulled away. "Careful there. Safety first."

Ben chuckled and untangled himself. "So what's our safe word?"

"Code word," Marlo corrected. "But you can call it a *safe word* if you want." She rested her chin on her hand and stared across the dashboard. "How about *Misty*?"

"You mean like 'It's getting misty out there, so we'd better head out'?"

"No, I mean like Misty Copeland, my pet fish. Ask me if I remembered to feed Misty today. She gets me out of all sorts of problematic situations."

"That sounds intriguing." Ben picked up the manila folder he'd brought to share with Chuck and Laura.

"I have my stories to tell too." Marlo winked and hopped out of the car.

Ben took a deep breath when he stepped outside. The air smelled like salt and cedar. Marlo slipped her arm around his waist and hugged him as they darted through raindrops to the house. Ben rested his arm around her shoulders, grateful for her reassuring presence.

The mahogany doors were fifteen feet tall and had cut-crystal windows that distorted the view inside. Marlo clasped the brass knocker and whacked; the knock echoed across the peaceful afternoon.

Laura opened the door a minute later wearing velvet yoga pants and a flowing green tunic. Her silvery hair was piled into a messy bun, and long crystal earrings dangled to her shoulders. "I was wondering when you two would arrive." She held out her arms for a hug. "Come on in. I've already opened the wine."

Marlo hugged her mother, and Ben held out his hand, unsure of how to greet her. Laura pushed his wrist away and embraced him, squeezing him with a surprising amount of strength.

"Have you been back to that farm lately?" Laura asked as she released him. "How were the goats?"

"Sorry. I've been too busy making pies." Ben tried to focus on Laura as he spoke, but it was hard because all his brain wanted to do was stare at the view out the back window. "Your daughter helped." Finally, he couldn't take it anymore and gazed over Laura's shoulder to the wall of windows framing Puget Sound. "Wow," Ben murmured. "What a view."

"Do you like it?" Laura linked her arm through Ben's and led him into the living room. The furniture was old but expensive looking, and the wood floor had dull spots in need of polish. But the floor-to-ceiling glass walls were spectacular.

"Is that Whidbey Island?" Ben stared across the water.

"Yup." Laura nodded. "And if you look to the right, you can see Mount Baker."

"Sometimes Mom and Dad see orcas." Marlo had sneaked up next to him.

"Only a few times," Laura admitted. "But we spot gray whales almost every year."

"And you should hear the sea lions." Marlo pointed down at the beach behind the train tracks. "They can be loud in the morning."

Ben guessed that the train must be loud as well but kept that opinion to himself. All of Harper Landing's waterfront properties dealt with coal trains barreling across the tracks twenty-four seven. At least he never had to deal with *that*, he mused. Or the risk of the coal trains derailing and causing an accident. It was a constant topic of conversation at city council meetings. The concern was that a train would crash and possibly explode, and then there would be no way for emergency service vehicles to reach the waterfront. The Jonas property was stunning, but it also had its drawbacks.

Ben breathed in a delicious aroma of roasted turkey. "Something smells good," he said. "Do I smell yeast rolls baking?"

"Yup, and Chuck took the turkey out right before you two arrived," said Laura. "It should be ready to carve soon." She waved for them to follow her. "Come on into the kitchen and help yourself to a drink. I'll need to make the gravy."

"I thought you'd have your famous hummus tray out," said Marlo as she walked behind her mother. Marlo reached back for Ben's hand and gave it a reassuring squeeze.

"I wanted to have appetizers." Laura's voice rose. "But your father said there wasn't enough time." She pushed a swinging door into the kitchen.

"That's because there wasn't time." Chuck stood behind an enormous carving board wearing an apron with the words COACH JONAS embroidered on the front. He sharpened a carving knife on steel. "You guys are so late that I almost pardoned the turkey."

"We're not late." Marlo put her hands on her hips. "You said dinner was at three thirty, and we're here thirty minutes early."

"Who arrives to Thanksgiving dinner with only thirty minutes to spare?" Chuck savagely slashed at the sharpening stick and glared at Ben.

"Don't blame Ben," said Marlo. "His family doesn't do a traditional Thanksgiving dinner."

"You don't?" Laura gasped. "You poor darling."

"We order takeout because Thanksgiving is such a busy week at the bakery that Thursday is my parents' only day off," Ben explained. "And I'm sorry if we're late." He glanced sideways at Marlo. "I didn't know we were expected earlier."

Marlo shrugged and stared out the window with a guilty look on her face. "We're here now. That's what's important." She picked up a bottle of Columbia Valley merlot and poured it into an enormous wineglass. "Would you like one?" she asked Ben.

He nodded. "Yes. Thank you."

"Why are you using that knife?" Laura asked in an annoyed tone. "I got out the electric carving knife that my mother sent us."

"I hate that one," Chuck grumbled. "You know that."

Laura picked up the box. "But Mother says—"

"I know what she says," Chuck thundered, "and I'll use it when she's here for Christmas to make her happy, but I hate the blasted thing."

"I don't know why you insisted on a turkey anyway." Laura's eyes took on an angry glint. "A Tofurky would have been equally delicious and wouldn't have involved a dead carcass on my marble countertop."

"The bird's not on your countertop." Chuck stuck the sharpening stick into the knife block. "I'm using a carving board."

"And there's death everywhere." Laura pointed at the juice. "For once, I'd like to celebrate a holiday that didn't involve the murder of innocent creatures."

"Oh boy." Marlo closed her eyes and massaged her forehead.

"You said something about gravy?" Ben asked. "Is there anything I can do to help?" He walked over to the sink, turned on the faucet, and washed his hands.

"You know how to make gravy?" Chuck arched his bushy eyebrows.

"I can make gravy and biscuits with sausage." Ben dried his hands on a towel he recognized from Dawn's shop with I BELIEVE IN FERRIES printed underneath a scenic shot of Harper Landing Beach. "But I've never made vegetarian gravy before," he said. Ben looked at Laura. "Could you teach me?"

Laura opened a carton of vegetable broth. "I'd love to." She turned on the stove underneath a cast-iron skillet. "I already sautéed the mushrooms."

"No, no, no." Chuck grabbed Ben's elbow and pulled him over to the roasting pan filled with turkey drippings. "Now that Ben's here, we need real gravy." He gave Ben a whisk. "Can you handle this on your own?"

"That's a whisk you'll have to take," said Ben. He grinned as Chuck belly laughed, and they began cooking together.

Two hours later, everyone was stuffed and sacked out on the faux-suede couches in the living room. Dinner had been a success, and Chuck had raved so much about Ben's gravy that even Laura had been talked into eating a bite. Unlike the Jonas family, Ben was still on his first glass of wine. Marlo had poured herself a second but wasn't drinking it. Chuck and Laura were halfway through another bottle, which helped explain why Laura's hand was on Chuck's thigh and why Chuck kept grabbing Laura's boob when he thought nobody was looking.

Ben winced every time he saw something he shouldn't have and tried to keep his focus on the view of Puget Sound instead.

"I ate way too much," Marlo moaned as she rested her head on his shoulder. "You'll have to roll me out of the house to the car."

"And you think your teaching schedule is too rigorous," said Chuck. "It's thanks to me you can eat like a trucker."

What the hell? Ben bristled. "Marlo doesn't eat like a trucker," he said with an edge to his voice.

"And the schedule isn't good for me, Dad." Marlo lifted her head from Ben's shoulder and stared at her father. "I'm sore and exhausted all the time. I feel like an old woman instead of a twenty-four-year-old."

"I told you Marlo's schedule was too intense." Laura took her hand off Chuck's thigh and wagged her finger at him.

"Keep moving forward." Chuck put his hands on his knees. "That's what the doctor said when he came out of your second surgery."

"What?" Marlo looked confused.

"The surgeon said that the key to your recovery was to keep moving forward and continually improve," explained Chuck. "Train longer. Train harder. Otherwise, your muscle would turn to fat, and the added weight would aggravate your knee injury."

"My knees will wear out if I keep up this crazy pace," Marlo protested. "That's why I want to make changes at the club."

"Hang on." Ben held his hand up and looked Chuck straight in the eye. "Marlo's weight is none of your concern. She deserves to be treated like a human being and not a machine."

"Don't tell me how to coach Marlo." Chuck folded his hands across his chest.

"She's not your soccer player; she's your daughter," snapped Laura. "And Ben's right—you have been treating her like a machine."

"And machines break." Marlo looked at the carpet.

"Not my daughter." Chuck's voice wavered. "My daughter can never break. She can never break again." His chin trembled. "Do you know how much pain I was in watching you collapse onstage when your ACL snapped? It was like my mom breaking her hip all over again. First her hip broke, and then she died of pneumonia in the convalescent hospital." He squeezed his eyes shut and shuddered. Chuck rose to his feet. "I can't ever live through something like that again. If I could have taken it all away from you, I would have." He looked up at the ceiling. "It should have been *my* ACL that ruptured, not yours." Chuck sniffed and wiped his nose on his sleeve.

"Dad . . . ," Marlo said in a soft voice.

Ben couldn't believe that Chuck was crying, but he was. Huge tears rolled down his cheeks. Laura handed her husband a tissue, and Chuck blew his nose with vigor. Ben looked at Marlo and saw that her eyes were wet too.

"I'm sorry I've been hard on you, baby girl," Chuck said in a watery voice. "Part of me thinks if I keep you going, you won't break again. The other part of me wants you to be invincible, and you prove that every time you teach another class."

"Oh, Dad." Marlo got up and hugged him. "I'm not invincible, and neither is the Cascade Athletic Club, but I've got some ideas on how to make both of us stronger." She looked over her shoulder at Ben. "And wait until you hear what Ben discovered. It'll feel like Christmas instead of Thanksgiving."

Ben picked up the file folder he'd brought with him. "Sometimes it helps to know a reporter." He waved it in the air and smiled.

"Now you've got me curious." Chuck cleared his throat and sat down next to Laura. "Forget you saw me blubber," he told Ben.

"Never happened." Ben nodded at Marlo. "You go first."

"Okay." Marlo launched in with all of her ideas for increasing revenue at the club. Family yoga night, Sunday bridge and brunch, swimming lessons, Facebook ad campaigns, and more.

"That all sounds great," said Chuck.

Laura nodded. "Especially family yoga night."

"But even if we scrap our ad account with Brittany, I don't see how we'll have the funds to get much of this started."

"You will with an extra one hundred fifty thousand dollars in your pocket." Ben grinned and opened up his folder. "The port commission is overcharging you by a whopping amount."

"*What?*" Laura threw out her arms, and her crystal bracelets clinked together.

Ben fanned out the papers. "There's an error in their math. They're charging every business in the marina a flat rate for the number of occupants per day, per building, that will use the new parking structure."

Chuck nodded. "That's right."

"But the other businesses are mainly offices and boating companies. They don't have the high customer turnover you do."

"Our members stay with us for decades," Chuck said, bristling.

"No, I mean in terms of parking," Ben clarified. "Your members park for one or two hours. A company like my sister's, Custom Aeronautic Plastics, has employees who park all day. So instead of the port charging you for the total number of guests you have all day, they should charge you for the total occupancy number of your building at any given time." Ben flipped through the paperwork. "Which is four hundred thirty-five, right?" He looked at Marlo for confirmation, and she nodded. "But the port commission is charging you as if you'll need three thousand parking spaces, which doesn't make sense."

"No." Laura reached for the data. "That doesn't make sense at all. How did we not realize that before?"

"I got the assessment bill, and I didn't think to question it." Chuck shook his head in disbelief. "The port commission must think I'm a sucker."

"Or that we need a new accountant," said Marlo. "I suggest George Fiege. Julia Harper highly recommends him."

"What we need is a business consultant." Chuck pointed at Ben. "You're hired." He thumped Marlo on the back. "You're a keeper, too, with your fresh ideas. You've talked me into all of it. I think you're brilliant. I hope you know that."

Marlo tucked her chin in. "Thanks, Dad."

"I'm not a business consultant, but I was happy to take a look when Marlo asked." Ben picked up her hand. "I think your daughter's brilliant too." He kissed Marlo's palm.

Chuck smiled broadly. "Do you see what happens when you listen to your father?"

"What are you talking about?" Marlo rolled her eyes.

"He's right," Laura burst out. "I see it so clearly."

"See what?" Ben asked.

Chuck pointed at both of them. "You two are equally matched."

Ben gazed into Marlo's eyes. "I agree."

"I meant on the attractiveness scale, son," Chuck said. "Try to be a little more humble."

Ben choked back a shocked laugh.

"Still," Chuck continued. "I see a promising future ahead of you."

"So do I," Ben said, staring at Marlo.

She lifted her lips to his and kissed him softly. When they pulled away, Marlo gasped.

Chuck and Laura were now full-on making out on the couch.

"I think you need to feed Misty, right?" Ben asked in a loud voice.

Marlo jumped to her feet. "That's right." She grabbed Ben's hand and yanked his arm. "Let's go do that."

"Goodbye, dear," Laura called from somewhere underneath Chuck's chest.

Ben stepped over entangled limbs as he scooted past the coffee table. "Thanks for dinner," he said.

When they reached the car, he and Marlo burst out laughing.

Ben swept Marlo up in his arms and lifted her off her feet. "We escaped." He kissed her loudly on the cheek, and she giggled. Then Ben set her feet back on the ground and leaned forward. He kissed her tenderly until every inch of his body yearned to be closer, and he found himself pressing her against the car. Marlo's arms laced around him, and her fingers kneaded into his back.

"I never, ever want to embarrass our children like that . . . someday," she murmured when they parted.

"Our children?" Ben raised his eyebrows and flashed his dimples.

Marlo blanched; instead of blushing, her face lost its color. "I mean . . ." She bit her bottom lip.

"I don't want to embarrass our children either someday." Ben brushed a lock of brown hair off Marlo's face. "But I sure as hell hope that thirty years from now, we're still making out on the couch."

"You do?" Marlo's bottom lip quivered.

Ben nodded. "I'm in love with you, Marlo Jonas, in all of your Leaping Lemur glory."

Marlo walked her fingers up Ben's chest and tapped him on the lips. "I'm in love with you too," she said. She grabbed him by the collar and pulled him closer.

EPILOGUE

New Year's Eve

The Harper Landing Yacht Club was the most elegant event venue in the entire town, and tonight it could rival the swankiest hotels in Seattle. Blue silk tablecloths glistened from the light of hundreds of candles glowing in mercury-glass votives. White and yellow roses scented the room with the faint fragrance of a floral shop. Waiters cruised through the crowds, holding silver platters laden with hors d'oeuvres. The award-winning Harper Landing High School Duke Ellington Tribute Band played one favorite after another and kept the dance floor hopping. At the center of the floor, right underneath the mirrored ball, Ben gazed into Marlo's eyes like they were the only two people in the room.

He wore his best (and only) suit and had polished his shoes until they shone like the waters of Puget Sound. Marlo wore the red velvet leotard she'd purchased at the Forgotten Hug and had paired it with a black satin skirt that swished out every time Ben spun her around. Her hair was long and flowing, the way Ben loved it, although he'd never dream of telling her how to wear her hair.

"I didn't know you could swing dance," Marlo said as Ben twirled her around in another circle.

"Simon taught me." Ben caught Marlo in his arms and pushed her away again, leading her into a quick procession of kicks. "He's a regular Renaissance man."

"So I've learned." Marlo looked across the floor to where Simon and Katelyn were dancing. They wore matching outfits, and Katelyn's pigtails had big bows. Dahlia and Mike slow danced next to them, completely ignoring the beat of the music, lost in each other's eyes.

"Uh-oh." Ben grinned. "It looks like your parents are recovering from an argument again." He saw Chuck and Laura pawing at each other in the corner.

"At least your parents aren't here to witness it this time." Marlo squeezed her eyes shut. "I don't know if your family will ever want to come over for Christmas dinner again."

"In your parents' defense, your dad had just promised your mom that the Cascade Athletic Club could sponsor a goat-yoga retreat next summer." Ben chuckled. "If there was ever a reason to start french-kissing in front of the rib roast, it would be *that*."

Marlo opened her eyes and giggled. "I thought your sister was going to die."

"Grace should loosen up. It would do her some good." Ben leaned Marlo back in a dip and then brought her back up for a kiss as the song ended.

"Ben, I have something to tell you," Marlo said as their lips parted. The band began playing a new song, a beautiful rendition of the Etta James classic "At Last."

"What is it?" Ben pressed his cheek against Marlo's and held her close.

"Now that the port commission fee is straightened out, the Cascade Athletic Club is making money again." Marlo took a deep breath before continuing. "All of my other ideas are going into effect, too, and revenue is pouring in. My parents are so happy they called their lawyer."

"Lawyer?" Ben breathed in the sweet fragrance of Marlo's floral shampoo.

"Yes, lawyer. They're giving me fifty-one percent ownership of the club starting tomorrow, with the intention that I'll inherit the rest of it later."

"Congratulations." Ben was proud of how far she'd come as a businesswoman already. "You earned it."

"I don't know about that." Marlo clung to him for support. "But it means that I can be a woman who supports my family and pays all of our bills." Her cheeks burned as red as her velvet leotard. "It won't matter what salary you bring home as a journalist. You'll never have to worry about money again. Our kids could be in childcare in the club, and I could visit them on my breaks."

Ben stopped dancing and looked at her closely. Butterflies the size of pterodactyls flapped in his stomach. "Are you saying you want to be my sugar mama?"

Marlo gulped. "Kind of. Yeah."

Ben rubbed the back of his neck and looked down at his polished shoes. His pulse quickened, and nerves coursed through him. "Well, that makes this awkward, because I happen to have stumbled across a stack of bridal magazines at the back of your closet, and I thought"—he dropped to one knee and pulled a jewelry box out of his pocket—"that you might consider being my wife instead."

Marlo stared at the diamond winking back at her and began shaking.

"Marlo Jonas, I love you with a love so big that words cannot express how deeply I want you. Your work ethic, your kindness, your grace, your beauty—I want it all, every moment of every day, for the rest of my life." Ben stared into her blue eyes and hoped against hope that she'd say yes.

The other dancers realized what was happening and paused on the dance floor to watch. Dahlia squealed and took out her phone to video-tape Ben's proposal. Katelyn and Simon held hands and smiled. Chuck and Laura stopped french-kissing and turned to stare. Chuck tucked in his shirt, and Laura adjusted the crystal necklaces she wore that had become tangled in Chuck's tie.

Ben took the ring out of the box and held it up. Grace had loaned him the money to buy it, in an astonishing act of sisterly love. "Marlo Jonas, will you marry me?" It felt like his heart stopped beating while he waited for her answer.

"Yes!" Marlo squealed and threw her arms around him. They kissed, and Ben slid the ring on Marlo's finger. The whole room erupted into cheers. Someone wolf whistled as Ben dipped Marlo back for a kiss.

Then, a loud *pop* exploded through the room, capturing everyone's attention. It was followed by three more *pop*s in rapid succession. Simon screamed and hit the floor. Ben shoved Marlo behind him. There, at the center of the balloon arch at the back of the room in the children's section stood Goldie, wearing bright-red clown shoes and her purple vinyl trench coat. Goldie ripped another balloon off the arch and popped it with a hairpin. When all eyes were on her, she opened one of her coat pockets and took out a balloon. She blew it up into a long skinny cylinder with three quick breaths.

"Uh-oh," Ben mumbled as Goldie blew up another balloon and twisted it into place.

"Why is that woman making a balloon sword?" Marlo asked.

"Ben, you've really got to deal with your crazy ex-girlfriend," said Mike.

"I thought I had," Ben protested.

Katelyn marched up to Ben and put something in his palm. "Here's a gift card to my old coffee stand with Hunter's phone number on the back. He doesn't believe in credit either—because it can be traced."

"They could be a cute couple." Ben put the card in his pocket. "Thanks, Kate."

"No problem."

Ben turned around and kissed Marlo's cheek. "I'll be right back," he told his fiancée. "I have a balloon duel to fight, and then I'm all yours. Forever."

ACKNOWLEDGMENTS

Thank you to my daughter, Brenna, for giving me permission to share about her dyslexia in all forms of my writing, including fiction. Before I was a newspaper columnist and author, I was an elementary school teacher. Like many educators, I learned nothing about dyslexia in teacher credentialing school. This is a shame, because according to the Yale Center for Dyslexia and Creativity, up to 20 percent of the population has dyslexia. Dyscalculia (related to numbers), dysgraphia (handwriting issues), and dyspraxia (motor skills) are often related.

My daughter is smart, witty, kind, and a gifted writer. She's also an incredibly hard worker who put in countless hours after school and on weekends with her tutor. My family was in the fortunate position to be able to pay for this extra help, but not every family is so lucky.

If you struggled with reading as a child or, like me, still battle spelling today, I honor your journey. Dyslexia requires a systematic, multisensory approach to upload phonemes—the building blocks of language—into the brain. If you had been given access to specialized instruction as a child when your brain plasticity was at its peak, your journey with language might have been easier. It has taken me years to realize that being a poor speller is not my fault. My brain needed a different way of learning that it didn't receive.

Thank you also to my son, Bryce, whose humor and creativity made writing this book easier, especially considering we were in the middle of a global pandemic. Every day when I turned on my computer, he was in the kitchen, filling our house with the aroma of freshly baked bread, bagels, english muffins, and more. He bravely tried complicated recipes that I would never dare attempt and contributed to the cozy atmosphere I envisioned when I pictured the Nuthatch Bakery.

My husband, Doug, has kindness and patience unmatched by any man I have ever met. Thank you for supporting my writing all these years and for encouraging me to buy a Peloton, which helped me channel my inner Marlo. If you're a fellow rider, my leaderboard name is #IBrakeForMoms, and you can count on me for a follow back and lots of high fives.

A big shout-out goes to three friends from school. Ben Wexler, thank you for letting me use your name. I haven't seen you in twenty years, and we were never childhood enemies, but in my mind the two names Ben and Wexler still go together. What a delight to discover—after I wrote the book and confessed what I had done—that you are a cyclist. Christy Varonfakis Henderson, thank you for your brilliant ideas for the Harper Landing Players, which you came up with instantly. Your third concept, *King Lear* performed by toddlers, would have been equally hilarious. Jean Elias, thank you for answering my questions about ballet, even my weird ones like choosing a career-ending injury for Marlo. You are my go-to person for torturing ballerinas.

Thank you to my literary agent, Liza Fleissig of the Liza Royce Agency; the phenomenal team at Montlake Romance, including Alison Dasho and Krista Stroever; and my writing group friends Sharman Badgett-Young, Laura Moe, and Penelope Wright. My writing is better because of you.

Finally, thank you to my readers. I love connecting with you on Facebook, Twitter, and Instagram. I hope your visits to Harper Landing lift your spirits and bring you joy.

ABOUT THE AUTHOR

Photo © 2020 Angie Langford/Verb Photography

Jennifer Bardsley believes in friendship, true love, and the everlasting power of books. A graduate of Stanford University, she lives in Edmonds, Washington, with her husband and two children. Bardsley's column, I Brake for Moms, has appeared in the *Everett Herald* every week since 2012. She also writes young adult paranormal romance under the pen name Louise Cypress. When Bardsley's not writing books or camping with her Girl Scout troop, you can find her walking from her house to the beach every chance she gets.

Sign up for Bardsley's author newsletter, and you'll receive Marlo's stir-fry dinner recipe: https://landing.mailerlite.com/webforms/landing/o1l7v3.